THE NEW WORLD

FINAL DAWN ✺ BOOK FOUR

T.W.M. ASHFORD

Cover design by Tom Ashford

DARK STAR PANORAMA

The *Dark Star Panorama* is a shared universe of sci-fi stories in which *Final Dawn* is the first series.

To hear about new releases and receive an exclusive, free prequel story set in the *Final Dawn* series, sign up for T.W.M. Ashford's mailing list at the website below.

www.twmashford.com

1

HOMECOMING

The *Adeona* lurched in and out of subspace. Her metal hull groaned. The view outside her cockpit windows went from planetary vista to pulsating nothingness and back again.

Jack, woken abruptly in his bunk by the jolting ship, rushed down the hallway and threw himself into the captain's seat.

"What the hell is going on?" he groaned, rubbing the sleep-dust out of his eyes. "Are we under attack or something?"

"Nope, nothing to worry about," the *Adeona's* speakers replied sheepishly. "Just experiencing a little turbulence. Go back to bed."

Jack raised a groggy eyebrow. Turbulence? There was no wind in subspace.

"Adi? What aren't you telling me?"

"She's malfunctioning," said Rogan as she climbed up the stairs from the loading bay.

That certainly woke Jack up.

"Oh, it really is nothing to worry about," she added,

noticing his panicked expression. "Engines, life support, shields – they're all stable. Even the coffee dispenser's working. Some of her auto-pilot wiring has been knocked loose, that's all."

Jack sighed and turned back to the dashboard.

"Why didn't you say anything sooner, Adi?"

"I didn't think it would be this much of a problem," the ship replied, before quietly following with, "and I didn't want to let anyone down."

"Oh, Adi." Jack shook his head and rubbed his hand over the console in front of him. "You've saved all of our lives multiple times over. Let us take care of you for a change."

"This must be from the battle at the Iris," she said. "I guess one of those Raklett missiles got a bit closer than I thought."

As she spoke, a camera feed showed one of her shielding panels rattle free from her starboard hull. It shot off into subspace behind them.

"Oh, bolts. I don't suppose I'll be getting that back any time soon."

Jack cast a concerned glance at Rogan.

"Okay, Adi." Rogan brought up a NavMap on the hologram table. "Let us take over for a while. You've earned a rest. I can monitor the skip drive while Jack acts as pilot... if that's all right with you, of course?"

A disappointed silence followed.

"I suppose that's best," the *Adeona* eventually replied. "Sorry. But... well, I can't rest without shutting all my systems down. If I'm not flying, I'm not sure what else I'm supposed to do."

"Why don't you hang out with Tuner for a bit?" said Rogan. "I'm sure he'll be glad to have some company."

"Yes, I'll go do that." Still, the poor ship sounded quite despondent. "Good idea."

Jack waited until the *Adeona* had gone quiet for a few seconds before he turned around in his seat to speak to Rogan.

"How *is* Tuner doing?"

"He's fine," Rogan replied, nodding. "A little glum he can't come up and join us, though. I think the novelty of being a walking tank is wearing off a bit."

Jack nodded. Up until recently, Tuner had been a pretty small automata – no more than a few feet tall and about as combat-effective as a filing cabinet. But his chassis was crushed during their escape from Krett. To save him, Rogan transplanted his data core into another model – a move considered controversial amongst polite automata society. Now he was four times the height and had a plasma cannon for an arm. He also couldn't fit up the stairs anymore, unfortunately, and was therefore confined to the lower deck of the ship – the cargo bay in particular.

"We'll have to get Adi looked at once this is over." Jack tightened his grip on the flight stick but, at least whilst travelling through subspace, there wasn't all that much he needed to do. "Another trip to Kapamentis might be in order."

"Or the moons of Ka'heet. They've got some great garages for sentient starships out there." Rogan paused. "Of course, we wouldn't need to go anywhere if Brackitt were still here."

"Yeah. Still doesn't feel right without him."

The tiny pinprick of light at the end of subspace's infinite tunnel shined bright. Waves of dark blue pulsed through the perfect black. It was almost as silent inside the cockpit as out.

"How are *you* holding up, Jack?" Only Rogan could simultaneously hold a conversation *and* programme faster-than-light travel. "After hearing that broadcast, I mean. Are you ready for what we might find?"

A few days after the battle at the Iris superstructure, the *Adeona* had received an emergency distress signal from almost the exact spot where they once found Jack floating helplessly in space. This alone might not have warranted much surprise or excitement, but the broadcast appeared to originate from the *Final Dawn* – the same Ark for which Jack had once risked his life to get tickets.

Despite Everett Reeves' attempt to create an insane, genocidal singularity ending in failure, humanity was somehow still alive.

"Yeah, I'm ready. I'm excited. These are my people. This is what everything we did was for."

"I'm excited, too. But remember what happened when you heard about Amber. Remember Earth. Please don't get your hopes up too high, okay?"

Jack took a deep breath and nodded.

"If even one other human made it out alive... well for hope, that's reason enough."

"WAKE UP, Jack. We're almost there."

Jack jolted upright in the captain's seat, momentarily disoriented. He must have nodded off. He and Rogan were still alone in the cockpit. Tuner was downstairs somewhere, and Klik presumably still slept in her quarters.

"When you say almost," he grumbled, stretching his arms above his head until the joints popped, "how soon do you—"

Rogan nodded at the windows.

"Coming out of subspace in three... two..."

Jack gripped the arms of his pilot's seat so hard he left curved fingernail marks in the leather. The prospect of reuniting with humanity again... the anticipation was almost unbearable.

"... one..."

From the perspective of those inside the *Adeona*, the ship came to an abrupt stop as it dropped out of subspace and back into regular space-time. In reality, she was still hurtling through space at hundreds if not thousands of miles per hour. And though the cosmic scene before them appeared to rush forward into existence like a tight elastic band being released, it was in fact *they* who had suddenly appeared.

"Oh my God," Jack gasped. He jumped to his feet and leaned forward with his hands pressed against the dashboard. "There she is. The *Final Dawn*."

The great Ark ship looked almost identical to how he saw it last. Two kilometres long and almost a kilometre in diameter, its cylindrical outer shell rotated slowly to reveal the giant letters of its name stencilled down its side. The only difference, in fact, was that it now appeared to be floating lifelessly on its side in space rather than standing stoic and upright on its colossal concrete launch platform.

That, and the torrent of electrical sparks which gushed out from a nasty gash on its backside.

"They're in trouble." Jack threw himself back into his captain's chair and yanked the straps across his chest. "We've got to—"

"Hold on, space ranger." Rogan pressed a button and the view outside the cockpit window magnified. "It looks like your friends have it covered."

The hull of the *Final Dawn* was even clearer now.

Hovering near to the gash in the hull – which on closer inspection was actually nowhere near as bad as Jack first thought – were two small, grey shuttles designed not dissimilarly to deep sea bathyscaphes. Roughly spherical and adorned with all manner of nodes and external cameras, they used their chunky, robotic arms to weld and bolt the exterior wall together. Jack couldn't tell if the vessels were manned or controlled remotely.

But they weren't what drained the colour from Jack's face. For a moment, he forgot to breathe. Tethered to an airlock door not far from the damage was an astronaut in a pristine white spacesuit. He or she appeared to be inspecting the damage and performing engineering work too fiddly for the larger vessels.

A human. His heart fluttered. He was looking at an actual living *human*.

This was even better than he'd dared hope.

"Okay, that's it." Jack pressed a button on the dashboard and the windows reverted to their normal view. He grabbed the joystick and ignited the *Adeona's* thrusters. "I'm taking us in."

Rogan marched to the front of the cockpit and pointed.

"Not if *they* have anything to say about it, you're not."

Slowly and with a heavy knot growing in his stomach, Jack came to realise that the *Final Dawn* was not the only ship out there. Not by a long shot. From behind the Ark emerged three enormous military battlecruisers. Their flanks were covered with artillery cannons. Jack read the words *UECS Invincible* written down the side of one cruiser and *UECS Constellation* down the side of another.

Who or what the UEC was, Jack hadn't a clue. He was much more concerned about the dozen or so gunships streaming out from inside the battlecruisers' industrial hangar doors.

Yep. Those he distinctly *did* remember working on back in the Pits.

"Erm, what do we do?" Jack's grip on the joystick remained steadfast, but his hands began to shake. "From their perspective, an alien ship just entered their airspace. Or space-space, or whatever. If we flee, they might shoot us down. If we stay here... well, humanity has never encountered an alien race before. They might shoot us down anyway."

"We came here because they sent out an emergency broadcast," replied Rogan, backing away from the windows. "So try broadcasting a message back out to them!"

Jack scrambled through the *Adeona's* various communication formats until he reached the option for radio wave. It was one of the most primitive systems on board, but he couldn't be sure that humanity was working with anything more sophisticated on their end.

"There are hostile ships coming towards us and we don't appear to be doing very much about it," said the voice of the *Adeona*. Jack jumped. "Are you sure you wouldn't like me to get us out of here? Or perhaps fire a couple of warning shots?"

"No!" Jack's finger hovered over the broadcast button. "No. Everything's under control."

God, he hoped the people flying those gunships spoke English. He didn't know if the translator chip could interpret any other human languages yet.

"Hello? Can anyone hear me? This is Jack Bishop broadcasting from the *Adeona*. We are not a threat. I repeat, we are not a threat!"

He released the broadcast button, but the gunships

didn't stop. They simply spread out and continued on their course to intercept them. Despite growing concern about his impending annihilation, Jack couldn't help noticing that some of the gunships were flying a little less graciously than the others. He wondered if any of the pilots had ever had the chance to fly a ship in space before.

"What should we do now?" he asked Rogan.

"Wait and see," she replied, sitting on a chair hidden at the back of the cockpit. "You wanted to check in with humanity. I suspect this is a risk you have to take."

"What are you sitting all the way back there for?"

"You said your kind has never encountered an alien before." Rogan ducked further out of sight. "If they look inside the cockpit, it's probably best if a chrome automata isn't the first thing they see."

"Good point." Jack gritted his teeth. "In that case, we'd really better hope Klik doesn't choose this moment to drag herself out of bed."

The gunships were surely within attacking range of the *Adeona* by now, but none of them had fired up their rotary cannons or launched any missiles. Not yet, anyway. They slowed to a stop – some more clumsily than others, Jack once again noticed – in an almost semi-circular formation around their ship. This told Jack one thing, at least. Lethal force was still very much on the table.

Nobody moved. Nobody said anything. Jack squinted at each gunship in turn, hoping to make out the face of a pilot inside its cockpit, but it was in vain. He considered magnifying the view, but this really wasn't the best time for curiosity. If evasive manoeuvres were called for in the immediate future, he needed a clear view.

Jack was hesitant to press the broadcast button again in case it surprised any of the gunship pilots into accidentally firing a rocket. But he was the one who jumped a second later as a loud, sharp message flooded the cockpit.

"Identify yourself."

The voice was undeniably human with no translation required. Jack thought he picked up a Scottish accent, in fact. It was the first human voice to address him other than Everett Reeves since... well, since that Stone fellow had helped him into his spacesuit ready for the wormhole test.

How had that only been three months ago?

"I've switched your comms to match their frequency," said Rogan, her head barely poking above her console.

Jack took a deep breath and held down the broadcast button again.

"My name is Jack Bishop. I'm human. I used to work in the Pits back at Sandhurst. Please do not shoot me."

He waited for a response.

"Your ship has no UEC registration number," replied the same pilot as before. Jack thought some of the fear had left his voice. "What did you say your name was?"

"Jack Bishop."

A much longer pause followed. Jack leaned back in his chair and anxiously chewed the skin around his fingernails.

"You are to be escorted down to the *Final Dawn*, Mr. Bishop. Do not change course or we will be forced to open fire. Do you copy?"

"I copy. Thank you."

The gunships formed a cage around the *Adeona*, blocking their escape. The ship in front led the pack forward and Jack dutifully followed, careful to keep his speed to an absolute minimum. He suspected he could outpace them easily, and he didn't want to give any of the (understandably nervous) pilots the wrong idea.

The *Final Dawn* grew larger outside the windows. My

God, it was majestic. Clunky, archaic and in desperate need of a paint job... but majestic all the same. The closer they got, the more Jack could pick out the specific details along its outer shell – antennae, vents and thrusters, and even the golden glow of lights radiating from inside porthole windows.

His heart rate quickened further. Earth as he knew it might be gone, but that much didn't matter. Home was wherever humanity was – of that, Jack was convinced.

And if humanity was alive, then maybe...

The gunship convoy descended – in so much as any ship in space can be said to descend, of course – towards a set of hulking great doors set in the side of the *Final Dawn's* rotating exterior. The doors shuddered open upon their approach to reveal a hangar within. Humanity might have mastered the basics of space travel, but apparently it was still miles away from developing forcefield tech.

"Land your ship in the bay directly ahead," came the Scottish pilot's voice. "Do not deviate or..."

"Or you will be forced to open fire," Jack mumbled to himself. "Yeah, I heard you the first time."

He carefully guided the *Adeona* into the hangar, keenly aware of the two massive cannons tracking the ship from either side of the doors. To his astonishment, marshallers in heavy duty spacesuits were beckoning him in to land. They were tethered to the hangar floor to keep from being sucked out into the vacuum of space.

Jack couldn't help but laugh.

"Something the matter, Jack?" asked Rogan.

"No, nothing. Just... Everything's so weirdly familiar, that's all. Different and yet the same."

The *Adeona* landed. Jack immediately switched off all of the engines and thrusters. The industrial doors behind them grunted to a close again. As oxygen was pumped back into the hangar, the flashing red lights on its ceiling and walls switched to green.

A whole squad of helmeted marines stormed out from a security door on the other side of the hangar and trained their battle rifles on the stationary ship.

"What's going on?" said Klik, wandering into the cockpit. "Did we land somewhere?"

"Stay back," Jack hissed urgently. He ushered her back out through the doors. "Don't let them see you!"

"Are we on a human ship?" Klik's eyes grew wide. "Woah! When do we get to look around?"

"*You're* not looking around anywhere. It's too dangerous. No offence, but you're a giant insect. They'd probably shoot you on sight."

Klik looked at Rogan, who shrugged in agreement.

"If it makes you feel any better, I'm not going out there either."

"Seriously? *Seriously?*" Klik threw her hands in the air. "Every time things get interesting..."

They watched her stomp back to her quarters.

"She'll get over it," said Jack. "Rogan, take Klik and Tuner down to the engine room. There aren't any windows there. We don't want to give anyone a reason to inspect the ship."

"Got it."

Rogan hurried after Klik as Jack climbed down the steps that led to the lower deck. He paused halfway.

"Oh, and Adi?"

"Yes, Jack?" came the voice of the ship.

"You're in charge while I'm gone. Raise your loading ramp as soon as I disembark. Nobody comes or goes without my say-so, okay?"

"Aye aye, Captain."

Jack reached the bottom of the stairs and stood alone in the empty cargo bay. Ahead of him, the loading ramp finished opening with a solid *clunk*.

This was it. This was everything humanity had been working towards ever since the first solar flare hit Earth all those years ago. The end of one chapter... and the beginning of another.

He took a deep breath and followed the ramp down.

2

THE FINAL DAWN

Jack stood in the hangar before a dozen semi-automatic rifles as the *Adeona's* ramp rose up behind him. Despite the threat, he couldn't help but smile. Twelve humans were less than ten metres away from him. *Twelve*. Or at least, he believed they were humans. With their dark helmets on, he couldn't actually be sure.

He'd considered wearing his own spacesuit and helmet – the set custom-built by Tuner, rather than the defunct one he first wore through the wormhole – but decided against it. The filters and shock absorbers needed fixing, and he didn't want to come across as too aggressive. He went out in his t-shirt and cargo pants instead.

The silence got awkward.

"So..." Jack twiddled his thumbs behind his back. "No 'welcome home' banner? Which one of you wants to give me the tour?"

None of the marines replied. The security door through which they entered slid open once more, and this time a lone officer entered the hangar. She wore a smart, black uniform. Her grey hair was pulled back into a tight bun.

Jack gasped. He actually recognised her... sort of.

"Captain Blatch?" He stared at her in disbelief. "Is that you?"

The woman approaching him through the crowd of marines certainly *looked* like the Captain Blatch he last saw overseeing the wormhole experiment. The same hard eyes, the same commanding stride. But like Everett, she was older than when they last met. *Much* older.

"It's Admiral Blatch now, thank you." Her eyes flickered between him and the *Adeona*. "And what did you say your name was?"

"Jack Bishop, ma'am. Don't you... Don't you remember me?"

Admiral Blatch studied Jack for a long moment. His stomach fell. But then the admiral's hard glare softened.

"My God. It is you, isn't it? How? We all assumed you were dead." She shook her head. "Hell, you *should* be dead."

"Tell me about it. I almost suffocated to death thanks to that experiment of yours."

"If I recall correctly, I did tell you it was a bad idea." She gestured for the marines behind her to stand down, and they lowered their rifles. "Do you realise how incredible this is? Of all the original trials, you were the only subject to be transported successfully. All of our FTL tech – it's based on the data you gave us. For you to be stood here now..."

She looked over his shoulder and nodded.

"Where'd you find the ship?"

"She rescued me."

"Who did?"

"The ship."

Admiral Blatch raised a grey eyebrow as she scrutinised the cockpit windows.

"And if I were to order an inspection of your ship, what would I find?" she asked slowly.

"Nothing that you nor anyone else on the *Final Dawn* needs to be concerned about," Jack replied firmly. "Everyone is safe, I promise. Let's just say there's a lot about the galaxy you don't know yet."

"I'm beginning to think you're right." Admiral Blatch returned her fascinated gaze to Jack and gestured to the security door. "Well, let's not stand around in the hangar all day. I have an office we can use. I'm sure we both have a lot of questions to ask one another."

"My ship." Jack stood firm. "Nobody touches it."

"You did tell me you were a pilot all those years ago, didn't you?" She nodded. "Don't give us a reason to go near it, and we won't."

Jack looked back at the *Adeona*. He thought of Rogan, Tuner and Klik hiding down in the engine room where they couldn't be spotted accidentally walking past a window and suddenly felt terrible. But humanity wasn't ready for them. Not yet. And this was something he had to do.

He followed Blatch to the security door while the marines stood guard around the hangar and got the green *All Clear* from a contaminant scanner. Jack took one last glance at the *Adeona* over his shoulder as the admiral ushered him into the transport shuttle beyond.

"Welcome back to humanity," she said as the shuttle doors closed behind them.

ADMIRAL BLATCH POURED two glasses and handed one to Jack. He took it with both hands as if it were a prized artefact.

"Is this bourbon?" he asked. "Like, actual *human* bourbon?"

She pulled an amused face.

"Of course. Is there any other kind?"

He took a sip and sank further into his armchair.

"Oh my God, that's good. I barely had any of this stuff even when I was back on Earth."

Blatch relaxed into her own chair on the other side of her desk and laughed.

"Well, savour it. It's not exactly much of a common commodity these days, either."

They were sat in Admiral Blatch's personal office. Had he not personally piloted a spaceship into the Ark's hangar, Jack might have believed he was back on Earth before the flares hit. Their armchairs were plush. The desk was made from solid oak. Bookshelves, certificates and military commendations lined the walls. She even had one of those globe-shaped drink cabinets, which Jack thought was sort of ironic, all things considered.

The shutters were down over the windows for the time being. Neither had Jack directly encountered any other humans on their trip to her office. He'd mentioned to Blatch in passing during their ride in the shuttle that she was one of the first humans he'd met in months, and she called ahead for security to clear the route for them. The words "you might find everything a bit overwhelming" hadn't been explicitly said, but the sentiment was definitely there... and it hung both ways, so to speak.

He could scarcely contain his excitement.

Baby steps, though. The pain of shutting down Everett's black hole and believing humanity to be wiped out forever wasn't something he'd forget in a hurry. He still found the idea of sitting down and sharing a drink with another human being a little hysterical. So maybe he wasn't quite ready yet.

Maybe.

He took another sip of bourbon to calm his nerves.

"So, erm... you look different?" he said.

Blatch let out a sharp laugh. "Older, I think you mean. It's been quite a while since you left us. Though I dare say not for everyone – how much time has passed for you?"

"Three months or so." He put his glass down on the desk. "But Admiral, the Earth..."

"Gone now, I assume." She took a large gulp of bourbon and shut her eyes. "Horrible to think about. Our scientists and engineers tell me the wormholes took us about twenty-seven thousand years ahead of our departure date. *Twenty-seven thousand years*. Christ. How is anyone supposed to comprehend that? I suppose everyone we left behind is long dead by now."

Jack said nothing. Everyone would learn about their husk of a homeworld sooner or later anyway. He had more pressing questions of his own to ask.

"So, what happened after the experiment?" He steepled his fingers in front of his face. "Tell me everything."

"Well, where to begin?" Blatch raised her eyebrows. "We thought you were dead, of course. None of the other test pilots survived and we couldn't find your body in the wreckage of the machine. We assumed that even if you *had* made it through alive, you wouldn't stay that way for long without a life support system. The powers-that-be ordered for the project to be shuttered and the funds diverted to other technological breakthroughs. Stasis chambers, Alcubierre drives – that sort of thing. None of which came to fruition, obviously. Only Reeves had the belligerence to comb through all the data your suit sent back and realise that the experiment had actually worked. In a manner of speaking," she added.

"But nobody would listen to him," said Jack, leaning further forward in his chair. The bourbon was warming his belly. "So he had to run the next experiment on himself."

"Yes. With disastrous results, unfortunately. He..." Admiral Blatch stopped and screwed up her face. "Wait. How the hell do you know that?"

Jack sat back in his chair.

"It's a long story. Remind me to fill you in later. Please, continue. What happened after Everett destroyed his machine a second time?"

"Nothing," Blatch replied, casting a curious eye over Jack. "He wasn't supposed to continue with his experiments in the first place. We launched an investigation into the misappropriation of military funds but quite frankly, I didn't see the point. Reeves was gone, and with him we'd lost one of the smartest minds in our fight for faster-than-light travel."

She paused in thought.

"What year did you leave us?" she asked. "Twenty-forty-one?"

"Twenty-forty-two," Jack corrected.

"Right. Twenty-forty-two." Blatch nodded. "Which means Everett vanished in twenty-forty-three. By that time things were starting to get worse. More terrorist attacks against Ark sites. Constant rioting in the streets from those who feared being left behind. Nobody could blame them, but... Well, the years after that were tough. Tough for all of us.

"I think it was twenty-fifty or thereabouts when the autonomy of individual nations was abandoned and the United Earth Government was reborn as the UEC, or United Earth Collective. The Arks had been an international effort before, but the UEC took everything one step further. They kept building and building and building. Recruiting, too. I presume you saw the battlecruisers on your way in?"

Jack nodded. "I think I recognised the gunships, but those battlecruisers – boy, we sure weren't building *them* when I was down in the Pits."

"With most of the Arks already complete, there wasn't much else for the world's population to do. The UEC took humanity from a species simply desperate to leave Earth to a military force ready to colonise the galaxy." Blatch chuckled without much humour. "Well, I say military. Most of our troops have never held a rifle before. God help us if we actually have to go to war with anything. But between enlisting as a marine or roasting to death on an abandoned planet, well..."

Jack took another drink.

"So, what happened? How come you're all here now?"

"Ah, yes." She topped up both their glasses. "Well as I said, our projects exploring other methods of crossing the cosmos didn't amount to much. Everyone was desperate. A whole new generation was being brought up on a dying planet, and the solar flares were only getting worse. But then somebody on the board of the UEC – her name was Kendis Walker, if I remember correctly – she came across Reeves' work and decided to reopen the wormhole project. A fresh pool of the world's smartest minds built on the work Reeves started, using the same data *you* brought back to us. I guess that's why we arrived only a few months apart from one another. It took more than a decade to get the wormhole tech to transport anything as big as an Ark or a battlecruiser, but the boffins managed it. July the sixth, twenty-seventy-one. That's when we finally took off. That's when humanity *finally* headed for the stars."

Admiral Blatch drained her bourbon in a single gulp.

"My watch tells me it's been thirty-one hours since we launched. But according to the universe, humanity's exodus happened twenty-seven thousand years ago! Christ. I can't wrap my head around it without a drink."

"Almost thirty years." Jack slowly shook his head. "How on earth did you keep going?"

Blatch returned a sad smile. Her wrinkles looked deeper than ever.

"Like I said, it was tough. But enough of the past. Humanity's future lies ahead of us... and I want to know what secrets lie on board that ship of yours."

Jack shifted awkwardly in his armchair.

"I don't know if you're ready for that yet. Everything you think you know will change."

"Try me. I doubt *you* were ready and yet here you are, mind still intact. Besides, I'm the admiral of a UEC fleet. Whatever you know, I'm sure I'll find out sooner or later."

"Okay." Jack chewed his lip. "But for now, everything I say stays in this room. I don't want everyone on the Ark heading down to the hangar to take a look."

He leaned forwards.

"We're not alone in the universe. Maybe we were before we left Earth, but we're not now. There are hundreds of thousands of alien civilisations out here, many of which are brought together in a galactic council called the Ministerium of Cultured Planets. My ship, the *Adeona*, isn't a 'she' because of any silly old naming convention – she's a member of our crew in her own right. There's Tuner, who used to be a scrappy little hacker but is basically now a war machine on legs, and Rogan, who's pretty much the smartest person you could ever hope to meet. They're both automata, which are basically robots but don't *ever* let them hear you call them that. And rounding off our little group is Klik – a refugee from the Mansa Empire. Oh, and she's a hormonal insect humanoid with acidic spit and bone blades that extend from her forearms, by the way. That's probably worth mentioning up front."

"Uh huh." Admiral Blatch smirked. "Very funny. Seriously, though. Which fringe group of humanity got to you first?"

Jack fixed her with a deadpan stare. Her smirk fell.

"Oh. You weren't kidding." She sank back in her chair, deflated. "Jesus. If I'd known you were going to say that, I would have saved more of my drink."

"Hell, I didn't even get to any of the weird stuff." Jack finished the last of his own bourbon. "But don't worry. An unregistered species suddenly turning up with a fleet this size? I'm sure you'll hear from the Ministry soon enough."

"A fleet this size?" Blatch perked back up. "Oh, Jack. You don't know the half of it. Almost every Ark has two or three battlecruisers as escorts. And though some of the Arks are still yet to arrive, we believe all one hundred and eighty four of them launched successfully. In fact, more are entering the star system as we speak."

"Bloody hell. How many people did the UEC manage to get off Earth in the end?"

"Spread out across all the Arks and cruisers? About a hundred million, give or take." She smiled. "It must feel pretty good to know it was your experiment that made saving them all possible. I only wish Everett Reeves were alive to see it, too."

Jack bowed his head and kept his mouth shut. Little did she know...

"So." Admiral Blatch rose from her chair as sharply as a woman in her mid-to-late seventies could. Jack hurriedly followed suit. "Given everything you've told me, I think you're ready."

"Ready? Ready for what?"

She picked a data pad up from her desk and tapped a button on the screen. The shutters covering her office windows began to rise.

"Ready to rejoin humanity, of course."

Jack's jaw dropped as the light from outside flooded in. He stumbled around to the other side of the large, wooden desk as if anaesthetised. A million different thoughts exploded across his brain in a synaptic supernova.

"Oh my God," was all he could muster.

A long, wide promenade stretched out directly beneath the admiral's office, eventually disappearing below the *Final Dawn's* curved horizon. Stars swept past small portholes embedded in the titanium ceiling as the Ark's barrel-shaped exterior rotated, generating the centrifugal force that simulated gravity on board the ship. A row of shrubs and rosebushes in soil-filled planters ran along the centre of the walkway, flanked by wooden benches on either side. And crowds of lucky citizens wandered up and down the gardened pavement, clearly anxious from the previous day's take-off yet many sporting smiles as big as crescent moons.

"It might be a long while before anyone here gets the chance to set foot on a new world," said Admiral Blatch, waving politely at a little girl below. "In the meantime, this is their home."

"It's incredible," Jack replied, his vocabulary still momentarily neutered.

"It ought to be. This is all there is now."

Jack watched in awe as a small bird – some kind of wren, possibly – hovered by the glass before fluttering down to settle on one of the planters. Not a hologram, not a robotic replica – a real bird of flesh, blood and feathers. Unbelievable. Many species had gone extinct, save for those protected in conservations or brought back thanks to extensive genetic cataloguing. And beyond that, Jack spotted something else he assumed had long ago died out – the neon signs of stores and restaurant chains and cola brands as the garden promenade assimilated into the Ark's extensive consumer district.

It was like being back on Earth.

No, that wasn't true. The Earth had become a miserable shadow of its former self long before he left it.

This was better.

Better... except for one important detail.

"Amber," he gasped, quickly turning back to face Admiral Blatch. "My wife, Amber Bishop. What happened to her? Is she here?"

The admiral opened her mouth as if to say something, then sighed and solemnly nodded her head instead.

"I think you ought to come with me," she said.

3

GOLDILOCKS

Admiral Blatch led Jack to an elevator, which shuttled them at high speed to a district on the other side of the *Final Dawn* that was off-limits to the general public. They disembarked into a pristine white lobby and wandered down corridors flanked by computer labs teeming with scientists and engineers. Not one of them looked up at Jack through the large glass windows. And why would they? They had no clue who he was. Still, Jack felt an insane urge to wave at each and every person he passed.

Actual people. He couldn't get his head around it.

"Everyone looks so... natural," he said. "It's like they've lived in space their whole lives. Didn't you only launch yesterday?"

The admiral smiled.

"The wormhole launch, yes. The Arks actually took off and left the Earth's atmosphere five days beforehand. It gave everyone on board a chance to adjust... and to make sure there weren't any unforeseen hiccups. Everyone got a double dose of promethazine to combat anxiety and nausea – one to take prior to take-off and another for 'the punch', as the FTL physicists like to call going through the wormhole. The latter was actually the gentler of the two launches, believe it or not. Besides, there's too much at stake for anyone behind the scenes to stop. There *have* been hiccups."

"Oh, yeah! I saw that sparking gash down by the Ark's thrusters. What the hell happened? Was that why you sent out the emergency broadcast?"

"Ah, yes." Blatch nodded. "Not as bad as we first thought, thankfully. We hit something coming out of the wormhole. Debris of some kind. Nothing to worry about, though." She raised a doubtful eyebrow. "Not yet, anyway."

They turned a corner towards a security door. A guard posted outside saluted with a snap when he saw Admiral Blatch approaching.

"At ease," she said, after returning the salute. "Just here to visit the archives. He's with me."

"Yes, ma'am." The guard entered a code into the keypad next to him and the door hissed open. "Right this way."

He escorted them into an unoccupied hall full of computer servers, then returned to his original post. The door hissed shut behind him. All was quiet, save for an idle electrical hum, and all was *very* cold.

"This much processing power has a tendency to run hot," she said, noticing Jack shiver. "Can't risk them overheating, especially on a spacecraft."

"Couldn't we have just logged in from somewhere else?"

"No. Access to this data is extremely restricted – for obvious reasons. This is a rare courtesy, for old times' sake. Ah. Here we are."

They stopped beside the only server in the hall with a keyboard interface built into its front. A blank monitor flickered to life upon their approach. Jack stuck his hands under his armpits for warmth whilst Admiral Blatch pressed one of hers onto the screen. A green glow flashed beneath her fingers as she was granted access.

After a brief hunt through the console's directories, she stepped aside and gestured to the terminal.

"Go ahead."

Jack's hands hovered over the keyboard. It had been a while since he used a computer interface that the alien chip in the back of his neck didn't need to translate. Classic QWERTY. But once his fingers got their bearings, he knew exactly who to search for.

"Amber Bishop," he mumbled to himself while slowly typing out her name.

The search returned thousands of results. He scrolled through the list, surprised. He never realised how common her name was.

"This is a database of every human who ever lived, going all the way back to when humanity's records first began." Blatch reached across Jack and pointed to a three-lined icon in the corner of the screen. "Press that. Try a sub-search using her date of birth. I assume you remember it."

Jack followed her instructions. This time only two results came up. One was an Australian citizen. The other was British. Jack tapped his finger on the latter.

His heart fell, just as he knew it would.

Amber's photograph – sourced from her old passport, Jack believed, before the flares – was the first thing he saw in her file. It was far from a flattering picture, but it didn't matter. Until that moment, all he had were his memories. She looked tired and serious, yet to Jack she was more beautiful than ever before.

It was her, all right.

Amber Bishop, born Amber Rogers, date of birth: 13/04/2015.

Date of death: 27/03/2064.

Cause: Radiation poisoning.

Jack sighed and suppressed a sob. Rogan had told him not to get his hopes up. And deep down he knew that she was most likely dead anyway, having all but condemned her to such a fate when he put a stop to Everett's black hole. Yet none of that took the sting out of seeing it typed out in an official document.

She'd gone on to live almost twenty-two years without him. If only she could have held on for another seven more...

But seven years is a long time to hold on when your sun is blasting out deadly solar waves every other day. And even if she *had* made it on board one of the Arks, their life together... It wasn't as if anything could have gone back to the way it was. Amber would have moved on. And besides, he was still only twenty-nine. If she'd lived, she would now be fifty-six. It wouldn't have worked – not for her, not after all this time.

Still. It would have been far, *far* preferable to this.

"I'm sorry," said Admiral Blatch, laying a hand on his shoulder. "I must say, you're handling the news pretty well. Better than I would."

"Let's just say I had time to prepare for it."

He started to scroll further through her file, to more deeply explore the details of her life after he vanished, when Blatch coughed rather deliberately.

"Sorry to cut this short, but I must get back to the bridge and I can't leave you here alone. You shouldn't really be here at all. I can get somebody to give you a copy of her file, if you'd like?"

Jack frantically wondered if there was anyone else he ought to look up before they left. Both of his parents had died long before the wormhole experiment, thank God – his mother when he was seven, and his father a year after the first solar flare hit Earth. He supposed he could search for Morgan and the other engineers who worked with him in the Pit, but that hardly seemed an urgent enough request to warrant delaying the admiral any further. He doubted any of them got tickets for the Ark anyway.

"Of course. A copy of Amber's file would be nice, thanks."

Blatch smiled and gently guided him back towards the door. The screen on the server switched itself off behind them.

"In the meantime," she said, "we'll have to decide what to do with you. I'm not sure we have any spare quarters available, but I suppose you've already got your ship. I'll arrange for someone to come and give you the full tour of the *Final Dawn* as soon as possible."

Jack gave this some thought. Stopping for a while *would* be nice. A few days not spent racing across the galaxy to stop a mad warlord from destroying a star system or wading through a criminal underworld to uncover a government conspiracy might even do him some good. His stomach rumbled, and he wondered if he could get a proper pub lunch anywhere on the Ark.

It wasn't as if he hadn't spent the last three months trying to find a way back to humanity, after all. Now that he'd managed it, he ought to enjoy the reunion as much as he could.

But...

But humanity was at its most vulnerable, perhaps even at its most ignorant. After everything he'd seen across the galaxy, he couldn't just sit back and watch them scramble in the cosmic dark.

They needed him. And he needed to help.

Because without a purpose, what else did he have left?

"Excuse me, ma'am?" Jack had momentarily fallen behind in the stark, white corridor, and he hurried to catch up with the admiral. "I don't mean to intrude, but... well... I was wondering if there was anything I could do to help. You're searching for a new homeworld for humanity, right? Or maybe I could reach out to the other, erm, *inhabitants* of the galaxy as a sort of ambassador, or something. I just can't bear to sit around feeling useless. Not right now. Not after everything."

Admiral Blatch didn't slow her pace. An urgent notification flashed on the data pad from which she was reading. For a moment Jack thought she was going to ignore him entirely.

"I appreciate the offer, Mr. Bishop, but we have professionals in place. I'm sure your continued survival alone will be inspiration enough once word gets out. Now, I really must get back to the bridge. I've got a missing drop ship to find and a rear Ark thruster that still needs fixing. Hardly the best start to mankind's new chapter, if you ask me."

Jack power-walked alongside her.

"Missing drop ship? That's easy! Just give me its last recorded location. My crew and I will go get them."

Blatch couldn't help smirking, even if she did look a little apologetic about it.

"With all due respect, we have an entire fleet of ships and marines at our disposal. You're a civilian, Jack. I'm hardly going to trust you and your foreign ship with a classified mission."

"With all due respect, *ma'am*, in the past three months I've battled rabid space pirates, stabilised collapsing stars and stolen dangerous technology from one of the most powerful empires in the galaxy. Tracking down a lost ship sounds like a quiet Sunday morning in comparison. *I'm* not the one out of my depth here."

The admiral stopped sharp and scrutinised Jack from head to toe.

"You've come a long way from the mediocre engineer I first met thirty years ago, haven't you?"

She carried on walking. Jack deflated with a sigh. Oh well. It had been worth a try.

"Well, what are you standing around for?" Blatch called back at him over her shoulder. "If you insist on helping, you'd better follow me."

THE BRIDGE of the *Final Dawn* was enormous, easily dwarfing that of Gaskan Troi's *Confession*. Scores of technicians, chief scientists and miscellaneous military personnel busied themselves at computer stations or stood debating the many complicated charts projected onto the chamber's wide, circular wall.

Jack looked up in awe as he entered. The ceiling above their heads *appeared* totally transparent, but in reality it was just a video feed from a wide array of cameras on the exterior of the ship. Had the dome been made of glass, a single stray rock could have wiped out the Ark's entire command centre. For the sake of a slightly crisper view, it was simply too great a risk.

The bridge was one of the few sections of the Ark based in its central column rather than its rotating outer shell. Whereas those occupying the shell were kept glued to the floor by its perpetual centrifugal force, the bridge at the tip of the ship had to continue functioning even (and indeed, especially) during moments of extreme acceleration. That meant its floor was technically the wall facing the rear of the ship. Jack guessed humanity had developed some form of artificial gravity generator in the years between 2042 and 2071, because the *Final Dawn* wasn't going anywhere fast while repairs to its thruster were ongoing, and he wasn't floating up to the ceiling yet.

Outside, a small green planet drifted innocently amongst a sea of black.

Admiral Blatch impatiently snapped her fingers. Already she seemed to regret her decision to bring him along. Embarrassed, Jack stopped his gawking and followed her to a command table in the centre of the hall.

"Attention on deck," one of the officers declared.

"At ease," commanded Admiral Blatch. The poor officer hadn't even finished speaking before she irritably waved the protocol away. "We don't have time for everyone to be getting up and down each time I step through the door. This is Captain Dyer's ship. I just decide where it goes."

A man dressed in smart uniform on the other side of the command table, who Jack guessed was the captain in question, pursed his lips but said nothing.

Jack looked down at his t-shirt and cargo pants and felt hopelessly underdressed. Perhaps he should have worn his battle-scarred spacesuit after all.

"Officer Simmons," said the admiral, turning to a fresh-faced officer with his nose buried in a data pad. "Give me a sit-rep on my missing drop ship. Where are fireteams Alpha and Sigma?"

He lowered the data pad from his face and shook his head.

"Nothing new to report, ma'am. We were just briefing Fireteam Omega on their last known location."

A gruff, chisel-jawed man in combat fatigues stepped forward with his hands clasped firmly behind his back. He gave the admiral a quick, curt nod.

"Sergeant Kaine, ma'am. Honoured for our fireteam to be chosen. We won't let you down."

"Right. Well, hold off on that a moment." With a swish of her hand, Admiral Blatch changed the image on the central display screen to a three-dimensional map of the planet outside. "Are these the coordinates?"

Officer Simmons nodded. "Yes, ma'am."

"This is New Eden, Mr. Bishop." She beckoned him closer. "It's a goldilocks planet – that is to say, it has the perfect climate for humanity's needs. Our astronomers discovered it decades ago and, as luck would have it, it's become no less inhabitable in the millennia it took us to get here. We intend for New Eden to become our next home world."

She pointed at a blinking dot close to the planet's equator.

"We sent a couple of fireteams down to scout the terrain in advance, but we lost contact with them shortly after they entered the planet's atmosphere. It might just be equipment failure, but I'm wary of committing to a full colonisation until we know for sure. If you really want to help, get down there and find out what happened to them."

"Ahem." Officer Simmons cleared his throat. He had Jack's file up on his data pad. "All things considered, are you sure Mr. Bishop is the right man for the job? I mean..."

Sergeant Kaine snorted. Jack crossed his arms.

"I can handle myself, believe me."

"Oh, I'm sure." Simmons nodded enthusiastically and apologetically. "It's not that, sir. Rather, your d—"

"Jack will be fine." Blatch's expression grew stormy as she

waved Simmons' concerns away. "I know it's unconventional, but unlike everyone else in the UEC fleet, this man actually has experience of traversing alien worlds. And if it *is* a tech issue, he's the only one whose ship might not be affected. Got something you want to say, Sergeant?"

Sergeant Kaine's stubbled jaw clenched even further.

"Apologies, ma'am. I just don't see why sending a lone civilian is preferable to a fully trained fireteam."

"Because if there's something dangerous down there, I'll gladly take the opportunity to avoid losing any more marines than we might have already," she replied. Jack's blood ran cold. "Patience, Sergeant. If Mr. Bishop here doesn't report back to us within twelve hours, your squad will go in afterwards. We have to take this planet... by any means necessary."

Kaine nodded, and Jack could have sworn he saw a tiny smirk flash across his lips. The guy looked eager for action, all right. Too eager.

"Make sure Mr. Bishop has everything pertaining to the Eden mission," she instructed Simmons. "Coordinates, flight plans, etcetera."

Simmons raised a careful eyebrow.

"Everything, ma'am?"

"Everything he *needs*," she stressed, turning back to Jack. "Actually, that's a point. You do have a data pad, don't you?"

He felt like he was getting asked that a lot lately. Jack pulled his pad out of his trouser pocket. Originally manufactured on Kapamentis long before Jack first set foot there, it was of vastly superior design to anything human technicians had built before. Simmons looked at it with a mixture of horror and awe.

"Just send the files over," Jack said with a grin, swiping

the screen to establish a connection. "I've got some friends who can make them work."

"Speaking of which..." Admiral Blatch pulled Jack away from the command table, out of earshot. "Intelligence sort of assumed we were alone in the universe, given we never made contact before leaving Earth. We never even picked up any suspicious radio signals. What you've told me... it sort of throws the entire mission for a loop. God knows how the UEC board will react."

She paused.

"That's partly the reason why I'm letting you go ahead of the reserve unit. Half our marines still have pimples. They're too jumpy for their own good. If there's any sign of life down on New Eden – advanced, *intelligent* life, that is – you'll be uniquely equipped to handle the situation. Tell me everything you find. We need to know what we're up against."

Up against. Jack wasn't sure he liked the sound of that.

"Erm, yeah. Sure." He pocketed his data pad again. "Whatever the *Final Dawn* needs."

"Not just the *Final Dawn*," she said, once again resting a commanding hand on his shoulder. "It's what *humanity* needs. Remember: New Eden is our last hope. I'm counting on you, Jack. We all are."

She turned back to the table and raised her voice.

"Officer Simmons. Keep Fireteam Omega on standby so they're ready to deploy at a moment's notice." She checked her watch. "Jack, you'd best be heading back to your ship. Your twelve hours have already started."

She held out a wrinkled hand. Jack shook it.

"Good luck." She smiled warmly but her eyes were stone cold. "And welcome to the UEC."

4

NEW EDEN

Jack lugged the heavy crate into the *Adeona* and her loading ramp closed behind him. He set it down on the floor of the cargo bay with a loud, metallic clang.

"Welcome to the UEC," he muttered in disbelief, stretching his arms and limbering up his shoulders. "Whatever the hell *that* is."

"What's in the box, Jack?"

He jumped. Tuner stood a few metres away, half-hidden behind one of the hull's support beams.

"Bloody hell, Tuner. For a big guy, you're sure good at sneaking up on people."

"Yeah, I feel a little bit like I'm becoming part of the furniture." He pointed at the crate with the more dextrous of his two hands. "So. Box?"

Jack undid the two clasps holding the crate together and then threw the lid open. Tuner stomped his way across the cargo bay and peered inside.

"Nice! Who are we going to war with this time?"

Jack lifted the first of three battle rifles out of the crate and inspected it under one of the *Adeona's* dim lights. Without so much as a scratch on its dark grey paintwork, it looked as if it had never been fired. Beneath the first layer of foam packaging was a stash of loaded magazines, attachable scopes and, to Jack's greatest excitement, a few packets of vacuum-wrapped military rations. It was months since he'd eaten anything specifically designed for a human stomach. He couldn't wait to tuck into something vaguely chicken-flavoured.

"Did I hear you say war?" Rogan hesitantly entered the cargo bay with Klik by her side. "Oh, Jack. What have you got us into this time?"

"No!" Jack delicately put the rifle back into its foam casing. "It's nothing like that at all. This is... it's just a precaution. The humans are in a spot of bother and, well, I kind of offered them our help." He scratched the back of his neck. "Sorry, I should have asked you guys first. I hope that's okay."

"That depends on what they need help with, Jack." Rogan crossed her arms and glared at him. "Explain."

"My species plans to colonise the nearest planet, but they lost contact with a scout team that went down there. I said we'd go look for their ship."

"And?" Rogan twirled her finger to indicate he should continue. "Then what?"

Jack shrugged.

"And that's about all there is to it. We find them, or we don't, and then we report back."

"Oh." Rogan's robotic features softened. She looked at Tuner and Klik. "That really *is* nothing, isn't it?"

"Wait, does this mean I get to leave the ship?" asked Tuner, his mood brightening again.

"Sure does, buddy." Jack patted the side of Tuner's hulking, metal torso. "No more hunched-over sulking for you."

"What about me?" Klik clacked her thin mandibles.

"You'd better not be leaving me behind on the ship again. And I'm not wearing no stupid mask or cloak this time, either."

Jack laughed, though it did raise the interesting question of what would happen if they *did* run into any lost members of Fireteams Alpha and Sigma. The automata were one thing, but a walking, talking bug? That was bound to get some trigger-fingers twitching.

"No, you're coming too. We all are. You'll just need to be especially careful if we run into any humans, that's all."

Rogan looked up at the ceiling.

"How are you feeling, Adi? Up for another adventure?"

"If it's important to Jack, I'm in." The *Adeona* sounded uncharacteristically hesitant for someone who'd been acrobatically dogfighting Raklett attack ships only days before. "But some of my systems are still... suboptimal. I suspect I won't be much use if we run into any trouble."

"There won't *be* any trouble," Jack insisted. "New Eden is unpopulated. These guns are just a precaution."

"All right. Pop the coordinates into the NavMap and let's get going."

Klik excitedly ran off to her quarters to get ready. Jack started to climb the stairs to the cockpit when Rogan grabbed his arm.

"How was it?" she asked. "Seeing your people again. Less genocidal ones, I mean. How are you holding up?"

"I'm fine." Jack's shrug suggested otherwise. "It was... kinda weird. Everything's familiar and yet it's all so different, too. So much has changed since I left. I guess it takes a while for a place to feel like home, right?"

Rogan smiled sadly.

"Still, I would have thought you'd want to spend as much

time with your people as possible. You're rushing off almost as soon as you got here."

"I *do* want to spend time here," he replied. "But after the rest of humanity has spent decades fighting to escape the Earth... I can't just sit back and not do my fair share, you know? I can't just *exist*."

"I don't know, Jack. You almost died going through a wormhole for them. You risked your life a second time trying to get back. I'd say you've probably earned a break."

"It doesn't feel like it. Not having to grow old on a dying homeworld like everyone else? If anything, it makes me feel like I've been taking the piss."

He paused, unsure whether he should continue. But there was no point skirting the issue. Rogan was far too smart not to figure out what was coming next.

"Besides," he said, "there'll be plenty of time to assimilate with humanity once they establish a new homeworld."

"And you know that the rest of us won't be able to stay, right?" Rogan cast him a sympathetic look. "That once you go to live with the humans either on the *Final Dawn* or on that planet, sooner or later we'll need to go our separate ways?"

"Yeah." Jack sighed. "All the more reason to stick together while we still can."

"All right." Rogan squeezed his shoulder as she brushed past him on her way up the stairs. "I'll go get the coordinates locked in."

"Thanks."

Jack lingered in the empty bay for a moment before he followed her to the cockpit. Something was bothering him.

He was doing his part to help humanity build a new home.

So why did it only feel like he was leaving one?

THE *ADEONA* SWEPT DOWN towards the coordinates Simmons gave them – a point on the planet's southern hemisphere about sixteen hundred miles from its equator. Jack sat in the captain's chair, ready to take over in case the flight proved too much for the ship to handle alone.

New Eden was beautiful. He could see why humanity had chosen it as its new home. It was ten, maybe fifteen percent smaller than Earth, but he supposed that would hardly matter given their severely reduced population. It was just the right distance from its star – itself quite similar to their own Sol prior to its unexpectedly early death cycle – for its climates to permit comfortable human survival. A goldilocks planet, they called it. Not too hot, not too cold – just right.

Brushstrokes of white cloud migrated slowly across its atmosphere, periodically masking the lush continents and marble-blue oceans beneath. There seemed, at least from where Jack viewed it, to be a greater ratio of land to sea than back on Earth, though evidently this never had any effect on the proliferation of the planet's foliage. The land masses appeared truly green, even from way up in the heliosphere.

But there was much more beyond that. A great, thin belt of golden desert stretched across New Eden's middle. And at the planet's poles were colossal caps of ice and snow – tundras of brilliant, dazzling white that, like the rest of the world, remained utterly untouched.

It really was like a new Earth.

A paradise for the survivors.

The *Adeona* rattled and shook as she broke through the upper layers of atmosphere and started her proper descent towards where the drop ship had sent its last broadcast. Jack couldn't help but grip the joystick as they headed down. He hoped the ship didn't take it personally, but the last thing anyone needed was for their crew to end up stranded on New Eden too.

The continents grew closer and closer, until all that was visible outside the cockpit windows was a great alien forest stretching from horizon to horizon. Some of the trees grew hundreds of metres tall with trunks wide enough to build whole houses inside. Others possessed hard canopies that spread out like mushroom caps, overlapping one another to form giant, winding steps in their bid to capture sunlight. And some blossomed into vibrant yellow and pink flowers, their velvety petals and antennae-like stigmas swaying in the jungle breeze.

"It's kind of like Krett," Klik said absent-mindedly, as she sat down in one of the chairs at the rear of the cockpit.

Jack smiled. In truth, the flora was completely different. But he supposed, having been to only three worlds in her lifetime – Paryx, Kapamentis, and Krett – that yes, it wasn't a million miles away from the rainforest moon on which her species first evolved. Trillions of *literal* miles away though, of course.

A dark shadow suddenly washed over the top of the ship.

"What was that?" asked Rogan, hurriedly initiating half a dozen scans of their immediate environment.

"I think some of the locals have come to say hello," said the *Adeona*, closer to her usual cheerful self than before. "Nothing to worry about. Yet."

"Woah," said Klik, stalking towards the front of the cockpit for a better look. "What in the galaxy have *they* been eating?"

Three massive creatures overtook the ship, swimming

through the air with the grace of blue whales gliding beneath the ocean. Their bodies were cloaked with dark, leathery skin – all save for their wings, which were shaped like a pterodactyl's yet covered with bright orange plumage. Four short limbs hung inertly from their swollen bellies. Each slow flap of the closest beast's wings sent a quiver through the ship's hull.

"How the hell does anything that big stay in the air?" Jack shook his head in disbelief. "Each one of them is almost the size of you, Adi."

"Good thing I'm a ship and not offended by that comment, Jack." The *Adeona* lowered her altitude so that they were practically skimming over the treetops. "I suggest we find a suitable place to land as soon as possible, however. We don't know how territorial these creatures get. They might have a nest nearby."

"Good idea," said Rogan. "We're near to the drop ship's last known coordinates anyway. Looking for a landing zone now."

"You'll be lucky." Klik peered out the windows. "This planet has been left to grow wild. Look at all the plants! You won't find an open field anywhere round here."

"But we might find a river," said Rogan, with a self-satisfied smirk. "Scans show one about thirty seconds to the north-east of here."

"Got it," said the *Adeona,* correcting her course.

She ducked beneath the canopies of some of the taller trees and slowed to a hovering stop above what was more of a shallow, rushing stream than a river. Still, the plant-life surrounding the wide brook was sporadic enough that she could get within a few feet of the ground.

"I can drop you off here," she said, "but I doubt I can land. The ground is nowhere near stable enough and

"Me?" Rogan crossed her arms. "You know how I feel about firearms."

"And yet you're so good with them." Jack winked as he handed her one of the rifles. "Just as a precaution. In case you need to save my life again."

"What about me?" asked Tuner, peering into the empty crate. "Don't I get one?"

"I think your hands are too big, buddy. Sorry. One of your arms does double as a plasma cannon, though."

Tuner gloomily flexed the fingers on his oversized hand.

"Oh. Yeah. I guess you're right."

He stomped off down the loading ramp. Jack and Rogan looked at each other, shrugged, and followed him down.

The water gurgled as it flowed around pebbles and rocks in the stream below. Birds tweeted in the nearby trees. Jack could feel the heat of the fresh, tropical air wafting into the ship and was already glad he left his suit behind.

It was only a four or five foot drop, but the ground was unstable. A bad landing could mean a twisted ankle.

"Who's going first?" asked Jack, uneasily.

"I will," said Tuner, quickly. "It's barely a step for me."

He hopped off the end of the ramp – which wobbled like a diving board upon his departure, Jack couldn't help noticing – and landed in the stream with a blunt splash. It was as shallow as it looked, barely reaching past the hulking automata's ankles.

"Come on," he said, waving up at them. "I'll help you down."

Rogan went first, then Klik, and then finally Jack. Tuner carefully lowered each of them onto a rock close to the riverbank, from which it was only an easy hop onto solid, grassy ground. Then he trudged out of the water himself.

"We're clear, Adi." Rogan spoke the words aloud for Jack

and Klik's sake, but truly spoke to the ship via an internal comm channel. "Go on, get someplace safe. We'll call you if we need you."

If the *Adeona* said farewell, Jack couldn't hear her without his helmet. She let off a few of her smaller air thrusters in what he knew to be a friendly gesture, however, before launching herself up towards the atmosphere. The water churned, the trees shook, and then she was gone.

All around them was still, and all was silent.

Jack took a deep breath and tightened his grip on his rifle.

"Right then," he said. "Let's go find us a drop ship."

5

DROP SHIP DOWN

Jack let Rogan take the lead when it soon became apparent he had no clue how to navigate an alien rainforest. For all he was grateful not to be roasting inside his spacesuit, he sure missed some of its bells and whistles. Notably its compass, but also its protection against all the goddamn bugs.

"How much further?" he whispered.

A couple of metres ahead of him, Rogan rolled her eyes.

"A *lot* further," she replied. "The coordinates you got from the *Final Dawn* are only of the drop ship's last known transmission, not where it ended up. I hardly expect it just fell out of the sky like a brick. We've probably got some ways to go yet."

Jack shut his mouth and kept on walking. He was the reason why they were pushing their way through miles of damp, prickly undergrowth, after all. And he didn't actually *mind* the trek. It was quite nice, really. The fresh, humid air was a welcome respite from the recycled, gasoline-soaked atmosphere of Kapamentis, that was for sure. He just couldn't ignore the way the skin on the back of his neck grew tighter the further they ventured into the forest, or the fear that behind the next set of trees could be... well, literally anything.

And for some reason, drinking deep from the endless well that was his own ignorance, he'd sort of assumed there would be a path.

"My trousers are drenched," Klik muttered, pushing a large, dew-speckled leaf out of her way. "Did it rain just before we got here? Or is it always like this?"

"I hope it doesn't rain," said Tuner, bringing up the rear like a miniature bulldozer. "I'm already sinking into the mud as it is."

While Rogan succeeded in navigating their small group via a path of least floral resistance, Tuner pretty much flattened everything he passed. Jack saw it as a blessing. At least they wouldn't have trouble finding their way back to the stream if they got lost. And if they came across anything too dense, they could always put him in front.

He hoped Tuner didn't get stuck, though. They didn't exactly have a brilliant track record of fishing him out of things.

Jack looked up and watched a pair of small birds flitter and dance in the meagre gaps of sunlight permitted to leak between the close-knit treetop canopies, singing sweet, chirping melodies to one another. Closer to ground level, something croaked deeply like a toad. He hoped they didn't need to wade through a swamp. Flies and mosquitos – none of which carried anything toxic to humans or Krettelians, Jack hoped – buzzed to and fro around their heads, barely visible amongst the shimmering, tropical heat haze.

So far they hadn't come across anything larger than a bird or a bug... and it was starting to give Jack the creeps.

"Well, this is it." A further ten minutes later, Rogan

stopped walking and looked around. "Apparently. The transmissions stopped... well, not here," she corrected herself, pointing up at the sky, "but a few hundred metres up there."

Jack brushed aside a purple flower with dozens of leaves like thin, spongey ribbons and climbed on top of a rotting log. It didn't help improve his view much, unfortunately, and was too precarious to stand on for long.

"Not to be a downer or anything," said Klik, "but I don't see a drop ship anywhere." She shrugged. "Unless human ships are made of plants."

"I guess we keep going," said Tuner, swatting a fly away from his plasma cannon's exhaust port.

"The question," said Rogan, "is where? Like I said, the coordinates only take us to where their comms cut out. Our best bet is probably to follow their original flight plan, but we've no guarantee they weren't forced to take a different route. We could wander this place for days and never find them."

"And there I was," said Jack, laughing awkwardly, "forgetting that locating somebody usually involves a bit of searching."

Rogan crossed her arms.

"Was that sarcasm?"

"No. Unfortunately, it was the truth."

Jack slowly turned on the spot, peering through the thick trees. He didn't know why he bothered. Out of the four of them, his eyesight was definitely the worst. If there was anything – or any*one* – out there, he was sure he'd be the last to know about it. And he certainly wasn't about to spot a parked drop ship out the corner of his eye.

"Hold this," said Klik, handing her rifle to Tuner. "I'll go get a better view."

Tuner cradled the weapon. It looked pathetically small in his oversized hands.

"You're not going up there, are you?" he asked, craning his clunky torso upwards. "Some of those trees are as tall as buildings. You'll break your neck if you fall."

"Yeah, Klik." Jack shook his head. "Don't be silly. We'll just call Adi back down and get her to do a quick sweep of the area or something."

"Oh, shut up." Klik rubbed her insectoid hands together and then pounced onto the elephantine roots of the nearest alien sequoia. "I had to climb all sorts of things back when I did supply runs for the resistance. Market walls. Sewage pipes. A big tree's just nature's ladder, really."

"Okay, but..."

Klik was already off. She scrambled up the bark and bounded from branch to branch. Twice she seemed to lose her footing only to swing herself up to safety, where she would crouch like a panther ready to strike. After about a minute she reached a point perhaps fifty metres above Jack's head – high enough to see past most of the surrounding foliage. His heart was in his mouth the whole time.

"Do you see anything?" he shouted.

Klik stood upright on her branch and peered across the rainforest canopies, shielding her black eyes from the hot sun. Unless she climbed another few dozen metres higher – something even she was hesitant to do – some of her view would remain blocked.

"Smoke!" she suddenly exclaimed. "I can see smoke! There's not much, and I guess it could just be a forest fire, but..."

"Well that *has* to be something," Jack said enthusiastically to Rogan. He turned back to Klik. "Where's the smoke coming from?"

Klik jabbed a finger towards the source.

"That way."

"Can you be more specific?" Rogan called up at her. "Can you triangulate the coordinates? Is it north-east, or more of a north-*north*-east?"

"How the frick should I know?" Klik's rose half an octave, and she jabbed her finger even more aggressively in the direction of the smoke plume. "It's over *there!*"

"I suppose that'll have to do," Rogan sighed. The aperture of her eye lenses contracted as she studied Klik's finger. "I should be able to calculate an approximate route from here."

"Sounds good enough to me," said Jack. "Come on down, Klik. And for God's sake, be careful!"

She took much more time coming down than going up, resembling someone trying to tackle a ladder with half of its rungs missing. When she was about midway through her descent, Jack heard a noise in the woods behind him. A crack like a twig being snapped in half.

He spun around, his battle rifle raised. Rogan and Tuner did the same.

"What is it?" Jack hissed, peering through the dense mass of greenery.

"I'm not sure," Rogan whispered back. "I'm trying a few different sensors, but I'm not picking anything up. Nothing sizeable, at any rate."

Klik reached the ground before any of them dared relax. She took her rifle back from Tuner and tossed its strap over her shoulder.

"What is it?" she asked, breathless from her climb.

"Nothing." Jack finally lowered his weapon. "False alarm."

"Just some local wildlife." Rogan started walking again, her eyes wary and stern. "Still, let's get moving."

The forests of Oregon were once filled with all kinds of beasts, Jack reminded himself as they pressed on. Bears. Moose. Even the New Forest had ponies, deer and the occasional badger. It was inevitable that the jungles of New Eden would be full of their own critters scurrying through the undergrowth. Some big; some small. Some predators, and others prey.

He just hoped nothing out there was thinking of them as the latter.

ROGAN HACKED her way through a bush bursting with luminous seed pods. She stumbled through the resulting gap, then suddenly stopped short.

"Huh. Well, I guess we found your drop ship."

Jack pushed past Klik towards the front, ignoring the way the bush scratched at his bare arms. He didn't like the tone of Rogan's voice. It wasn't exactly overflowing with "mission accomplished" optimism.

"Oh, Christ." He froze beside her. "What the hell happened?"

There was no mistaking the drop ship, even if the model had improved somewhat from those he'd once welded together in the Pit. The letters *UEC* were even stencilled along its side in pale grey. But it was little wonder nobody up in the *Final Dawn* could get through to them. The ship had dropped, and then some.

Its nose was buried five or six feet in the ground – so deep, in fact, that the ruptured soil now crept up across the cockpit's cracked and shattered windows – and a twenty-metre long furrow had been carved through the earth in its wake. Smaller trees were felled; further back, upper branches and whole canopies had been sheered off as the ship dive-bombed into the forest. One of its thrusters had been sheered off in the crash and lay in a crumpled, dented mess amongst the ferns. Even if it hadn't, there was no way this ship was ever going to fly again.

And neither would its pilots.

One dangled halfway out of the smashed cockpit window like a dish cloth hung out to dry. The other was still fastened into his seat, but it hadn't done him much good. The whole left side of the ship had buckled inwards, crushing his chest like a coke can. The sheer amount of dried blood both inside and outside the cabin told Jack that checking either of them for a pulse was futile.

"Oh, that smell does *not* improve in the heat," said Klik, following them into the small clearing once Tuner had crushed a suitable path for her. "Well, this is a shame. It would have been nice to go back with good news."

"Or people," said Tuner, tilting his substantial body. "Going back with *people* would have been even better."

Jack crept around the ship, surveying the damage. The smoke plume Klik had spotted stemmed from an electrical fire in one of its rear exhaust ports. It was still spluttering and sparking, but any rage it once boasted had long since gone out. At least the smoke might scare off any curious fauna, he supposed.

"Hey, guys." Jack hurriedly waved the rest of them over. "The sliding door – it's been opened a crack. We can take a look inside."

The sliding plug door occupied most of the drop ship's flank, but the gap in question was only just wide enough for a single person to squeeze through. He peered into the gloom but couldn't make anything out. The sun shone from the other side of the ship, unfortunately.

"We *can* take a look inside," said Klik, still wincing from the smell of blood baking into the earth. "But should we?"

"Somebody might have survived the crash." Rogan grabbed the door and strained to push it along its runner. "If so, they probably need our help."

"Let me," said Tuner. He gently nudged Rogan out of the way, then pulled at the door as if he were tearing the tape off a hostage's mouth. The whole thing ripped loose from its runner. Tuner looked at the warped chunk of metal in his hand, shrugged with his entire body, and then tossed it into the shrubbery.

"I'm not sure anyone can help this lot." Klik swatted the flies away from her face as the gloom inside the drop ship's fuselage dissipated.

"Oh, I'm not sure," said Jack, soberly. "Maybe an undertaker."

Three bodies were sprawled across the interior. Their glassy eyes stared without sight. Each marine wore a similar set of military fatigues to that which Jack saw on Sergeant Kaine back on the bridge of the *Final Dawn*. Like the pilot's seatbelt, their helmets hadn't improved their chances much. One of the poor sods barely had any head left to hang his on.

"Look at the slashes across the door on the other side," said Rogan. She was the only one with the stomach – or lack thereof – to step inside the wreckage. "They're enormous. I wonder if whatever caused this ship to crash is responsible for them as well."

"What could have even done that?" asked Tuner. "Those flying creatures we saw?"

"Maybe. If that's the case, it's probably a good thing Adi didn't hang about. But I don't recall them having particularly large claws or teeth..."

besides, those bloated pterosaurs are still circling overhead. I don't think we should antagonise them further if we can help it."

"Are you sure?" Jack hesitantly got up from his seat. "Will you be all right on your own?"

"Of course. I'll hang around the upper atmosphere where nothing fleshy can go, and I'll keep track of your signal so I know where to come pick you up. Don't worry about me," she added. "*You're* the ones going into the unknown."

"All right. Everyone down to the loading ramp, pronto."

They hurried downstairs to the cargo bay whilst the *Adeona* kept herself level above the water. The ramp was halfway lowered by the time they got there.

"Oh, hello," said Tuner, being deliberately glum. "Nice of you all to join me."

"Adi's not hanging around." Jack threw open the doors of a cabinet near the stairwell. "We've got to drop down."

Inside the cabinet was his spacesuit, which still hadn't been repaired since its temperature filters got fried back on Krett. He needed Tuner to give it a proper fix – presuming he still could in his new, tank-like form. Whilst its shock-absorbing armour was still just as effective as ever, he hardly liked the idea of weighing himself down with extra layers in an already hot climate. He shut the doors without taking anything and hoped nothing on New Eden decided to take a shot at him. Or fancied him as some kind of afternoon snack.

Behind him, Klik popped open the weapons cache.

"I assume we're taking these?" she asked with a grin.

Jack sighed. "Yes, take one. Rogan and I will take the others."

Jack got as close as his gag reflex would allow. The other side of the drop ship wasn't just crushed and crumpled – the metal was torn to ribbons, too.

"Erm, guys?" Klik wandered over to one of the few trees still standing in the immediate clearing. "I think one of the humans made it out of the ship. He didn't get much further, though."

Sat up against the tree trunk with his chin slumped against his chest like he was asleep, was a marine. His helmet lay upside-down in the grass beside him. A deep, bloody gash stretched down his ribcage. Jack guessed that whatever mauled the ship was responsible for this, too.

"I wonder if he had time to realise he was the first human to ever set foot on this world," he said, kneeling beside the soldier. Seeing a human face that wasn't Everett's still fascinated him. "I guess he probably had more pressing things to think about."

"So that's it, then." Klik raised her arms dranatically, then let them fall back to her sides. "We found them. They're dead. Sucks. Do we go back to the stream and call the *Adeona* to come get us? Or do you reckon she could land here?"

"Hold on a second." Jack pulled his data pad out of his pocket and opened up the files on each of the missing marines. A lot of the content was redacted, not to Jack's surprise. "We've found the two pilots and four soldiers. But the UEC sent two fireteams down here. If everyone's dead, there should be ten bodies in total."

One by one, he tried matching the corpses to the photos in the files. It wasn't always easy.

"Jesus. Tough break."

"What is it?" asked Rogan.

"The dead marines all belong to Fireteam Alpha. I could be wrong, but I don't see anyone from Fireteam Sigma here."

Rogan peered back inside the drop ship.

"Makes sense, actually. Look at where the marines were sitting – right next to the lacerated hull. Aside from our friend over by the tree, I suspect they were dead before the ship even crashed."

"The door *was* ajar before we got here," Tuner added. "I doubt the dead guy over there could have got it open all by himself."

Jack put his data pad away and brandished his rifle.

"So the others must still be alive, then!"

"Or dead elsewhere," said Klik, deadpan.

"Or dying and in need of our help," said Tuner, charging his plasma cannon for dramatic effect. "Why don't we find out which one of us is right?"

"There's just one problem," said Jack, the wind leaving his sails. "None of us is exactly an expert tracker. We've no idea where they went from here."

"Oh, I wouldn't say that." Rogan pointed at a second winding trail of crushed bracken leading further into the jungle. "We just follow the path they left us."

6

RED CLIFFS OF CLAY

Jack took a greedy bite from one of the ration bars and winced. It was as rubbery as bath sealant and tasted about as good, too. After the bourbon he shared with Admiral Blatch, he'd expected the food to be halfway decent. If anything, he thought he preferred the slop they handed out as ration packets back when he worked in the Pit.

Judging by the expression on Klik's face, she wasn't any bigger a fan. And she was from an enslaved species, for crying out loud. It wasn't as if she was fussy.

"Is this what all human food tastes like?" she said through a mouthful of stodgy gunk.

"I hope not." He stuffed the second half of the bar back into his pocket. "God, I could kill for a lamb madras right now. I wonder if anywhere on the *Final Dawn* serves curries..."

Klik threw the rest of hers on the ground. Aghast, Jack grabbed the wrapper and told her to pocket it until they got back on the ship.

"This is going to be my future home," he said, shaking

his head. "We're on an untouched paradise. Don't throw litter on it!"

"Oh, I've seen what fleshies do to new worlds," said Tuner, stomping along behind them. "This whole planet will be trash soon enough."

Up front, Rogan smiled and shook her head.

They'd walked for another half an hour after leaving the drop ship, and still they hadn't encountered a single member of Fireteam Sigma – alive or dead. Jack supposed this was about as promising a sign as he could currently hope to expect. But it also meant the marines could be headed anywhere. If they weren't too badly hurt in the crash, they might even be pulling ahead of them.

And they didn't even *really* know that Sigma were the ones who left the trail they were following. Boy, could they be in for a nasty surprise.

Something nuzzled against his trouser pocket. Jack glanced down and almost fired his rifle in shock.

"Woah! What the hell is that?"

The squat, bipedal reptile sniffing Jack's leg sprung back from him in equal surprise. It was not much bigger than a young husky, but its scaly skin and long, bony tail suggested it had a closer relative in the crocodile or alligator than any dog. Its hind legs were short and stocky, its front pair small and weak like those of a Tyrannosaurus rex. In a way, it kind of resembled a large, prehistoric bullfrog.

It fixed one of its yellow, thin-slitted eyes on Jack and let out a low, croaking growl.

"Stand back!" said Klik, aiming her rifle. "I'm gonna shoot it!"

"No!" Jack waved his hands about in warning. "Don't shoot! I think it's just hungry, the poor thing."

As if it could understand him, the animal's snake-like

eye rolled in its socket to stare at Jack's pocket. Jack slowly reached down to retrieve the ration bar inside, then hesitated.

"I mean, I'm still kind of hungry," he said.

"Let him have mine," said Klik with a sigh. "He'd be doing me a favour."

She tossed it over to Jack. The reptilian creature leapt up far more spritely than any of them expected, snapped the bar out of the air and gobbled it down – plastic wrapper and all.

Jack expected it to rush back off into the undergrowth now it had been fed. Instead, it gave the air a fresh sniff and started stalking towards Jack's pocket again.

"I think it's still hungry," said Rogan, backing away.

The tiny dinosaur growled even more menacingly than before.

"Right, that's quite enough of that." Tuner revved up his plasma cannon – the inside of its substantial barrel glowed a fiery, otherworldly purple. "Scram before I turn you into jungle-paste."

The reptile took one look at the heat haze coming off Tuner's hand-cannon and scarpered off into the trees.

"Jungle-paste?" asked Jack, his eyebrow raised.

"Oh, I don't know." Tuner powered down his plasma cannon. "I couldn't come up with anything more threatening in the moment. And it was kind of adorable until it thought about biting your leg off."

"Everyone, keep your guard up." Rogan nodded to Jack's rifle before she continued down the makeshift path of squashed grass and hacked bushes. "If it comes back with friends, I suspect we'll need more than Tuner's harsh language to scare it away."

WATERFALLS SPILLED from high red clifftops, evaporating into a fine mist on their way to form pools amongst the rocks below. More of the grand, swollen-bellied pterosaurs they saw before flapped through the bright, subtropical sky, followed by swooping flocks of smaller, brightly-feathered birds. The rainforest below was filled with the sound of excited animal cries.

Jack stood on the edge of the cliff to which the lost marines' path had led, lost in awe at the powerful vista. For a moment, he quite forgot what they were even out there for.

"How does it compare to Earth?" asked Rogan.

"Before the flares started?" Jack bobbed his head from side to side. "Just as beautiful. Maybe more. I never got the chance to see most of it, unfortunately."

"Well, you're one of the first to see this one. Come on. It's all rocky up here. If we don't move quickly, we'll lose their trail."

Jack lingered a second longer before finally tearing himself away from the view. Amber would have loved it there. She was once so glued to a sunset on their American West Coast road trip that they'd lost their dinner reservation by the time they finally rolled into town. He smiled to himself. Thank God for drive-through takeaways.

"Get over here, guys." Tuner stood with Klik further along the cliff's edge. He sounded concerned. "Correct me if I'm wrong, but I don't think *that's* supposed to be here."

A narrow ravine separated their clifftop from the next. Wedged in the crook between, and balanced precariously above the lip of another giant waterfall, was a crashed ship. It was a few times bigger than the *Adeona* and relatively circular, albeit with a blunt nose-cone at its front and a pair of large thrusters jutting out from the back. Its weathered, grey hull formed an inclined bridge between the two outcrops.

"Huh." Rogan crossed her arms. "I don't think that ship is supposed to be *anywhere*. I haven't seen anyone fly that model for at least a couple of hundred years. The G-300 series had dodgy fuel injectors. Most were returned or traded in for scrap. Those that hadn't already blown up, that is."

A couple hundred years. Jack shook his head. Considering how much more advanced she looked compared to other automata, it was easy to forgot how old Rogan actually was.

Come to think of it, he'd never properly asked.

"Maybe the pilot fixed it himself," said Jack. "Could this have been what brought the drop ship down? Before crashing too, I mean."

"Doubtful. Look at the way vines have grown over the hull. I reckon it's been here for a few decades at least."

"Only one way to know for sure," said Klik, a beaming smile spreading across her face. "Let's go take a look!"

"We're not here to explore," Rogan replied in a tired and stern voice. "We're here to find Jack's missing fireteam, in case you need reminding."

"What, and you think a bunch of humans who've never seen a spaceship before didn't go and check it out too?" Klik replied testily. "Besides, where else could they have gone?"

"She's got a point, Rogan." Tuner shrugged his whole body. "Either they fell off the cliff or they crossed the ship to get to the other side. And I don't see any bodies below."

Rogan politely pulled Tuner back from the edge before he could topple to his death. The poor guy still wasn't accustomed to his new size and weight.

"Fine," she sighed. "But don't come crying to me when

we lose track of them and have to go back to the Ark empty handed."

A cascading slope of rocks formed a natural staircase down to the base of their cliff and therefore to the lowest end of the ship itself. They followed it slowly to avoid slipping where the river of the waterfall had splashed. The crashed ship looked even more imposing up close. The vines Rogan pointed out earlier snaked through cracks in its hull like a trap net. Black and yellow-spotted flowers bloomed amongst thorny stalks running along their length. The whole craft groaned as parts of its metal shell expanded in the heat, which suggested the rainforest got cold at night. Jack reminded himself to get back to his own ship before darkness fell.

"So, do we climb over it?" he said, nervously peering up the ship towards the clifftop across from them. "I guess it's safe if the marines already came this way..."

The angle of the wedged spacecraft wasn't particularly steep, and there were plenty of crushed rocks around its base from which they could start their ascent. He couldn't help noticing how far the tip of the ship's cockpit dangled over the edge of the waterfall, however...

"Don't be so sure they did," said Rogan. She followed the ship around towards the back, away from the edge. "Look here. The airlock door is already open."

Door was a stretch. The doors themselves were missing – rather, a perfectly square hole was set in the side of the spacecraft. Any power supply the ship possessed had dried up long ago, and all the interior lights were off. Everything was a deep, oppressive, and ultimately silent black.

"Are you saying Jack's fireteam went inside?" asked Tuner, already measuring himself against the height of the doorway to see if he'd fit.

"Somebody had to open it." Rogan shrugged. "And who knows? Maybe Klik's right. Maybe they're still in there."

Jack chewed his bottom lip. He wasn't sure if going inside the ship was any safer than clambering across its hull. But if the marines were injured and looking for somewhere to hole up...

"We've got to make sure," he said. "Besides, we need to get to the other side either way."

"After you, then." Rogan gestured to the foreboding airlock. "If we bump into any of your fellow humans skulking about in the dark, the first face they see had better belong to you."

7

THE VISITORS

Jack may have left his customised spacesuit back on the *Adeona*, but he wasn't so foolhardy as to not bring a flashlight. Heavy dust drifted across its curious beam.

The crashed ship reminded Jack of an ancient, undisturbed tomb. The only sounds were that of their footsteps against the hard floor and the occasional wounded groan of the ship's metal frame flexing in the rising heat. A particularly sharp bang made Jack pause and turn to Rogan.

"There's no chance those dodgy fuel injectors can still go off, right?"

"Not unless somebody tries flying this wreck," Rogan replied, studying the derelict walls. "By the look of things, I think that opportunity has passed."

Jack doubted the G-300s had been a particularly flashy model to begin with, but its corridors were certainly nothing to write home about after a few decades gathering moss on a rainforest clifftop. The pipes, cables and gaskets that ran along the dark, industrial walls were openly exposed, and many of the floor panels had come loose. Water dripped from holes in the ceiling. Everything was tight, functional and cheap. If the corridors got any more narrow, Tuner was going to struggle.

"Assuming the marines came through here," Klik whispered, "where do you think they went?"

"Rogan?" Jack kept his flashlight on the claustrophobic corridor ahead as he spoke. "You knew about this ship already. You might be best placed to answer that question."

Rogan shrugged.

"Nothing special about this model, aside from its tendency to blow up without a moment's notice. It was marketed to businesses that wanted a productive office space whilst travelling between systems, but it was too cheap for any reputable corporations to consider buying. The cockpit up front is actually fairly small for a ship of this size – definitely not enough space for four adult humans to rest comfortably. I believe there should be a sizeable conference room somewhere towards the rear, however."

"Then that's where we'll start looking," said Jack. He made no effort to hide his relief that they were headed in the opposite direction to the edge of the waterfall. The cockpit teetered enough as it was without their added weight.

They took a left when they came to the next crossroads and passed a small room with a locked door. Jack shined his flashlight through its small window. Two pairs of large bunks were stacked inside. He couldn't make out any occupants – not that he imagined anyone lying down would still be sleeping, of course.

Jack coughed. The air wasn't just thick with dust – it was stale and sour, possibly even toxic. There was no telling what gas was once pumped through the original crew's atmospheric generator. Even diluted over the years by the planet's oxygen, it could be enough to knock him out if he wasn't careful. Once again Jack wished he had his spacesuit and helmet, and resolved to tell Rogan if he started feeling dizzy.

Something burst out from an overhead vent and scuttled down the corridor away from them. Everyone jumped and trained their rifles on the click-clacking sound of its spindly legs. Without his flashlight raised, Jack suddenly couldn't see a thing.

"Just a critter," said Rogan, whose night-vision sensors and telescopic eye-lenses gave her the best vision out of everyone in their group. "All sorts of creatures must have taken roost in here over the years."

"Let's get a move on before we run into any more of them," said Jack, waiting for his heart to settle. "This place is seriously giving me the creeps."

Luckily, the conference room Rogan mentioned wasn't much further. They passed through an open doorway – either the crash or the power cut had disabled any mag-locks on the ship, it seemed – and into a circular hall, the centre of which was dominated by a round table ringed by a dozen high-backed chairs. Computer servers and terminals, relics even by the *Final Dawn's* standards, stood as lifeless monoliths against the walls.

Everything was covered in a thick layer of dust.

"It doesn't look like anyone's been in here for a while," said Tuner, studying the enormous footprints he left in the floor. "Not the best place to lie down if you've got any open wounds, either."

"Tuner's right," said Rogan, shaking her head. "Your marines didn't come through here."

"Damn." Jack deflated with disappointment. "They must have climbed over the top of the ship, then. They'll be long gone by now."

"Then we may as well take a look around while we're here," said Klik, cheerfully. Jack suspected she didn't care too much about finding the marines one way or the other, just so long as she wasn't stuck on board the *Adeona* for a while longer.

"I'm going to try and jump-start one of the computers," said Tuner, before quickly adding, "That won't set anything off, will it?"

Rogan smiled nervously.

"Probably not. And the fuel cells have probably all turned to slush by now, anyway. But be careful what you turn on, all right?"

Tuner unravelled an auxiliary cable from a compartment built into his side and plugged it into one of the servers at the back of the conference room. First, a few blue LEDs lit up on the computer. Then the backup lighting for the whole ship kicked into life with a passive electrical hum.

Jack blinked as his eyes adjusted.

"Well that makes everything a little less creepy, at least."

"You sure about that?" asked Klik.

Buckled into one of the chairs around the conference table was the skeleton of an eight-foot alien. Most of its long, black robe was either rotten or torn, and all of the flesh beneath had been eaten away. Its elongated skull curved back behind its bony shoulders. One of its arms had become detached and lay half-submerged in the dust-tundra carpeting the floor.

"They must have died in the crash," said Rogan. "I don't see any obvious signs of trauma, but it could have been blood loss or excessive G-force. Hard to tell with only bones to go by."

"I wonder what brought them to New Eden," said Jack. "Smugglers making a secret layover, perhaps?"

"Or maybe all their engines conked out and the planet's gravity pulled them in," Klik suggested.

"They were from the Ministry," said Tuner, reading through the old comm messages. "I guess that explains why their ship was so crap."

"The Ministry?" said Jack. There was no mistaking the corpse's uniform now that Tuner had pointed it out. "What the hell were *they* doing here?"

"Can't say for sure. Could have been a cartographic mission that went wrong, or something." Tuner sounded strained, as if he and the computer were engaged in a digital tug-of-war. "All the files in this thing are either redacted or corrupted from the crash. And I can't..."

Tuner gave up whatever fight he and the terminal were engaged in and yanked his auxiliary cable free.

"Are you okay?" asked Rogan, hurrying around the table to him. "You're not scrambled, are you?"

"No, of course not." Tuner punched the ceiling. Jack winced as the panel above their heads swung open on a single rusty hinge. "It was just messy in there, that's all. And weirdly empty. Look up there."

Jack peered up into the dark and dusty floorspace.

"I don't see anything," he said.

"Exactly!" Tuner gestured to other panels and cabinets all around the conference room. "It's all missing. There's *supposed* to be a comm scrambler up there, an early NavMap processor over there, and a thermal regulator over by the engines. But they're gone. This whole ship has been stripped for parts."

"Maybe raiders got the jump on them." Rogan watched the doors as if she expected a tribe of space pirates to charge in on them at any moment. "That would go some way to explain the crash *and* the missing equipment."

"Unless they crashed *because* all their equipment got stolen." Jack gave his idea a bit more thought, then shook his head. "No, forget it. That's probably unlikely."

A terrible clattering echoed around the conference room. They all turned to discover Klik standing beside the dead minister's skeleton – what remained of it, that is. Their bones now lay in a pile upon the seat, their curved skull rocking back and forth on the hard floor like a seesaw.

Klik shrugged and offered them an embarrassed smile.

"I think we've seen everything this ship has to offer," said Rogan. "The question is, do we keep going in search of those marines? Or do we call it a day and head back?"

"How long do we have until sundown?" asked Jack.

"A good four hours and fifty-two minutes, according to my calculations. Plenty of time before we need to think about returning to Adi, if that's what you mean."

"Okay, let's keep going." Jack followed the sloping floor up to the other side of the hall. "If I have to go back empty-handed, that's fine. But at least I'll be able to say we did everything we could."

"Sure. I'm in." Klik stretched out her arms. "But let's not stay out *too* long, all right? My feet are starting to ache."

"I can't believe they pulled it right out of there," said Tuner, mourning the broken cables left dangling from the compartment overhead. "That's half the market value gone straight away."

He slammed the panel shut.

The whole ship groaned. Everyone froze.

"Tuner?" said Jack. "What did you do?"

"Nothing! I just—"

The ship made another sound – this one louder, longer and forlorn, like a mother whale mourning her calf.

"You bolt-bucket!" Rogan gestured for everyone to head

up through the ship. "You just shook the ship loose from the rocks. Move!"

"I'm sorry!" Tuner moaned as he chased after them.

They fled up the corridor opposite to that through which they came. Jack felt the ship start to shift beneath his boots. It started as a faint rumble and then grew into a barely perceptible (yet no less unsettling) nausea in the pit of his stomach, as if what he saw through his eyes didn't *quite* marry up to the sense of balance in his ears. The faster he ran, the more his legs complained about the increasingly steep incline.

"Which way?" screamed Klik. "Everywhere looks the same!"

"The ship's design should be symmetrical," said Rogan, keeping pace with her. "So take a left and then a right. There should be an airlock straight ahead!"

Jack was almost a full corridor behind the women and in front of only Tuner. His words came out in a dry wheeze.

"See anything?"

"No!" came Klik's panicked voice from up ahead. "It's all just walls and pipes and—"

"I've got it!" said Rogan, followed by a loud, metallic smashing sound. If the airlock wasn't open before, it was now.

Jack turned the corner and squinted as harsh, natural light glared through the airlock. He raced towards it, almost pulling himself up the tilted floor with his hands. But despite all his fear and determination, he could feel the calves in his legs cramping up.

The ship jolted with a bang and a crunch.

Jack lost his balance and pinwheeled his arms around, looking for something – *anything* – to grab onto. His fingers brushed the exposed pipes on the walls, but he couldn't get any purchase. They came back brown with rust. He fell backwards towards the deck.

Tuner caught him around the waist without slowing down and charged towards the airlock, the pistons in his legs pumping and hissing.

"Don't worry, buddy. I've got you."

Tuner leapt from the opening just as more of the rocks under the crashed ship gave way. The two of them went sprawling through the mud on the clifftop outside. Klik helped Jack to his feet while Rogan helped knock some of the dirt off Tuner's chassis.

More of the waterfall's peak crumbled beneath the G-300's shifting weight. Another metallic clunk and groan started... and then the ship grunted to a stop.

They all looked down at it.

"Well, that wasn't so bad," said Tuner, sheepishly kicking the dirt. "Look, it didn't even—"

Suddenly, the entire rock face beneath the ship collapsed. Everybody took a quick step back from the edge of their elevated clifftop as the red earth spilled away like an avalanche. Boulders rolled. Trees fell. The large spacecraft tipped over the edge of the stream and disappeared screaming into the dense forest below.

None of them saw the crash, but they sure heard it.

Jack turned to face Tuner, failing to suppress a grin. It wasn't that the situation was remotely funny. At this point, he was just happy to be alive.

"What were you saying, mate?"

"Sorry." Tuner bowed his entire body. "Guess we're not going back that way, then."

"There's some good news, at least." Rogan pointed at the muddy trail leading away from them. "The rain must have been heavier up here. Do those boot prints look human to you, Jack?"

At least two pairs of boots – one much larger than the other – had sunk deep into the fresh mud. The prints they left behind looked to be of Earthly origin.

"They sure do," he said. "And if they didn't know somebody was following them before, I'm sure they do now."

"In the meantime," said Rogan, carefully walking around the footprints, "everyone keep an eye out for somewhere suitable for the *Adeona* to land. As Tuner said, we won't be heading back that way any time soon."

Jack went to follow, then paused. He turned back towards the cliffs on the other side of the ravine, back to the spot where they themselves had stood prior to making their treacherous crossing.

He could have sworn he saw something moving amongst the trees. Was something watching them from afar?

Jack shrugged and chased the rest of his crew down the muddy path. It was probably just good old paranoia playing tricks on him. That or dehydration.

And besides – after the racket they just caused, he'd be surprised if the whole damn forest wasn't keeping a careful eye on them.

8

SEEKING SIGMA

The muddy clifftop path led Jack and the rest of the *Adeona's* crew down to a freshwater river. Its banks were thick with dark, slushy soil and abundant with luscious, fruit-bearing plants. Jack didn't know whether it had rained before they began their expedition or not, but judging by the ominous clouds forming in the previously tranquil sky, it was sure threatening to pour down now.

"Is it just me," asked Tuner, "or is it getting harder to find a suitable landing zone the further into the forest we walk?"

The trees were bunched up closer together, and the bushes of prickly ferns grew even thicker. There wasn't even a path anymore – if they didn't have the occasional human footprint in the mud to guide them, they would have been totally, utterly lost.

Not that any of them had any clue where the footprints were going, of course. They knew they were in the right place... they just didn't know where the right place was, exactly.

"It's not just you." Rogan pulled her metallic foot out of the mud with a comical plunger sound. "We're never going to find somewhere suitable round here. We should have reached out to Adi while we were still up on that cliff."

Jack kept his mouth shut. He probably shouldn't have suggested they push on after their close encounter in the crashed spacecraft. But everyone else had agreed to it, hadn't they?

Something stirred in the river to their left. Jack turned his head just in time to see a six-foot black and bone-plated tail slither into the water from between two mangrove trees. A second later, only the tiniest ripples on the river's dark surface hinted that something deadly had been there at all.

Yeah, they should have gone back. In fact, Jack was starting to think they should have left the whole rescue mission to the professionals after all.

Not having a huge desire to be dragged into the river by a hungry alien caiman, Jack gave up on following the bank and started trekking through the thick foliage instead. Tuner, unable to walk through the mud without sinking and oblivious to the bushes' thorns, bulldozed a path for them. Klik, never one to not take full advantage of a situation, was riding piggy-back.

"It's getting dark," she said, clacking her mandibles impatiently. "I thought you said we had hours left til nightfall."

"We do," sighed Rogan. "Or we should, based on the velocity of New Eden's rotation on its axis. It's just the storm clouds overhead. Not much sunlight gets down here as it is, given how thick the tree canopies are."

The sunlight may have had trouble reaching the forest's humid understory, but the rain sure didn't. A big drip splattered against a large, waxy leaf a few inches from Jack's head. Then another, and then another.

"It's not New Eden's monsoon season, is it?"

Rogan glared over her shoulder at him.

"We're on an uncharted world," she replied. "For all we know, it's *always* monsoon season."

"If we can't find a suitable landing site, should we be looking for some kind of shelter? Like a cave, or something?"

"Yes, that's not a bad idea. And somewhere elevated while we're at it. We don't want to get caught in a flood."

Jack shivered. Especially not with that scaly beast he saw lurking in the water.

"Do you think you could climb another tree, Klik?" he asked. "Tell us the highest point nearby?"

"In this weather?" Klik scoffed. "Don't make me laugh."

"Sorry." Frustrated, Jack bit his lip. "How stupid of me. Hmm. Maybe we—"

"Flash."

Rogan, Jack, Tuner and Klik – all four of them stopped dead in their tracks.

"Which one of us said that?" asked Jack, slowly raising his rifle.

"Don't look at me," said Klik. Rogan shook her head without taking her eyes off the trees in front of her.

"Flash," the voice whispered again, a little more urgently this time. With the pattering of rain growing steadily louder, it was hard to tell exactly where in the forest the word was coming from.

"Fireteam Sigma?" Jack whispered back. "Is that you?"

Four figures leapt out from the flora all around them, their own rifles raised and trigger-fingers at the ready. The closest was barely six feet from where Jack stood. Their faces were deliberately obscured with thumb-streaks of mud, though there was no masking their contorted expressions of panic beneath.

"Who are you?" the man in front shouted. The white of

his large, terrified eyes shone bright amongst the gloom of the forest floor. "Identify yourself!"

"I'm a friendly!" Jack spluttered, dropping his rifle and raising his hands. "We're here to—"

"What in Christ's name is *that?"* the marine screamed as he noticed Klik for the first time. He swung his rifle round towards her.

"No!" Jack rushed forward. "Don't shoot!"

He shoved the man's rifle just as he pulled the trigger. The shot went wide, perforating an unlucky orchid, but Klik went tumbling backwards off Tuner all the same. The marine slammed the butt of his gun into Jack's stomach in retaliation, winding him.

"Everybody stand down," yelled Rogan.

At a distance and with the light being as poor as it was, Jack didn't think any of the marines were yet to realise the metallic automata wasn't human. None of them took a shot at her – or at the completely motionless Tuner, for that matter – but they didn't exactly do as she commanded, either.

Bunched over double, Jack looked up to discover the muzzle of a rifle hovering inches from his face.

"Explain," the marine growled. *"Fast."*

"Admiral Blatch sent us," Jack gasped, inching backwards with one hand on his stomach and the other raised in defence. "From the *Final Dawn*. Told us they lost radio contact with fireteams Alpha and Sigma not long after you entered the planet's atmosphere. We found Alpha. I take it you're Sigma. We're here to bring you back."

"Bullcrap." Yet despite the man's words, his grip on his rifle loosened. "You don't even know your call-signs. You're not military."

"No, I'm not. *We're* not. But we know a hell of a lot more

about this galaxy than you do, and we came here to help. So do you reckon you could try not to kill us, please?"

All four marines stiffened again as Klik re-emerged from the ferns, stumbling with an insectoid hand clutched to the back of her bug-eyed head. Jack winced.

"That moron tried to shoot me," she snapped. "Are we gonna pretend like that's okay?"

"Have you got an explanation for that thing, too?" said a female marine towards the back of the squad, her voice on the verge of breaking.

"Everybody calm down," Jack pleaded. "I will explain everything, I promise. She's a friendly... unless you keep pointing that rifle at her, that is. Look, there isn't much time before they send down another fireteam. And that Kaine fellow didn't seem half as friendly as I am."

"Sergeant Kaine?" The marine in front of Jack lowered his rifle and gestured for the rest of his fireteam to do the same. "They're sending Fireteam Omega down after us? Jesus Christ. Not *that* blockhead. We'll never hear the end of it."

The rain grew heavier. By this point, Jack's shirt was glued to his chest. The fireteam leader gave the sliver of sky above them a cursory glance.

"You got a way off this planet right now?" he asked.

Jack shook his head.

"We were looking for a suitable landing zone when we ran into you," he replied, keeping one eye on Klik to make sure she didn't do anything stupid in retaliation for her bumped head.

"Then you'd better come with us." The marines started walking in the direction Jack's own crew had been headed, though none of them turned their backs. "We found a spot of shelter not far from here. But keep your squad on a tight leash." He eyed Klik with terrified disbelief. "Boy, have you got some explaining to do."

Jack thought back to the massive claw marks slashed through their drop ship's hull.

"Yeah. You and me both."

FIRETEAM SIGMA'S "SPOT OF SHELTER" was little more than a dozen giant, overlapping rubber-plant leaves, but even as the rain grew from a shower to an all-out onslaught, it seemed to do the job. The eight of them sat amongst the gnarly, winding roots of a colossal, ancient sequoia. One of the marines even lit a small fire where the soil was dry.

Not because it was cold, mind. But because as the daylight receded further, they sensed the creatures of the rainforest closing in to fill the gap.

Jack finished off the last of his ration bar as soon as they sat down. It was only after stuffing the wrapper back into his pocket that he realised nobody around their makeshift camp was saying anything to one another. All four of the marines were staring at Klik and Rogan as if they were horror movie villains come to life.

"Why are they looking at me like that?" asked Klik. She nervously clacking her mandibles together. "It's freaking me out."

"What did the insect say?" asked the fireteam leader, his eyes flicking from Klik to Jack and back again.

"Don't you understand her?"

"They don't have translator chips, Jack." Rogan kept her voice hushed. "Klik can understand English because of the chip her father had implanted in her as an infant, but she still speaks Paryxian."

"Paryxian? I didn't know that was her language." Jack turned to Klik. "I always assumed you spoke Krettelian."

"Krettelian?" Klik laughed sarcastically. "As if the Mansa would let us keep *those* languages alive after they put us in chains."

"Translator chip?" The largest of the soldiers, whose arm and forehead were tightly bandaged, scrunched up his face. "What the bloody hell are you on about?"

Jack leaned over to Rogan and whispered.

"How come they can understand *you*, then? I thought you spoke in binary, or something."

"Automata do, usually. But our chips are directly integrated with the rest of our systems, and we have speakers rather than vocal cords. We can 'speak' in whichever language we choose. I tend to speak English whenever I'm around you." She rolled her eyes. "Thanks for noticing."

"Oh. Sorry." He turned back to the marines and sighed. Their expressions were even more bewildered than before. "Perhaps some introductions would help calm everyone's nerves. Congratulations, by the way. As far as I'm aware, you all come joint third in regard to meeting an extraterrestrial species. Not bad, eh? Let's start with the *most* extraterrestrial, shall we?"

"Oi!" said Klik.

"This is Klik. She's a Krettelian, a race of insect humanoids enslaved by the powerful Mansa Empire, who I'm sure the UEC will run into sooner or later. She's not much different from you and me, really. Minus the sword-arms. And the mandibles. And..."

He sighed and started again.

"Well, you'd better get used to aliens pretty quick. There are plenty of civilisations out here that look a hell of a lot weirder than her."

Klik smiled sheepishly at the two female marines. Only one of them – a dark-haired hispanic woman who Jack reckoned was the youngest member of Fireteam Sigma – gave her a hesitant wave back.

"And then we come to our two automata," said Jack, gesturing to Rogan and Tuner. "They're—"

"I get this one," said the beefy soldier. He jabbed a thick finger at Tuner. "It's some sort of battle mech, right? Mind-blowing engineering, man. Remote controlled or autopilot?"

"Neither, thank you very much," said Tuner, rotating his considerable body to face him. "I'm quite capable of thinking for myself. I used to be customised for electronic defence breaching and invasive network disruption, but I... erm... I had a small transplant."

"Small?" Rogan laughed. "I replaced your whole body, Tuner."

"But it was only my data core that got transplanted," Tuner insisted. "And that's tiny!"

Jack smiled and shook his head.

"And this is Rogan," he said, laying an affectionate hand on her shoulder. She covered his hand with her own. "The smartest person you will ever meet. Ask her literally anything about the galaxy. I bet she knows the answer."

"Oh, I don't know about that." Rogan lowered her gaze. If she hadn't been made of metal, Jack might have thought she was blushing. "*Most* things, maybe."

"So, *she's* an alien," said the marine who waved at Klik, "and you're... what? Robots?"

Jack bit his lip. Rogan shook her head.

"Not robots. Robots are mindless drones that at best only create the *illusion* of consciousness. We're automata. We may come in a thousand different models, but we're one people."

The marine crossed her arms and leaned back on her root.

"If you say so."

"It's a lot to process," her fireteam leader added. He nodded to Jack. "And what about you? You haven't told us who you are."

"Me?" Jack shrugged. "I'm just Jack. I came through a wormhole from Earth long before you guys in the UEC did. Would have died if it hadn't been for Rogan and Tuner – and our ship, the *Adeona*. They've been stuck with me ever since."

Jack leaned towards the fire. Its crackles and pops were lost in the heavy rain.

"But enough about us. We've been tracking you for hours and we don't even know your names yet. I suppose I could just look up your files on my data pad but given how we're stuck here for the time being, I'd much rather hear them from you."

The fireteam leader nodded.

"Well, since you were sent by the good Admiral anyway... Yes, we're Fireteam Sigma. Trained specially for scout and recon missions. I'm Sergeant Yates. Pleased to meet you. *All* of you," he added diplomatically, before jabbing his thumb at the hispanic marine sat next to him. "This here's Private Flores. She's our markswoman. We call her Ghost."

Ghost gave Jack a curt nod. Now the Sergeant mentioned it, Jack noticed that the scoped rifle laid across the root next to her was considerably longer than those of her companions. She also had a submachine gun holstered against one hip and a knife strapped to the other.

"Why Ghost?" he asked.

"Because in combat field training," said the beefy marine, "she picked off the other fireteams without them ever knowing she was there." He stuck out his hand for Jack to shake. "Hey. I'm Private Sampson, but everyone calls me Duke. Demolition expert."

Much to Jack's surprise, Duke then extended his handshake to Rogan and Tuner. He was a little more hesitant when it came to Klik, but in the end he shook her hand too.

"And why Duke?" asked Rogan, echoing Jack's question out of politeness.

"Can I assume you've never heard of the late great David Bowie?"

Jack chuckled to himself. Rogan warily shook her head.

"Shame," sighed Duke. "I'm a big fan."

"Too big," said Ghost. "It's all I ever hear coming from his bunk room."

"Not my fault you're too crass to appreciate the classics."

"Pfft. *Gordita...*"

"What about her?" asked Jack, nodding to the only other marine left. "What's her deal?"

The last of the four marines was sat with her boots up on her root and her back partially turned to her fellow squad members. She was alternately cleaning out the dirt from her sidearm and fixing Klik with a look sharp enough to cut bone.

Duke gave her a friendly nudge in the ribs with his elbow.

"Oh." She gave Jack a nod even more curt than Ghost's. "Name's Ginger. Pleased to meet you."

Then she went back to cleaning her gun and staring at Klik. To her credit, Jack had taken much longer to adjust to being around the automata, and they'd given him plenty of warning before he set foot on Kapamentis. All things considered, the marines were taking meeting a bunch of extraterrestrials for the first time pretty well.

Ginger, though. He might need to keep an eye on her.

"So what happened, if you don't mind me asking?" said Rogan, directing her question to Sergeant Yates who, with the possible exception of Duke, seemed the most approachable of the marines. "With your drop ship, I mean. What made you crash? And why didn't you call for help?"

"Call for help?" Yates turned to Ghost, who scoffed. "Calling for help was the *first* thing we did. Tried the radio in the ship after we landed, but we had no more luck than the poor pilots. None of our comm units down here work, either."

A knot formed in Jack's stomach. He quickly turned to Rogan.

"Have you tried reaching Adi since we got here?"

She slowly shook her head.

"I assumed she wanted some peace and quiet. I'll try getting hold of her now."

"Who's Adi?" the sergeant asked.

"Our ship," Tuner replied.

"Keeping your pilot on standby," said Duke, nodding sagely as if he hadn't misunderstood Tuner completely. "A smart move, normally. Today, maybe not so much."

"Nothing." The aperture of Rogan's eyes grew wide. "I can't get through to her at all."

"Keep trying. I'm sure she's fine. We probably just need to get to higher ground or something. Maybe it's the storm."

"Or maybe there's something about this planet that's blocking our signals," Ghost muttered. "Polar magnetism, or whatever?"

"I hope not," said Jack. "Otherwise they'll keep shipping people down here until they figure it out. Speaking of which... why'd you crash?"

"Wish we knew," said Ginger.

"We were closing in on the forest canopy a few klicks out from the landing zone our drones had picked out when something hit us," said Sergeant Yates. "Don't know what, exactly. First the whole left side of the drop ship buckled inwards. I assumed it was some sort of atmospheric pressure adjustment the techies overlooked. Going from the vacuum of space to burning through re-entry to, well, normal. But then something... some *thing* tore through the metal as if it were paper. Whatever it was, it took out our engines, too. We started spinning as we dropped, so none of us got a good look at it."

"We saw some pretty big flying beasts on our way down," said Tuner. "None of them looked capable of causing the sort of damage we saw on your drop ship, though." He shrugged. "I guess you never can tell."

"Well whatever it was, it came out of nowhere and damn near killed us. Wiped out the whole of Fireteam Alpha, God rest their souls. I hope to high hell we don't run into it again."

Deep in the dark rainforest, something howled.

Sergeant Yates checked his watch.

"It's getting late, both here and in old Earth-time. Besides, we're not going anywhere fast in this weather. We ought to get some rest and look for a way to call your ship tomorrow. I'll take first watch."

Klik cast Jack a wary glance. He didn't blame her for feeling uncomfortable, considering the way Ginger and the other marines had been staring at her. Luckily, Rogan seemed to share her concerns.

"Tuner and I will stay up as well," she said rather adamantly. "Automata don't need to sleep."

"Even better." Yates lowered his helmet's night-vision goggles. "You take this side, I'll take the other. Everyone else, try and get as much shut-eye as you can. Long day tomorrow. We'll wake you if we need you."

Klik sidled up to Jack so that they both rested in the hollow nook of two overlapping roots. Jack guessed that even with Rogan and Tuner looking out for threats within as well as outside of their new group, she felt safer sleeping by his side than alone.

He couldn't imagine falling asleep himself. Yet with the warm fire crackling beside them and the steady drumming of rain in his ears, Jack drifted off before long.

9

CLEVER GIRL

Sleep may have come fast, but it didn't last long.

"Jack!" came the whisper. Something grabbed his shoulder and shook it hard. "Wake up, you idiot!"

He blinked himself into consciousness, then suddenly sat bolt upright. Rogan was leant over him with a panicked look on her face. He almost headbutted her in his surprise.

"What?" he half-mumbled, half-gurgled. "Why? What time... What's happening?"

Jack wasn't so tired that he couldn't recognise the urgency in Rogan's voice. He fumbled beside the giant sequoia's root for his rifle and squinted around for Klik, who no longer lay in the nook beside him. He had a terrible feeling one of the marines – that Ginger woman, most likely – might have done something to her.

But Klik was wide awake and squatting on the mangled root above him with her own rifle clutched in her hands. Her bare, carapace-topped feet flexed nervously against the wet bark. For a moment, Jack relaxed... and then he remembered the wide lenses of Rogan's eyes.

"What's going on?" he repeated.

"Be quiet!" Rogan hunkered down beside him; she too had her rifle at the ready. "Something's out there!"

Jack peered into the rainforest. Enough hours had passed that he found himself able to see through the silver-black twilight gloom well enough, but not so many that any pencil-strokes of sunlight broke through the gaps in the trees. He found himself woozily wondering if New Eden's night sky had a moon, and bit down hard on his lip to stop himself from nodding off again.

The marines were all awake, too. Duke and Ginger rose from their disturbed slumbers around the same time as Jack did, and neither looked much better for the rest. Sergeant Yates stood up front with Tuner, their respective battle rifle and plasma cannon trained on the trees ahead of them. Ghost had climbed to a spot on the tree even higher than Klik. From the way she kept pulling her eye from the scope and tutting, Jack guessed she wasn't having much better luck spotting anything.

The rain continued to drum against their rubber-plant rooftop. Someone had snuffed their fire out. The smoke made his nostrils itch.

"I don't see anything," he whispered, inching towards the front. "I don't hear anything, either."

"That's because you have crap ears," Klik replied. Kind of ironic, Jack thought, considering she didn't even have any.

"None of us will hear anything if you don't shut your damn mouths," growled Sergeant Yates. "Your robot friends will back me up. Something big came scurrying past here a couple of minutes back. But I can't for the life of me pick anything up on the sensors. No heat signatures, nothing."

Jack felt the hairs on his arms stand on end.

"Erm, just out of interest," he said, "can you pick up Klik with those things?"

"These?" Yates impatiently pointed to the smart-goggles attached to his helmet. "Sure, when they're set to night-vision. Not getting much heat off her, though. Why? You reckon your bug friend went for a midnight stroll?"

"Oh, I wish." Jack let out a long and staggered sigh. "No. If I'm right, it's much worse than that."

"What?"

"Reptiles."

The ferns in front of the tree rustled. All eight of them snapped their weapons to aim at the shaking clump of rain-sodden leaves ahead. The tension amongst their group was so high, Jack was surprised they didn't turn the poor plant into a crater.

A heavily scaled and irritatingly familiar bipedal creature came shuffling out. It raised its head, blinked at Jack with a pair of yellow, thin-slitted eyes...

...and sniffed.

"Oh, thank God," said Jack, relaxing. "It's just this—"

Yates fired a single shot that rang out through the storm like a thunderclap. The curious little critter fell on its side, convulsed twice, and then died.

"What did you do that for?" yelled Jack. "It was only looking for food!"

"Sure." Yates lowered his rifle. "And when it finds some, what do you think happens next? It goes back to its family with the good news. The next thing we know, we've got a whole pack of daddy dinos on our arse. No thanks."

Rogan and Jack shared a worried glance.

"Yeah," said Klik, nervously hopping down from her root. "But that's the thing..."

"We already *did* feed that little guy," said Tuner, charging up his plasma cannon again.

The foliage further back began to tremble. Yates slowly turned back around, tightening his grip on his rifle.

"Oh, goddammit."

Five hulking beasts stalked towards them from the undergrowth, their heads lowered like predators on the hunt. Daddy dinos indeed, thought Jack, almost tripping over the root behind him as he took a terrified step backwards. They reminded him of goddamn velociraptors. The muscles of their thick hind legs bulged as they stomped through the dark flora. Having grown to full adults, their swollen bellies were now lean, and their long, spiny tails swayed back and forth behind them for balance. Their wide heads were covered in dark, bony ridges and filled with teeth the size of pocket knives.

Judging by the guttural growls brewing deep in their throats, none of them were all too pleased about the death of their young scout.

"Light 'em up, boys and girls," said Sergeant Yates.

The four marines opened fire on the advancing creatures. Their rifles roared; Ghost's submachine gun rattled. Even Rogan and Klik joined in the shooting, while Tuner's plasma cannon reduced whole trees to wooden shrapnel. Jack fired a few shots but, if he was honest, he couldn't really see what he was shooting anymore.

They stopped a few seconds later when the only sound besides that of the falling rain was the harrowing click of their empty magazines. All but one of the five theropods emerged from the smoke and debris, bloody and scarred.

Jack didn't think reptiles could look any more angry than they usually did. He was wrong.

"Fall back," Yates said quietly.

"Where?" asked Ginger.

"Anywhere!" he yelled. "Move!"

They started running... and so did the raptors.

Everyone headed in a different direction to everyone else, sprinting through the trees in a blind panic. Jack kept decent pace with Rogan and Klik for a little while, at least; Tuner tried to keep up but quickly fell behind. The marines stuck closer together but were little better organised, despite their military training. Jack couldn't help wondering if they'd even been in the field as much as he had the past three months.

The theropods chased after them, far quicker and more accustomed to the jungle terrain than any of their other-worldly prey could ever hope to be. They leapt over thick bushes and fallen logs in their stride as if they were nothing. The sound of their clawed feet hitting the mud pounded like tribal drums in Jack's ears.

One closed in on Jack's group and another on the marines. The other two surviving raptor-creatures disappeared into the trees to either side. He had a horrible suspicion the beasts were smart enough to try and flank them.

God, did he wish he'd put up with his sweltering spacesuit now. But even the suit's armour may not have been enough to withstand the teeth on *those* carnivores.

Over in the other group, Duke fumbled at the various satchels and inventory hanging around his waist.

"Tossing a frag!"

He pulled the pin on his grenade and, after cooking it in his hand for a couple of seconds, lobbed it over his shoulder. It disappeared amongst the floor of fallen leaves and no doubt sank into the thick mud beneath.

For a second, nothing happened. In his gut, Jack was sure Duke had thrown a dud. But then suddenly it went off, painting the twilight forest with a brief, orange flash. Something small almost clipped his ear as it whizzed by. A shard of bark, perhaps. Maybe a piece of the grenade itself.

He risked a glance over his shoulder. Either Duke got lucky, or he really *was* an expert with explosives. The blast hadn't killed the reptile on the marines' tail – nobody was *that* lucky – but it certainly knocked the steam out of it. It thrashed its disoriented head from side to side as it hobbled back the way it came.

One down. Only three giant, bloodthirsty lizards to go.

Something caught his eye. Jack looked over his other shoulder and discovered another raptor only metres behind him and closing fast. As it prepared to bite, the horrid beast looked like it was smiling.

Despite Tuner being the slowest member of their party by far, the raptor ignored him completely. Jack supposed it made sense. The raptor probably saw Tuner as machinery rather than a person, and he certainly wasn't food.

It lowered its skull, arched the shoulders of its short, reptilians arms, and leapt.

Jack winced, but the raptor never made it to him. Tuner swung a fist the size of a workout kettlebell into the creature's side. The punch was hard enough to knock it out of the air and into the side of a pink blossom tree. Almost felled the tree, too. Its petals floated to the ground like feathers.

Now the raptor noticed Tuner. Staggering back onto its hind legs, it turned towards the automata and snarled.

"Run, Jack!" he shouted, moments before the raptor pounced onto him. "Run!"

Jack stayed frozen to the spot as Tuner toppled into the ferns with the theropod hanging off the front of his chassis, slashing at him with its claws. Then he turned and fled.

God, he'd never complain about going up against Rakletts again.

Rogan and Klik were nowhere to be found. He hoped they'd reached someplace safe – whatever the hell *safe* meant in a tropical nightmare like New Eden. He was starting to think humanity hadn't made a wise choice of homeworld. They should have found somewhere cold and drizzly with no indigenous wildlife that could kill you. England, basically.

He couldn't see any of the marines anymore, either. That, he wasn't so worried about. They could look after themselves. And if they couldn't, all it meant was he'd have to deliver a slightly different report to Admiral Blatch when they got back to the *Final Dawn*.

If any of them got back.

Jesus Christ. Why the hell couldn't they get hold of the *Adeona?* They could really do with an exit plan right about now.

He pushed through a curtain of vines ahead of him and immediately pulled his hand away when he heard something hiss. All of a sudden, the whole planet seemed full of death traps. A second later he came close to face-planting a giant prickly shrub when he stumbled over a coiled root lying across the floor. Or what he hoped was a root, at least.

It was still too dark to see anything, too rainy to hear much beyond his own laboured breathing, and the mud was making his boots stick. Panic and bile rose in his chest. He hadn't a clue what to do.

Something stirred in the forest to his right, so he darted left instead. Immediately Jack came across a sheer wall of rock flanked on both sides by stone avalanches and fallen branches. He tried climbing it, but he couldn't pull himself even a few feet off the ground. The rain made the rocks too slippery.

He dropped to the floor and heard a low, snarling growl behind him.

One of the reptiles had caught up with him. It advanced into Jack's enclave slowly and let out a sharp, almost bird-like bark that made his heart shudder. He tried to retreat, only to discover his back was already pressed as far against the rock face as it would go.

No way out. He was trapped.

The monster lunged...

...and suddenly Jack was launched high into the air.

His first thought was that the raptor was playing with its food. The merciful lack of agony was either down to shock and adrenaline, or because he was already dead. But then the pain stayed gone, aside from a slightly uncomfortable tugging sensation around his ankle. And though he still scrunched his eyes shut, he didn't *appear* to be falling back down again.

He heard the violent snapping of jaws below him. Given that those same jaws didn't appear to be tearing chunks of flesh off his bones, he finally dared open his eyes again.

The raptor was still down on the ground. Jack, on the other hand, wasn't. It was leaping up towards him but missing by a good three or four feet each time. Not far enough, if anyone were to ask him. He shivered. It looked like an angry alligator bursting out from midnight swamp water.

He turned his attention back the other way, towards whatever was tugging on his ankle.

There was a rope tied around it like a noose. Better than a snake, Jack supposed. He instinctively bent over – or in this case, upwards – to untie himself, then had second thoughts. Whatever had caught him in its trap couldn't be any worse than the beast down there.

He glanced at the branch across from him and almost jumped another dozen feet into the air.

Perhaps he spoke too soon.

A strange figure squatted upon it, obscured by the shadow of the storm clouds. It looked lanky, exaggerated, deformed. Jack couldn't tell if it wore any clothes or what colour its alien skin was, but there was no hiding the starlight twinkling in its massive eyes.

It extended one long, bony arm. Clutched inside its simian hand was a little pouch crafted from leather scraps and silkworm thread.

Jack struggled against his bind as the bag came within a foot of his face. He wanted to swat it away, but that would mean touching it. He didn't want to. It smelled putrid.

"No," he begged as he tried swinging himself out of the way. His upside-down head felt heavy with blood. "Please, don't..."

The alien squeezed the pouch.

A noxious gas puffed out.

The world fell into an even greater darkness.

10

TIES THAT BIND

Jack woke to warm, dry air and the sound of creaking floorboards. That, and an elbow digging into his ribs.

"Hey. You awake?"

A groan escaped his lips as he struggled to open his eyelids. His whole head felt like it had been filled with children's plasticine. When the gas went off, he thought he was dead. He wasn't sure if the hangover was much of an improvement.

"Wake the hell up, man!"

Jack shook his head clear and turned to the owner of the voice beside him. It was Ghost, Private Flores – whatever her name was. She had a fearful and frustrated look in her dark eyes.

Her feet were bound together with the same type of frayed rope that had pulled him up into the tree and away from the raptor. Her hands were tied behind her back, too. He tried reaching across to undo her knots and soon discovered he was in much the same predicament.

"Where are we?" he asked groggily.

"No idea. I woke up in here just like you did."

His temples pounding and his vision swimming, Jack took stock of their surroundings. They appeared to be held captive in some sort of large, semi-spherical hut. Delicate rugs and tapestries hung from the wood-woven walls, which curved inward to a central point about twenty feet above the boarded floor. A thick pillar ran through the centre of the hut. Jack had to squint to study the intricate carvings in its dark wood, as blinding white light pierced through chinks in the wattle and daub panels around them.

The other three marines lay slumped together about six metres to Jack and Ghost's left. Just knocked out, he hoped. The bandage around Duke's head looked much more blood-soaked than before, and there was another quite nasty gash down his forearm.

"I don't suppose you've got any aspirin on you, by any chance?" Jack asked, as a fresh flash of pain shot through his grey matter.

"Only morphine, and that might be overdoing it." Ghost stopped trying to wriggle out of her binds and shrugged. "Not that it matters. They took all our guns and supplies anyway."

"Who did?"

"Whoever did *this*, you idiot. They knocked me out too, remember? Why don't you ask your robot friend over there?"

Rogan and Klik sat on the opposite side of the hut to the marines. They looked healthy enough, and though Klik was out cold like the rest, Rogan's mechanical nature meant she was immune to the knockout gas. She watched the far side of the hut expectantly. Jack was relieved nobody had fallen victim to their reptilian pursuers, but suddenly he was overcome with a new worry. Tuner was nowhere to be seen.

"Rogan," he hissed. "Rogan! What happened? Did you see who grabbed us?"

"Shh!" she replied.

"Rogan, did you—"

"Be quiet! Someone's coming!"

A rickety old door creaked open on the far side of the hut to them. Jack and Ghost bowed their heads in tandem and pretended to be unconscious, though Jack kept his eyelids slitted open just enough to see what was going on.

Once again, the sunlight from outside was much too bright for Jack's semi-anaesthetised brain to handle. All he could make out were two black silhouettes standing in the doorway, each approximately the same size and shape as the weird alien who gassed him up in the branches during the storm. They carried something large and cumbersome into the hut, let it drop with a floor-shuddering smack, and then slammed the door shut as they hurried back out.

Jack slowly raised his head and let out a gasp.

"Jesus, Tuner. What did they do to you?"

Tuner was a mess. Half the midnight blue paint had been scratched off his body, three jagged grooves were slashed across his metal chest, and some of his wiring hung loose. He looked like a pile of scrap.

And he wasn't getting up.

"Tuner?" Rogan desperately struggled to climb to her feet. "Please tell me you're all right."

He suddenly jerked upright.

"Sorry, guys. Had to play dead. I saw them tying you up and figured things might go easier if they thought I was just an engine part or something."

Jack and Rogan let out sighs of relief. Tuner casually prodded the ugly grooves in his chassis.

"Hmm. Those lizards really did a number on me." He

shrugged melodramatically. "Uh oh. I guess you'll have to resurrect me all over again, Rogan."

Rogan chuckled.

"You miss your old body," she said. "We get it. Now hurry up and untie us, will you?"

Tuner stomped across to where Rogan sat and clumsily released the ropes from around her wrists and ankles. Rogan then freed Jack and Ghost, who got to work rousing her fellow marines.

Jack hurried over to Klik, wincing at how the floorboards groaned under his boots. She looked to be in a deep, deep sleep. He laid a soft hand on her shoulder, praying that the knockout gas wasn't fatal to Krettelians.

"Hey. Can you hear me?"

Klik woke with a flash. She instantly deployed the bone blade of her right forearm, cut through the rope binding her wrists together, and pushed its flat length against Jack's neck. She looked into his face with large, fearful eyes, breathing heavily.

"You're awake, then." Jack's words came out in a squeak. "Good."

"Crap. Sorry, Jack." Klik retracted her blade. Her breathing grew calmer as he got to work untying the knots around her ankles. "I was having the worst dream. Some weird ape thing was carrying me through the trees in a net."

"Yeah, about that. You might want to try waking up again."

Klik looked around at the wooden hut and groaned. Once free, she first stretched her legs and then helped Rogan release the ropes around Sergeant Yates' wrists. The more Rogan tugged at them, the tighter and more painful the knot became. Klik snuck behind his back and, careful not to frighten the man any further, used one of her blades to sever the knot clean in two.

The only one of their number still not awake was Duke. No matter how much his fireteam shook him or slapped his face, the best response they got from him was a choked moan. Jack guessed the big guy's injuries were as bad as they looked. This was a problem. None of them, besides perhaps Tuner, could possibly carry him out. But it wasn't as if they could just leave him behind, either.

"Where are your smelling salts?" Ginger asked Yates.

"With the rest of my med kit, wherever the hell *that* is," replied the sergeant. "Same place as your rifle, most likely."

Ginger looked around for her gun, then swore loudly.

Three clay pots stood in a line beneath one of the banners hanging from the wall. Jack checked inside them. One was empty. The other two were half full with a clear and odourless liquid. Probably water. He gave it another sniff, just to be sure.

Oh well. They had to wake the guy up somehow.

He picked up one of the half-full pots, waddled over to the crowd of marines, and dunked the contents out over Duke's head.

"Wha...?" The giant of a man spluttered back to life before anyone in his team could protest. "What's going on? Why am I so wet?"

He scrunched up his face and raised a trembling hand to the wound on his head.

"*Christ*, that hurts. Be honest. How much of me is left?"

"Only the worst bits, I'm afraid." Ghost put his arm around her shoulders and helped him climb to his feet. "Nah, friend. You're all right. Just some blood loss and a concussion, that's all."

Duke swayed. One of his knees buckled. Sergeant Yates

quickly ducked under Duke's other arm and kept the barely conscious man from toppling back onto the floor.

"He needs proper medical attention," said Yates, straining against Duke's weight. "Even if we find our equipment, the stuff in my med kit might not help for long. We need to get him back to the *Final Dawn*."

"I still can't get hold of Adi," said Rogan. She looked more concerned than ever. "I really hope nothing's happened to her."

Jack got to the door of the hut first. It had crude hinges but no handle. He got ready to shoulder-barge it open.

"It could just be the forest still," he said. "Blocking our signal, like you said. We'll get out of here and find somewhere high and open to call for help. I'm sure we'll get through to somebody."

He turned to the marines.

"Ready?"

Sergeant Yates rearranged Duke's arm to make himself marginally less uncomfortable. He glanced at Ginger and Ghost, then nodded.

"As we'll ever be."

Jack steeled himself for resistance, then charged through the door. He quickly stumbled to an abrupt stop.

"Woah," was about as articulate an observation as he could manage.

He expected the wattle and daub hut to be on the ground – perhaps part of some barbaric, tribal village – but that assumption couldn't have been further from the truth. Jack swayed on his feet as vertigo kicked in. He grabbed a sturdy-looking flagpole for balance.

Their enclosure stood at the very peak of a tree growing a hundred metres from the rainforest floor below. The pole running through its middle had been carved from the trunk of the tree itself. The floorboards of the hut, kept in place by two of the tree's grand, arching branches, groaned as a strong wind blew by, shaking the leafy canopies and rippling Jack's t-shirt around his chest.

Had the fancy treehouse been a one-off, that would have been impressive enough. But it wasn't alone. There were *hundreds* of them, all connected to one another by an intricate network of boardwalks and rope bridges, ranging in size from small pens and huts all the way up to multi-storey longhouses. Ladders and pulley-drawn elevators led down to the dark world of the forests below, while flags and tapestries fluttered in the clear blue sky.

This wasn't some primitive village. This was a goddamn jungle city.

"Woah, indeed," said Ginger as she filed out of the doorway behind him.

"Jesus Christ." Sergeant Yates' face grew even more stern. "How are we supposed to get down from here?"

Tuner pointed to their right.

"Erm, why don't we ask them?"

A horde of aliens raced along the rickety bridges towards them. Jack recognised them as the same species that captured him from their shape and gait alone. Their legs were shorter than their arms, which were gaunt and gangly and hung almost to the floor. Each creature was perhaps a little shy of five feet tall, and their skin was a dull shade of green that blended perfectly with the leaves of the trees and bushes all around. Their four black eyes – one pair the size of saucers and swimming with intrigue and emotion, the others further up and no bigger than shirt buttons – occupied a great deal of their round, hairless heads. Twin yellow fins flared out from along their spines, shimmering in the sunlight.

They carried no weapons. But even with Tuner's plasma cannon, Jack knew their group would be too quickly overrun.

"Okay, you got us." He threw his hands in the air. "We surrender."

"Erm, Jack?" Rogan slowly pulled one of Jack's hands back down. "I don't think we're their prisoners."

"No?"

The alien crowd stopped short of the hut, muttering in an unidentifiable language and sharing anxious glances with one another. One of the shortest amongst them – a child adorned head to toe in a frock of brightly-coloured flowers – stepped forward and offered them a hand-picked bouquet. Rogan bent down and accepted the gift.

"No." She looked over her shoulder at Jack and raised a mechanical eyebrow. "I think that we're their guests."

11

THE FLO'WUD

The treetop city merged the natural with impossible feats of mechanical engineering. Alien relatives of palms, oaks and sequoias blended seamlessly with complicated systems of rope pulleys and wooden cranks. Whole gardens of fruits and vegetables grew from open rooftops. Huge carvings of majestic, long-tailed falcons had been chiseled into the side of giant trees. And no matter how hard the wind blew, not a single structure toppled from what ought to have been a precarious position upon the upper branches of the forest. They creaked and groaned, yet remained perfectly still.

The rope bridges were an utterly different story.

"Oh, I don't like this," said Jack, halfway across one of them when a fresh gale chose to batter their group. "I don't like this *at all*."

Inevitably, he looked down. This was a mistake. The gaps between the bridge's planks were too wide and too common. What may have been comfortable for a species with arms like an orangutan was a death trap for the average human.

He swayed above the jungle floor. Or rather, above the intricate criss-crossing branches and wooden galleys below. The ground was too dark and too distant for Jack to make out with his naked eyes alone. His stomach gurgled and his vision swirled.

"Keep moving," said Sergeant Yates, still carrying Duke's weight with Ghost. They weren't having half as much trouble crossing as he was, even with the big man's arms slung around their shoulders. "We need to get this guy to a doctor, pronto."

Jack jerked his head up again and continued to cross the bridge, only glancing down to make sure his boot didn't disappear through any of the gaps. He gripped the ropes to either side the whole time. His hands were red and raw when he finally reached the other end.

He joined Klik, Rogan and Tuner while the marines caught up. If Duke was fading before, he was practically translucent now. Yates was right – they *did* need to find him a doctor. But Jack wasn't exactly confident they'd find one here.

A crowd of the green simian folk waited just ahead, eagerly waving at them to follow. *Where* they were following the indigenous creatures, nobody knew. It wasn't that they hadn't thought to ask. Rather, none of the locals had translator chips and, without synchronising their language, nobody else could understand a word they said – and vice versa. Rogan was running a translation algorithm as they walked, just as she had when the automata first met Jack. It was taking considerably longer to sequence and, even if successful, the locals still wouldn't understand a word Jack or Klik said back to them. The marines would remain forever clueless either way.

The aliens beckoned their group to follow them into a

building larger than most of those surrounding it – about fifteen metres in height and perhaps a hundred metres in diameter, the mud and stick walls domed inwards to a central spout from which steam billowed. At least it wasn't smoke, Jack thought to himself. The last thing a city like this needed was a fireplace.

Unlike the structure in which they'd been detained – or rather unconventionally held as exalted guests, as Rogan would have everyone believe – this hut had no solid door. A curtain of multi-coloured stone beads blocked anyone outside from witnessing whatever transpired within. The head of their gangly congregation once again gestured for them to follow, then disappeared through the curtain. The beads soon fell still again.

"I guess we're supposed to go inside," said Rogan.

"Sure." Jack crossed his arms. "After you. If I hear the sound of metal being sawn in two, I'll know to run the other way."

Rogan rolled her eyes with a tired smile, then ducked through the bead curtain. Jack nodded to the marines to make sure they were still on board, and then followed.

If they were being led into a trap, it wasn't a particularly threatening one. Fine beds of straw and feathers were laid out in an orderly grid, their frames simple yet as ornately carved as the pillar Jack first saw upon waking. Above them hung more beds and more wooden walkways, which could be raised and lowered using a network of ropes spun into a spider's web under the ceiling. And in the centre of the hall was a ring of ancient black cooking pots – it was the steam from these that Jack saw billowing out from the roof before entering.

Locals occupied many of the beds, either sick or wounded. Others hurried from patient to patient, serving them some kind of soup or remedy from the pots. Jack guessed they'd been brought to the treetop city's infirmary.

"Erm, I'll wait outside, guys." Tuner pushed the curtains aside and peered miserably through the opening. He was too big to fit. "Or maybe I'll take a look around. This place is a technical marvel. Could learn a thing or two."

"All right, buddy," said Jack. "But don't go too far, okay? Who knows how quickly we'll need to leave."

"Chooka chooka," said their guide, jabbing a long, slender finger at an empty bed nearby.

"I think he wants you to set your friend down over there," Rogan said to Yates and Ghost.

"I don't have a good feeling about this," replied Yates, though Jack noticed the man wasted no time in leading his friend to the bed in question. Ginger waited back by the entrance, eyeing the aliens in the room with the same wary disdain she once showed Klik.

Jack sighed. Would every human behave like this around their new galactic neighbours?

Duke let out a groan as Yates and Ghost lowered him onto the plush straw. At six and a half feet tall, all of his lower legs stuck out past the end of the bed. Under different circumstances, it would have looked almost comical.

The eldest of what Jack assumed was the treetop civilisation's equivalent of doctors hurried over. Her skin was wrinkled, her pace slower and knuckles raw. Stars almost seemed to swim in her big, obsidian eyes as she gazed up in awe at each of her visitors... stars that then scattered when she realised she had a new patient to whom she must attend.

With hands that moved as delicately as if she were delivering brushstrokes to a canvas, the doctor unwound the bandages on Duke's arm and head. The more she unravelled them, the darker red they became. What they revealed was worse than Jack realised – perhaps worse than *any* of them realised. Duke's wounds had already begun to fester.

But the doctor didn't look worried. She turned to her colleague and casually muttered a series of words – or syllables, or *sounds* – that Jack still couldn't understand. He in turn shuffled off towards the cooking pots and quickly returned with a small bowl filled with a steaming white substance. The old doctor dipped a pair of fingers in it. It stretched away from the bowl with an elasticity similar to that of wet plaster.

"What's she doing?" asked Ghost, standing as close to Duke as she dared. "That stuff might kill him!"

"Let her do whatever she wants," Duke mumbled, barely conscious. He flapped the hand of his good arm nonchalantly. "I feel as good as dead anyway."

The doctor added a little more of the glue to her fingers and then, with the same delicate strokes she used to unwrap his bandages, applied the substance to the gashes on his arm. Everyone bristled as Duke took a sharp intake of breath... but relaxed when he subsequently sighed with comfortable relief.

She then started on the gash across Duke's skull. His wince as she got started was more restrained even though the injury was arguably worse. By the time she finished, the sticky substance on Duke's arm had already dissolved into the blood and cleaned the wound. Not only that, but Jack swore he could see the surrounding flesh slowly stitch itself back together as if with a thousand microscopic needles and thread.

Apparently Rogan saw it too.

"That's incredible," she whispered. Jack had never seen her so in awe of anything before. "Their understanding of natural remedies rivals any technology developed elsewhere in the galaxy. And all without the use of stem cells or diagnostic scans..."

The doctor's assistant came back with half a dozen more bowls cradled in his gangly arms. These were older, cracked, in need of a good varnish. Something orange and lumpy floated in each of them.

"Now hold on a second," said Yates, finally stepping forward with his hand outstretched. "No sticking any more of your weird gunk in my friend, you hear me? Jesus Christ. What's even in that stuff?"

Jack peered down into the contents of the bowls.

"Kwagua?" he asked, cautiously.

"Kwagua!" replied the doctor's assistant, breaking into a beaming grin.

Jack couldn't tell if it understood him or if it was just parroting the word back. Still, he unburdened the creature of one of his bowls and gave it a sniff. It smelled familiar, though it had been a good few months since he last tried it. And there was no guarantee he and the alien were talking about the same thing.

Even so, he *was* hungry.

He fished out one of the fleshy orange lumps and, much to the surprise of the marines, popped it into his mouth. Its unusual flavour – mango, passionfruit, clementine and angel cake – flooded his senses and banished all his aches and pains. Ah, the kwagua berry. The heavy-duty aspirin of fruity soups. The automata had once given him some after a bounty hunter shot him just above the heart.

The assistant eagerly held out the bowls to everyone else in their party... including Rogan, bless him. The marines stared at the food with transparent apprehension.

"Give it a go," Jack said through a second enthusiastic mouthful. "Trust me. It's good."

"OKAY. I think we're almost done."

Rogan and one of the gangly aliens sat on small, wooden stools set a few feet apart from one another in a hut not far from the treetop city's infirmary. Her translation algorithm had done a pretty good job of sequencing the key words in the local language, despite it sharing no common ancestry with anything in her database. One short and admittedly stilted conversation was all she needed to prepare it for conversion into English and a few dozen million other galactic languages.

Jack, Klik and the three upright marines – Yates, Ghost and Ginger – stood waiting by the door. Tuner was still absent, having been invited on a tour of the city like some sort of tin-can god.

The alien said something Jack found totally incomprehensible. Then Rogan nodded and stood up.

"Right, that should do it. I'll sync the data with your translator chips now. Normally it would automatically go out to everyone across the galaxy, but not while we're stuck in this no-comm zone."

The alien on the stool continued to talk as if anyone was listening. He seemed content enough.

"*Chooka nuu deebra si*—honestly, it's so nice to meet you all. We so seldom get any visitors."

Jack jumped as the chip in his neck translated the alien's language into words he could understand. Klik let out a yelp as her own chip did the same.

"What's happening?" asked Yates, uncrossing his arms and stepping away from the door.

"Nothing to be alarmed about," said Jack. "I... I understand him now. I've spoken to thousands of different aliens before... but for some reason, this time it feels different. Weird."

"It's probably because no outsider ever *has* understood them before," said Rogan. Jack could hear the pride in her voice. "You should probably introduce yourself."

He crossed to the empty stool and sat down. The alien smiled blankly at him.

"Hello. I'm Jack. Pleased to meet you."

The alien's blank smile remained steadfast. He looked from Jack to Rogan and back again.

"Sorry," he replied, "but I haven't a clue what you're saying."

"Wait." Jack bit his lip. "This guy doesn't have a chip. He can't understand me. Do you think you could...?"

"Translate for you?" Rogan replied with a smirk. "Of course."

She repeated Jack's message, using her vocal speakers to communicate in the alien's own language. His little face lit up.

"Pleased to meet you, Jack!" He gave Jack an over-excited nod. "My name is Benet. You might remember me from when I caught you in my trap and saved you from the Rippers."

"That was you?" Jack barked out a laugh. "I suppose I owe you my life. Thanks, Benet. I could have done without the knockout gas, though."

Rogan relayed the message.

"You are most welcome," Benet replied. Apparently the translator chip still had a few kinks to iron out. "We thought it would be the quickest and most comfortable way to get you up to the city. Our most humble apologies for leaving you all tied up, however. We didn't want a repeat of last time."

"Last time?"

Benet nodded.

"Yes, last time. The last visitor who came here got so freaked out when he woke up that he sprinted right off the balcony to his death." He sombrely shook his head. "That was quite a while ago, though. Long before I was born."

"How long have your people lived here?"

Benet shrugged as if confused by the question.

"Forever. There was no time before. We are the Flo'wud, and we have always lived in the forest."

"The Flo'wud? And what's the name of this place? This city?"

Rogan patiently translated Jack's message into Flo'wudian, or whatever their language was called locally.

Benet paused before he answered.

"We do not give the city a name." Each word carried the delicate deliberateness of a champion moving a chess piece from one square to another. "Only what is alive can bear a name. Given that some trees must die in order for us to build our home, it would be quite an affront to name it. But I suspect what you're truly asking is whether this is the *only* place our kind lives, correct?"

Jack nodded, a little embarrassed. That *was* the question to which he'd been leading. They may not have mastered faster-than-travel flight, but Benet's species was sharp.

Benet smiled and shook his head.

"Far from it. Though we're all self-governed with strict territorial boundaries, you can find Flo'wud tribes, clans and cities for as far as the forest grows. Some have travelled further still, the elders say. I haven't gone past where the rivers end, myself. Not that I can't," he hurriedly added as if he'd said something utterly abhorrent. "I'd be perfectly welcome. The Flo'wudian people haven't spilled so much as a drop of blood in generations."

"And these other towns and cities," said Jack. "They're all up in the trees, too?"

"Indeed. They're well disguised, of course. We have to build them up high so the Rippers can't get us."

"I'm sorry," said Rogan, hesitant to interrupt. "Did you say the Flo'wud people haven't spilled a drop of blood in decades? None of you, across the whole rainforest?"

"Centuries, most likely," Benet amended with a smile. "Why would we? Food, shelter, medicine – we all have everything we need and more. There's no reason for us to fight."

"What about the, erm, what did you call them...?" asked Jack. "The Rippers? Surely you've had to kill one of them from time to time."

Benet's eyes grew wide. He shook his head.

"Certainly not," he said, aghast. "We may not like dealing with them, but they belong to the forest just as much as we do. There have been incidents of bloodshed against the forest fauna during moments of self-defence, I will admit. *Rare* incidents. And we do sometimes use the hides of animals that have naturally passed for our roofs and mechanisms. But every precaution is taken to ensure that no living creature is harmed for our own benefit. That's why we caught you in the traps. Both you and the Ripper that wanted you dead are still absolutely fine."

"Zero violence *and* a surplus of resources," said Jack, turning to Rogan. "Humanity was right. New Eden really is a paradise."

"Unfortunately for humanity, this paradise is already

taken." Rogan crossed her arms. "That Admiral Blatch of yours is not going to be pleased."

"Hold on a second," said Sergeant Yates, stepping forward from the doorway. "What do you mean, already taken? Are you saying humanity can't live here?"

"It's not for me to say," Rogan replied. "But the planet does appear to have a few existing tenants."

"Well, where the hell else are we supposed to go?"

"New Eden isn't entirely covered in rainforests," said Jack, rising from his stool to stand between them. "They're a peaceful lot. Maybe we could find somewhere else on this rock to set up sticks."

"Like the polar ice caps or the desert belt?" said Ghost, rolling her eyes. "Yeah, we did our homework. Prime real estate right there."

"I think I'd rather stay on the *Invincible*," Ginger added with a sigh.

"Goddammit." Yates marched back and forth with his teeth gritted and his hands balled into fists. "This whole mission's a right bloody mess. The UEC board members are gonna be *pissed*."

A spark shot up Jack's spine.

"What time is it?" He stared wide-eyed at the sunlight pouring through the open doorway. "Blatch only gave me twelve hours to find Fireteam Sigma and report back. They don't know this planet is occupied. If we don't get in contact with the *Final Dawn* soon, they'll go ahead with a full invasion."

"Starting with a fireteam led by Sergeant Kaine," said Yates, pinching the bridge of his nose. "Hardly the most diplomatic soldier in the UEC."

"It'll be a massacre," said Klik. "Just like when the Mansa came to Krett."

"Is everything okay?" asked Benet, still sat on his stool with an uncomprehending smile plastered across his face. "Can I get you anything to drink?"

"We've got to find a way to reach the fleet," said Jack, growing more desperate the longer the conversation went on. "Whether we radio in or fly back and tell them directly, the UEC has to know the rainforest is off-limits. They *have* to!"

"But we can't, Jack." Rogan cycled through her channels to no avail. "All of our long-range comms are still out. Without them, there's no way of getting hold of the *Adeona*, either. We'll have to fix that problem before we can even think about helping anyone else."

"Yeah, about that." Everybody jumped as Tuner squatted down on the other side of the hut's doorway. "You're going to want to come see this."

12

SILENCE IS SAFER

Tuner led everyone – save for Private Sampson, aka Duke, who still lay recuperating in the Flo'wudian infirmary – up a series of rickety wooden walkways that wound towards the highest point in the city. A bowl-shaped platform nested amongst the tallest trees like the tower of some grand forest castle.

Waterwheels screwed into the titanic sequoias and oaks clicked as rain collected in the upper canopies turned their paddles and got funnelled down to the levels below. Higher, above even the most skyward-reaching branches, the wind blew more wooden paddles, these ones laid on their side, which rattled like a baseball card stuck in the spokes of a child's bicycle.

Emerging from the leafy camouflage of the canopies, Jack felt more exposed to the elements than ever. A crowd of Flo'wud citizens bustled around the junction at which their winding walkway started, but none followed. Only Benet and a couple of older aliens guided them to the top.

"There had better be a point to this climb," grumbled Sergeant Yates.

"Oh, it'll be worth it," said Tuner, when they were almost at the top. "Trust me."

Sergeant Yates pulled a face that told Jack the day when Yates trusted the word of a walking vending machine would be a very dark day indeed. Ghost and Ginger looked no less wary.

They were free to leave the city, of course. None of them – not Jack and his crew, nor the Flo'wudians – would stop them. But with Duke on the mend and the "Rippers" no doubt still skulking around the jungle floor, it wasn't like they had much in the way of options.

"Here we are," said Benet. Unlike the huts elsewhere in the city, the platform actually sported a proper set of barn doors. They were curved to match the rest of the platform's bowl shape. When closed, they appeared as just another panel along its considerable circumference. Benet creaked them open. "Please head inside."

"Go on," said Tuner, ushering them all forwards. "It's safe, I promise. They're only showing you up here because I asked them to."

Everyone filed inside. The platform had no roof and despite the hot sun, the floor was still a little slippery from the previous night's storm. It was also almost completely empty. Only a single metallic device stood in the centre of the platform. It was the size of a bookcase and the shape of a triple-A battery, and it looked totally out of place amongst the city's otherwise natural aesthetic.

Jack laughed nervously and shook his head.

"Is that what I think it is?" asked Rogan, approaching it as if it were a bomb.

"What?" Klik impatiently nudged Jack in the ribs. "What am I missing?"

"It's the stolen comm scrambler," Tuner said in an

ecstatic tone of voice. "The Flo'wud must have salvaged it from the crash. They brought me up here because they thought maybe I'd like to chat with it. I guess they think we might be cousins or something."

"How is it even powered?" asked Rogan, studying the cables running out from its base. There was a faint yet audible hum. "Its internal backup power should have run out decades ago."

"Electricity," said Benet, enthusiastically. "You really should try it. It's useful for all sorts."

"The wind turbines and waterwheels," said Tuner. "They build up a small charge which the Flo'wud use to power the scrambler. They've got the NavMap running a few towers over. It's a whole field of study here, apparently."

"But... why?" Ginger glanced across at the two older aliens, who were watching the group with obvious anxiety. "What use could these people possibly have with tech like this?"

It was a good question, even if not very elegantly put. Rogan relayed it to Benet in a language he could understand.

"At first we didn't know what it did," he replied. "We only wished to learn more about the people who sometimes fell from the sky. Through it we heard a chorus of voices – some sounded friendly, others much less so. We couldn't understand any of them, of course. Intrigue soon turned to fear. If we could hear them talking – could they hear us, too? We used the scrambler to return to the silence we knew before. Silence is safer."

"You don't want to join the wider galaxy?" asked Jack.

"Gods, no." Benet's face turned cold and frightened. "We know there are other worlds out there. Other people like yourselves. Please! We're not ignorant. But whilst we certainly enjoy the company of the occasional visitor, all we want is to be left alone. I hope that doesn't seem rude."

"Makes perfect sense to me," said Klik. Rogan nodded in agreement.

"I completely understand," said Jack. "We all do," he added, glancing at the three uneasy marines standing clumped together near the barn doors. "But unless we do something soon, I'm afraid you won't have much choice in the matter. My people – the humans – are looking for a new place to live, and we're desperate. Our own planet is... well, it's gone. Too hot for anything to live on. Unfortunately, they've chosen this world to be their new one. They don't know that anyone lives here already. If I don't get hold of them, they'll send a whole army down to take it."

Rogan translated the message using her vocal speakers. Benet's face went from a beaming smile to a rictus of abject terror, as did those of the two elder Flo'wud tribe members who'd escorted them up to the towering platform. Jack felt a knot of guilt grow in his stomach, which didn't seem altogether fair considering he was the last human to be informed of humanity's plan.

"They want to take this from us?" Benet's eyes swam. "But we've always lived here! We always will!"

"I'm sorry," Jack replied, bowing his head.

"We can stop them, Benet." Rogan stepped forward and rested her hand on his shoulder. Much to Jack's surprise, the Flo'wudian didn't so much as flinch. Rather, his eyes, already swimming with tears, now glistened with a desperate hope. "We can stop them," Rogan continued, "but we'll need to switch off your comm scrambler if we've any hope of reaching them."

The elders erupted in a cloud of cantankerous indignation.

"Only for a little while," Rogan said to them, "and I can show you how to activate it again once we're done with it. I promise."

"This could be part of their plan," grumbled one of the elders.

"A trap!" snapped the other.

Benet turned to them.

"Entra, Ventri, please," he said, tangling his fingers into knots. "If what they say is true, we have to try."

Jack sighed. The poor, naive lad put too much faith in his would-be colonisers. But somehow Benet's innocence seemed to work. The two elders grumbled and mumbled and shook their heads... but still they reluctantly gestured for Rogan to do her work.

"Thank you," Rogan replied. "Now come closer and I'll talk you through everything I do."

"Don't patronise us," muttered the one Benet had called Entra. "We got it to work once before. I've no doubt we can get it to work again."

"Come on," said Jack, escorting Benet over to where Klik, Tuner and the three marines stood. "Let's leave them to it."

AFTER ABOUT TEN MINUTES, during which the three marines asked young Benet all manner of random questions – translated back and forth by an ever-patient Tuner, of course – Rogan cried out in triumph.

"I've done it! It's old tech and I had to circumnavigate some quite frankly *baffling* firewalls that shouldn't have been there in the first place," she added, shooting an accusatory glance at the two nearby elders, "but the comm scrambler should be off now."

Jack hurriedly pulled his data pad out of his pocket. The officer on Admiral Blatch's bridge had given him a tonne of data pertaining to the mission – much of it redacted, to Jack's complete lack of surprise – and access to a number of restricted comm channels, too. He *could* reach out to the admiral directly, but...

"The range on this data pad probably won't extend to the *Final Dawn*," he said. "I might be able to bounce the message off Adi, or—"

"Adi!" Rogan quickly checked in with their ship. "How are you doing? Please tell me nothing bad's happened to you."

"There you are!" said the *Adeona*. Rogan played her response out loud so that everyone could hear. "I lost you down there – couldn't track your positions or anything. I was worried sick. Are you okay?" She didn't wait for an answer. "Nothing much has happened on my end. Just floating about up here in near-orbit, taking in the view. Jack's human friends certainly seem to be gearing up for something big, though."

Jack's insides shrivelled. From the sound of it, he was almost out of time.

"Okay," said Rogan, her voice growing urgent. "We've still got some work to do down here. Keep staying out of trouble, all right?"

"Not a problem. Call me if you need me."

Rogan turned to look at the data pad in Jack's outstretched hand, then shook her head.

"Don't worry about that. We can use the scrambler itself as a comm unit, just like the Flo'wud people did when they first salvaged it. Just tell me the channel we need to use."

Jack read out the long string of numbers assigned to Blatch's channel. Everyone inched closer to the scrambler in the centre of the platform – Yates, Ghost and Ginger most of all.

"Did it work?" asked Klik.

"Give it a moment to warm up," said Rogan. "It hasn't been used since long before any of you were born."

A cacophony of alien voices suddenly spilled from the tinny speakers on the side of the comm unit. Jack's brain turned to mush as the translator chip fought to separate and convert all of the different languages at once – few of which seemed to be discussing anything of real importance, and none of which were in languages that had originated back on Earth. The humans covered their ears. Rogan quickly set the scrambler to "send" rather than "receive" and the voices stopped.

"Transmit whenever you're ready," she said.

Sergeant Yates instinctively stepped forward, no doubt desperate to report back to his superior officers. But Jack was closer to the machine. He started speaking before Yates could get any further.

"Admiral Blatch? Captain Dyer? Can anyone on board the *Final Dawn* hear me?"

Rogan switched the scrambler back to "receive" again. Thankfully, the verbal assault had vanished. Now that the machine had calibrated itself properly, they would only hear from those communicating via the channel whose code they'd input... so long as there was somebody on the other end with whom to communicate, that is.

They waited.

"This is the *Final Dawn*," said a calm, professional voice through a cloud of static. "You're speaking on a restricted channel. Who is this?"

"This is Jack Bishop," said Jack, taking over the controls

from Rogan. "Admiral Blatch sent me down to New Eden to find your missing fireteams. She told me—"

"Hold, please."

The line went silent. Jack was about to try reaching out again when a familiar voice took over.

"This is Admiral Blatch. Who's speaking?"

"It's Jack, ma'am. Jack Bishop. I found—"

"Where on Earth have you been the last eleven hours?" she said. "The fleet is on standby and my arse is on the line. Tell me you've got good news."

Jack took a deep breath.

"It's a bit of a mixed bag, ma'am. On the one hand, Fireteam Sigma are all present and correct..."

"This is Sergeant Yates, Admiral." Yates barged Jack out of the way in his eagerness to speak. "Fireteam Sigma reporting in. Something big took down our bird, ma'am. Lost both our pilots in the crash. All of Fireteam Alpha, too."

"Goddammit." Admiral Blatch sounded as pissed off as she did relieved. "Well, I'm glad to hear somebody made it, at least. We'll send a drop ship down to your location – get you fixed up and ready for the second wave."

"About that," said Jack, elbowing his way back to the microphone. He wasn't half as effective in doing so as the gruff Sergeant Yates. "You need to call off the invasion. There's been some sort of mistake."

Jack expected a contemplative pause. The reply he got was as sharp and instant as a lion tamer's whip.

"Sorry, *what?* What the hell are you on about, Mr. Bishop?"

"New Eden," he gasped. "It's not uninhabited like humanity believes. There's a whole civilisation living down here. You can't invade the planet. Or not the rainforest, at least. We need to look someplace else."

Now he got his pause.

"There is nowhere else, Mr. Bishop." When the admiral spoke again, her voice was cold and calm. "You know how important this colonisation effort is for our species. For our *survival*. It doesn't matter what you found down there, just so long as it won't be a threat to our new colonists."

"You don't understand, ma'am." Jack chewed his lip as he fought to stop all his words from flooding out of his mouth at once. "This planet is *already* colonised by the Flo'wud people! There are whole cities down here amongst the trees, populated by... well, it must be millions of aliens. *Peace-loving* aliens. If you send more troops down here, then..."

His words slowed to a trickle, then a stop. A worrying idea had dammed the flow. What had Admiral Blatch said to him just before he left the *Final Dawn*?

We need to know what we're up against.

"Wait," he said into the microphone. "You already knew there was something down here, didn't you?"

Another thoughtful pause. It told Jack more than words ever could.

"We suspected," she eventually replied, sending a shiver down Jack's spine. "Our drones could only fly so low before we lost contact with them, and our telescopic photographs came back too blurry to know for sure. But yes, we knew it was a possibility from the moment we reached orbit. Yet it changes nothing. There is no other option."

"And was that why you agreed to send me down ahead of Fireteam Omega? Because I have experience dealing with... with... with *extraterrestrials*?"

"Among other reasons, yes."

Jack shot a sharp look at the three marines.

"Did *you* know?"

Beside him, Sergeant Yates shook his head. At the same

time, his hand instinctively went for his sidearm... which, of course, was no longer there. Klik raised her arms, ready for a fight.

"We had no idea," he whispered. Though his eyes were shadowed with fear, Jack felt inclined to believe him. "We're specialised in reconnaissance. We were ordered to scout the terrain and identify possible threats, that's all. We were as much in the dark about this as you, I swear."

Jack went back to the scrambler.

"Please, Admiral Blatch. Listen to me. I know there's nothing I can do to stop you if you choose to go ahead with the invasion. I know how desperate humanity is for a new home. But don't do this. You've no idea the level of destruction this will bring."

"It is no longer your concern, Mr. Bishop," she snapped. "Thank you for returning our fireteam safely, but your services are no longer required."

Admiral Blatch disconnected. Jack tried to reply but got nothing except static. Her team on the bridge must have closed the channel.

Everyone stood in appalled silence. Benet looked around at them all with a slowly shrinking smile.

"What did we get ourselves into?" said Tuner.

The curved wooden doors of the bowl-shaped platform swung open again behind them. Duke climbed through, escorted by the doctor's assistant. His bandages were fresh and unbloodied, and colour had returned to his face.

"Hey, guys! Will you take a look at this place? It's incredible!" His big, toothy grin started to fade. "Erm... what's up? What did I miss?"

"Oh, not much," said Ghost, giving him a hearty slap on the back. "I think humanity just declared war, that's all."

"Not war," said Jack, bowing his head. "Genocide."

13

LAST WORST HOPE

Jack sat on the wooden floor of the scrambler's platform and stared solemnly through the cracks. He could just about make out a nest of branches below.

"Well, I guess that's it," he said. "It's going to be a slaughter."

"What did he say?" Benet asked Rogan, his upturned face writhing with anxiety. "His chat with the scrambler didn't sound too good."

"He said he needs to come up with a new plan," Rogan replied. "One that means you all get to keep your home."

"As bloody if," Jack replied, chuckling in disbelief. "You saw the fleet out there. That was just a fraction of what humanity brought with them! Besides, this isn't some Raklett battlecruiser we can blow up with zero weight on our conscience. These are... you know... people."

"Exactly," said Ghost, though clearly she hadn't the slightest clue what a Raklett was. "This is the last remnants of humanity we're talking about. Who cares if a few aliens lose their treetop village?"

"Well, I wouldn't go *that* far," said Jack, climbing back onto his feet. "It's not like—"

"Ghost is right," said Sergeant Yates. "I don't like it any more than the rest of you, but if this is the only way humanity gets a new world to live on, so be it. Whatever it takes, right?"

"What?" Klik stepped forward, her mandibles clacking furiously. "Because us 'aliens' matter less than you, is that it?"

"Jeez," said Ghost, quickly backing away from the insectoid. "Don't take it personally. It's not your planet getting steamrolled."

"Ghost!" Duke looked appalled. "Have a little respect, will ya? If it weren't for these little green guys, I might not be standing in front of you right now."

Ghost bowed her head and sighed.

"Yeah, I guess you might have a point. Sorry."

"I mean, I get it." Duke put his hand on Ghost's shoulder. "Humanity *has* to find somewhere to settle – we can't float about in space forever. We're not built for it. Let's be honest – our *ships* aren't built for it. But whatever it takes?" He shook his head. "Sorry, Yates... but I'm not sure I'm okay with that. Not if it means displacing people. Or getting them killed."

"Yeah, me neither." Yates clenched his jaw. "Not really. But it doesn't matter what we are or aren't okay with. We all knew humanity would need to make some uncomfortable decisions before we settled somewhere. Hell, how many people did our Arks condemn to die when we left Earth? If the UEC wants to colonise New Eden, that's what they're gonna do. How one fireteam feels about it really doesn't factor into the equation."

He finished talking. Everyone remained silent.

"It sucks, all right?" Yates threw up his hands. "What else

do you expect me to say about it? Yes, I'd rather it was them than me. But... yeah. It sucks."

"Not for us, it doesn't." Jack nodded at the Flo'wudians. "We feel guilty for a bit and then we forget about it. We adjust. But what about these guys? What will they do? And what the hell are we supposed to tell them?"

The elders were muttering amongst themselves and casting circumspect glances in the direction of their group.

"I bet they wish they hadn't rescued us now," said Tuner.

"Nah, that's what makes it so awful," said Duke. "I reckon they still would. Goddammit. Why couldn't they be psychopaths or something?"

Benet awkwardly approached their circle of discussion and tapped Rogan's chrome body with the tip of one extremely slender finger.

"So... what *is* the plan? How *do* we get to keep our home?"

Jack suddenly felt very hot and red, and he suspected it wasn't just sunburn from standing above the canopies for too long.

"Listen, Benet." He scratched the back of his neck as he spoke. "I know your people forbid violence under any circumstance. But is there any chance you might make an exception? When it's a matter of life or death?"

"Don't be ridiculous," said Yates, taking a long and laboured breath. "They can't win. Even if every man, woman and child amongst them was willing to defend their city, they still wouldn't have the numbers. And what would they fight with? They don't even wield clubs, and they'd be going up against tanks and machine guns."

"You can't knock out a tank with sleep powder," Tuner added. "I should know. Didn't work on me."

"My goodness," said Benet, once Rogan had translated

Jack's last question. "Absolutely not. We never even hurt the Rippers if we can help it. I can't imagine why we would change our entire ethical philosophy just because a few more of your friends show up."

"But Benet," said Rogan, "their friends might not be so... friendly."

"If you don't leave the city, they'll probably kill you," Klik added, just in case the threat wasn't clear enough.

"Then that is on them," Benet snapped. "This is our home. This is our way of life. Nothing a bunch of stupid outsiders do is going to change that."

"I think you might be wrong about that," Yates muttered to himself as he paced back and forth.

"Maybe they don't have to stop the invasion," said Jack, tapping his finger against his chin. "Maybe they only have to slow it down."

"What do you mean?" asked Ginger.

"Yeah, what good would slowing it down do?" Duke shrugged. "Way I see it, that's only dragging out the inevitable. Unless... unless you're just talking about relocating everyone?"

Jack shook his head.

"No relocation. This is their home – the Flo'wudians stay here." He turned to Rogan. "The scrambler – how far can it send a signal?"

"Quite far. Further if we bounce it off a few relays. The real question is how long it'll take for anyone to reply. This system is pretty remote."

"Let's worry about one thing at a time." Jack unlocked his data pad and handed it to her. "Can you contact this comm channel and tell them everything that's about to go down? As an automata, it'll be quicker for you to send them a direct message than if I try calling myself."

Rogan looked at the name under which the comm channel was listed and raised an incredulous mechanical eyebrow.

"Sure. If you really think it'll make any difference."

"Hey," said Tuner, waddling across the platform to peer over her shoulder. "It's better than nothing."

"Barely."

"In the meantime," Jack continued as the two automata got to work on the scrambler, "we need to figure out what we're going to do when the rest of the UEC forces get here."

"Hitch a ride back to the *UECS Invincible*, probably," said Ghost. "Take a shower, neck a bottle of gin and try to forget this whole sorry day ever happened."

Duke tutted and gave her a playful punch on the shoulder.

"I don't know who you are or what you've done to think you can take on the UEC," said Sergeant Yates, "but you can't. Not on your own. And no matter how much we might dislike what our government has planned, Fireteam Sigma won't go against orders. Dishonourable discharge doesn't mean going home with your head held low, you realise. It means going out a goddamn airlock."

"I understand," said Jack. "Seriously, I do. Back when I was welding ships in the Pits at Sandhurst, I wouldn't have risked disobeying orders either. But I'm not sure you fully appreciate the gravity of humanity's decision here. Look at Klik. Or the automata. This galaxy isn't just made up of humans and a few million friendly tree-folk we can push around. There are hundreds of thousands of planets and species and empires. How do you think *they're* going to react to us throwing our weight around the moment we arrive?"

"You worked at the Sandhurst facility?" asked Ginger. "Funny. Never saw you there."

"It was a little before your time," Jack said with a humourless smile. "Come on, guys. There's a bigger picture here. If humanity does this, we risk getting blacklisted from the galactic community before we even get the chance to join it. And you do *not* want some of these civilisations as your enemy, believe me."

"You might be right," said Yates. "Hell, I'm sure you are. But we're marines, Jack. It's not our call to make."

Jack grunted in frustration and turned back to Benet. Tuner returned from the scrambler to translate.

"Are you really telling me that there's never been a time when any Flo'wudian has had to defend themselves? Not once in all of your people's history?"

Benet opened his mouth to answer, then snapped it shut again. He shot the pair of elders a nervous look.

"Hold on a second," said Jack, straightening up. "I saw that. You made an exception, didn't you? Well, why the hell won't you make one now?"

Benet glanced between Jack and the other aliens. His little simian face scrunched up in indecision and he wrung his hands together as if he were stretching taffy.

"No, *we* never made an exception," he eventually replied, withering under the heat of the elders' glares. "Our people pledged to live by this mantra long ago, and we'll forever stand by it. But..." He looked down at his feet and balled his toes into fists. "But not *everyone* chose to follow the same path as us."

"Benet!" He flinched as one of the wrinkly aliens hobbled over to him on her knuckles. "Kindly shut your eager mouth. That is not your story to tell."

"Then whose story is it?" asked Jack. "Because if they don't start telling it soon, that story's likely to end up forgotten. Humanity doesn't have a great track record of honouring the cultures it wipes out."

"They're outsiders," the old woman hissed in Benet's ear.

"They're offering us help," said Benet, shuffling away from her. "And... And I think we might need it."

The elders grumbled and cursed as they filed out of the wooden bowl-platform in protest.

"Please," said Jack, gesturing to Benet. "Elaborate."

"Well, many generations back – long before the time of anyone alive in the city today," he quickly added, "some of the Flo'wud communities decided they... that they didn't..."

"Come on," said Klik. "Out with it."

"They decided that they no longer wished to follow the same rules as the rest of us," Benet finally managed, fighting through the words as if he were revealing some dark and twisted secret hiding deep inside himself. "They wished to hunt still, to live on the ground amongst the beasts as predator and prey, and..."

He physically shuddered.

"My apologies, but I did not lie before. They are not Flo'wud. They haven't been for a long time. We call them the Forgotten now."

Jack clapped his hands together in triumph.

"Well, okay then! These Forgotten – would they fight for this rainforest, if we asked them?"

"Gods, no!" Benet's mouth dropped open. "They have no honour, no creed, no morals. They would not understand this otherworldly threat even if you tried explaining it to them. Not that you'd get the chance. They'd slit your throat and drink your blood before you uttered so much as hello."

"Then what on earth did you mention them for?" Jack cried, throwing his arms in the air.

"Because of what the Forgotten guard!" said Benet, excitedly. He dropped his voice to a whisper and checked the wooden door as if fearful that the older Flo'wud had returned. "The elders speak of a legendary beast that slumbers in the great lava caverns north of here, with blackened wings that eclipse the sun and a tail that curls around whole mountains. It has lived on this world far longer than any Flo'wud clan. For aeons it protected our forests. But the Forgotten moved into the caverns a dozen lifetimes ago, and ever since then sightings have become less and less frequent. Those heathens have it on some sort of leash, I'm sure of it. If perhaps we could free it..."

"What did he say?" asked Duke. Jack, shaking his head in both disappointment and disbelief, relayed the message.

"Jesus wept," said Ghost. "That's what they're going with? A myth? A campfire story? Fat lot of good that'll be."

"Steady now," said Yates, crossing his arms. "Don't be so quick to dismiss it. *Something* tore through our drop ship. I'm not saying it was this creature the locals believe in, but whatever it was must have been damn big. Big, and not exactly keen on visitors."

"I've seen stranger things," said Ginger, giving Klik an odd look again.

"Yeah, well, it makes no difference." Ghost shielded her eyes with her hand and peered up at the blisteringly hot sky. "Another drop ship will be coming down to extract us soon. They'll probably zero in on that scrambler you called from. You and the locals can do whatever you want, but us? We're out of here."

Duke gave her another punch on the shoulder.

"What?" she asked. "Those are the orders. Yates said so himself. Isn't that right, *Sarge?*"

"That's right," he replied, matter-of-factly. He was checking a new message on his clunky, archaic data pad. "Official orders finally came through. 'Remain on-site and wait for extraction' – just like Ghost said. This city's gonna be ground zero for the invasion by the sounds of it."

"So all we've managed to do is cut the Flo'wud's time here even shorter," said Jack, fighting to suppress a frustrated scream. "Brilliant. Just brilliant."

"Well, we'd better decide on a plan soon," said Rogan, rejoining their group. She handed Jack's data pad back to him. "The twelve hours your admiral gave you were almost up when you called. I can't imagine they've got much reason to delay the invasion any further."

"I know this sounds a bit heartless," said Klik, "but I vote to get out of here *before* the shooting starts. Just for once."

"The right thing would be to stay and help," said Tuner, but Jack noticed that even he had a note of hesitation in his robotic voice. "But it's also the most likely to get us killed. For once, we're not responsible for this. At all. The invasion would have gone ahead regardless of whether we answered the *Final Dawn's* distress call or not."

"Tuner's got a point," said Rogan. "As does Klik. But humanity are your people, Jack. We understand how torn you must feel right now. Whatever you choose, we're with you."

"For once," Jack sighed, "I wish it wasn't up to me."

He turned to Benet.

"Be honest. Do you really, truly believe this protector of the forest exists? That if freed from this Forgotten tribe, it'll come to the defence of the Flo'wud?"

"Oh, absolutely." Benet nodded enthusiastically, his eyes wide and brimming with hope. "Why would our elders

Jack, anxious to get a move on. They didn't really have time to discuss this. "I'm heading back there afterwards, anyway."

"Well, don't take too long. Though I suppose we've lost six good soldiers already – one more gone AWOL isn't gonna make much difference. I'll try to let you know if we get transferred back to the *Invincible* before you arrive."

"Thanks, Yates."

"Yeah, well. You owe me. Big time."

"Speaking of which," said Tuner, "I'd better stay behind, too."

"You're not coming with us?" asked Rogan, visibly shocked. "Why?"

"If the rest of the marines are staying at the Flo'wud city for the time being, *somebody's* got to translate for them," he replied. "Besides, nobody except Benet here seems to fully comprehend the danger they're in. I might try and convince them to evacuate, at least."

"If you're sure," said Jack, wishing Tuner would change his mind. "But don't be a hero, buddy. Humans haven't seen automata before, remember? When the shooting starts, get the hell out of here."

"Hey. You're the ones heading into the lair of some giant lava-dwelling monster. Worry about yourselves, please."

"We'll take care of him," said Yates, apparently forgetting that Tuner had a cannon for an arm. "At least until Fireteam Omega turns up," he added somewhat hesitantly.

Klik let out a loud and impatient sigh.

"So... are we going or what? I'm starting to feel pan-fried standing up here in the sun."

Jack's head was starting to throb, too. He gestured to the platform's wooden door and everyone started climbing out. Benet didn't follow.

"Aren't you coming, Benet?" asked Rogan, popping back

through. "We'll never find our way to the caverns without you."

"Me?" The poor creature's face grew steadily more mortified as the reality of his own suggestion dawned on him. "Oh. Oh dear. I didn't think this through at all."

14

THE ROAD TO HELL...

They bid a bunch of awkward farewells at a lush tropical garden on the edge of the lofty Flo'wud city. Ginger gave a hearty forearm-handshake to each of her fellow marines in turn while Rogan wished Tuner her best. Everyone promised to return safely.

Their weapons and satchels were returned to them, though not without considerable hesitation on the locals' part. Jack suspected that they didn't really know what the rifles did exactly, only that it wasn't for anything good. Not that they had anything to worry about, of course. Humanity as a whole might be willing to do anything for a new home, but Jack knew the members of Fireteam Sigma were good people. It was just a shame they had to follow orders.

The elders appeared to give Benet a fair bit of grief, though Jack couldn't tell if it was for telling the outsiders a story the Flo'wud considered sacred or for being stupid enough to guide them so far beyond the city limits. Perhaps they simply feared this protector of the forest being disturbed from its slumber. But whatever their reasons, none of them forbade Benet from leaving. Maybe that was against their creed, too.

A large and curious crowd hung around the gardens to see them off, enthusiastically waving and cheering. There were far too many smiles for Jack's liking. Tuner was going to have his work cut out for him if he planned on getting everyone there to leave within the next few hours.

"Shall we?" asked Ginger, once all the goodbyes were done. Jack nodded, they flung the straps of their rifles over their shoulders, and Benet nervously led the way.

The cavern in question lay about an hour or so to the north, so long as everyone kept a quick pace. Rogan estimated the actual distance at about five or six kilometres. It would have taken them much longer had they been crossing the dense rainforest floor, but thankfully a seldom-used series of bridges connected the city to the base of the craggy mountain in question.

Or so Benet claimed. For the most part, their group had no view other than the next band of creaking boards ahead of them. The bridges tunnelled through the treetop canopies, invisible both from the sky and the undergrowth far below. This came with two benefits – they were shielded not just from the harsh sun, but also any form of nauseating vertigo. It didn't do much to distract Jack from how derelict the planks and frayed the ropes of the bridges were, however.

"I still don't see why we couldn't have just flown to this cavern in the *Adeona*," Klik grumbled. "Would have been a lot quicker."

One of the boards groaned beneath Jack's boot. A hairline fracture began to snake from one end to the other like a crack across thin ice. He quickly hopped to the board ahead before the ancient wood could snap in half.

Thank goodness Tuner chose to stay behind, Jack thought to himself. He would have plunged right through.

"I told you why," Rogan replied from near the front. Built almost entirely from metal components, she was studying the planks harder than any of them. "We're going to this cavern to find a creature that swats drop ships out of the sky. I hardly think it sensible to bring Adi anywhere near it."

"Not unless you want to wind up like Fireteam Alpha," said Ginger, shuddering. Following Jack, she matched each of his steps like-for-like. "Never been more terrified in my life. And now I'm going out of my way to see the damn thing."

"Welcome to life out in the galaxy," said Jack. "Seems to be made up of one mad decision after another."

"You make it sound like you've been out here a long time."

"Three months or so. Long enough, let me tell you."

"Huh. Does it get any less intense?"

"Not really. Well, maybe a little. This expedition is a nice change of pace, if anything."

"Bloody hell." Ginger paused. "And there I was thinking this was the worst of it."

"Maybe it will be, for you. But I wouldn't count on it. Not if this UEC of yours is so intent on starting a war."

Ginger snorted.

"You keep mentioning the UEC as if you've never heard of them before. Where have you been the past twenty years?"

"Long story." Jack laughed to himself. "And one that's probably still classified, come to think of it."

Rogan spoke up before Ginger could probe any further.

"Hey, Benet. Does this mythical creature of yours have a name?"

Benet, far more fleet in foot than everyone else, waited for them further ahead. He hung from one of the ropes suspending the bridge from its neighbouring branches as if he were as light as the rays of sunlight that sliced through gaps in the leafy canopy. Looking at him made Jack's palms even sweatier.

"Why, of course," he replied. "Its name is Jörubor. Some of the younger children call it the Sky Devil, though if you ask me, that's a little disrespectful. The Jörubor is sacred. As old as the world itself." He shrugged. "But I suppose they don't know any better yet."

"You said the Forgotten guard it," said Jack. "Are they likely to give us any trouble?"

"I really couldn't say." Benet tilted his head from side to side. "It's been a couple of lifetimes since anyone made proper contact with them. It's as much worshipping as guarding, though. Maybe they'll keep their distance when they see a bunch of outsiders approaching."

"Or maybe they'll slit our throats and drink our blood before we even get the chance to say hello," said Klik, sarcastically.

"Yes." Benet's face turned a lighter shade of green. "Or that."

"Don't worry," said Klik, grinning as she passed him by, "you can always inhale some that knockout gas of yours. That way you won't feel a thing when they kill you."

"Never mind her," said Rogan. She stopped beside Benet as he gracefully hopped down onto one of the ropes running lengthways along the bridge. "How much further do we have to go before we reach this place?"

Benet's fingers fidgeted, and his fins flattened.

"We're about halfway, probably? I can't say for sure."

"Haven't you been to the caverns before?"

"Oh, yes. Once or twice. But that was quite some time ago. And I've only ever gone as far as the end of the bridge. I've never made the climb."

"Then it'll be a first time for all of us," Rogan replied, sending Jack a concerned glance over her shoulder.

Jack ignored her and spoke to Ginger again instead.

"So, Ginger. You said you trained at Sandhurst. What's it like there now? Or what *was* it like, I guess."

"I dunno." Behind him, Ginger sounded flippant. "Same as every other Ark base, probably. Hell of a lot better than off-base, though. Come on, you should know. You were there only a few months ago."

"Let's just say it feels a lot longer than that. Humour me."

"Is this some kind of UEC test, or something?"

"No test. Just interested."

Ginger sighed.

"Well, it was busy, especially after they started recruiting marines. Before then it was mostly essential personnel – the scientists in the labs, the grunts in the Pits, the soldiers guarding the *Final Dawn*. I grew up in Sandhurst, but I actually spent most of my training closer to Basingstoke. If you could call it training..."

Grunts. Jack stifled a laugh. It probably wasn't the best time to mention he used to be one of them.

"...pretty much had to build a wall around London," Ginger continued. "First the riots. Then the bombings. Didn't really matter that the UEC started offering people a way out through enlisting. By that point, the city was kinda already lost."

"Ah, yes." Jack nodded. "I remember the riots. Even then, hard to keep people civilised after you tell them their civilisation is coming to an end. Is that why you signed up as a marine? For a way out?"

"Of course. Nine out of ten soldiers in the UEC will give you that exact same answer. Having said that, I think Yates always wanted to serve. Same with our Staff Sergeant, Baker, though he's a little older than the rest of us. But yeah, that's why I signed up. Didn't have the skills or the money to qualify for one of the few tickets still going on board the Arks, and it sure beat dying a slow, cancerous death back on Earth. With both my parents gone, there wasn't all that much tying me to the place anyway."

"Doesn't sound like a lot's changed since I left," said Jack. "The Arks always were pretty exclusive. We never had the fleet back then, though. It's incredible how many humans the UEC managed to save in the end."

"Yeah, I guess. They're far from perfect, but there's no ignoring the fact the UEC turned a crisis into an opportunity. What do I know, though? I was pretty young when they took charge, so not sure I know any different."

Ginger fell into a short, thoughtful silence.

"It's just a way off that forsaken rock for me," she eventually added. "I've spent my whole life in limbo waiting for the day we'd leave, not even knowing if I'd be going with them. As soon as humanity finds somewhere to settle, I'll actually have the chance to live a life. A *real* life. Well. Once my term of service is up, that is. However long the UEC sees fit to keep me."

"It's as good a plan as any."

"What about you? You're obviously not with the UEC, so what will you do when we establish the colony?"

It was a good question, and one too complicated to answer while navigating the bridge's fragile boards.

"I really don't know," was all Jack could say.

JUST OVER AN HOUR PASSED, in fact, before they came to the bridge's end. The canopies grew thinner, as did the trees to which they belonged – gnarly branches snapped like statues of ash at Jack's touch. And though he couldn't yet see the ground below their feet – not even through the many gaps where boards were missing – something in his stomach told him their path had been slowly heading downwards for quite some time.

"Smell that?" he asked, wrinkling his nose.

"Smell?" gasped Klik. "I can *taste* it. It's like Krolak eggs."

"Sulphur," Rogan replied, curtly. Jack knew she couldn't smell in the human sense – she had to be isolating the chemicals in the air through filters instead. "It's common to areas of volcanic activity. The ground here is probably rich with the stuff. Could be whole lakes of it, too."

"Forget about the geology lesson," said Jack, covering his mouth with his hand. "Is it safe to breathe?"

"Oh, it should be. It sounds like the Forgotten haven't had any problems, though of course I haven't a clue what a Flo'wud's internal physiology is like. Just try not to eat any of it, I suppose."

"Thank goodness you told me. You know what I'm like. Always munching on rocks these days."

"Hey. You asked."

"Please be quiet," Benet whispered from up front. His anxiety hadn't improved. "I don't know how close the Forgotten come to the forest these days. They might hear us."

"Killed before we even get there," Jack heard Ginger mutter behind him. "That would be typical."

The tunnel of brittle branches and dead leaves continued to thin until eventually only a skeleton of vines and twigs encaged them. Jack discovered he could jump to speak of it if it weren't so? Besides, some of us have seen its shadow coasting high above the clouds."

"Could have been a passing freighter," Rogan whispered to Jack in English. "Every culture has its myths. Would you like to know the percentage that turn out to be true?"

"Let me guess. Zero?" Jack chewed his lip. "But legends... legends usually have at least a nugget of truth at their centre. Tell him we'll go to these lava caverns, if he'll guide us. But if this beast of his turns out to be make-believe, or if it won't help us slow the invading force down in any meaningful way, we're out of here. I don't need any more death and destruction on my conscience."

"I'm coming with you," said Ginger, suddenly.

"What?" said Yates, uncrossing his arms. "No you're not. You heard the orders from Command. We're to remain here until Fireteam Omega arrives with the first wave."

"We were sent down here to do advance recon," she replied. "We made contact with the locals who told us about a giant, flying monster that protects the rainforest the UEC is *about to invade*. Don't you think we ought to send *someone* to report back on a potential threat to our troops? It's our job, after all."

"Christ almighty," he said, pinching the bridge of his nose. "You realise Blatch will have my balls in a vice for this, right?"

"Not if we tell her that Ginger left for the caverns before the order came through," said Duke. "Right, Ghost?"

"Hey, you know me. I don't snitch." Ghost gave Ginger an intrigued look. "You'd better come back with some actionable intel though, you hear me?"

"I'm more concerned she won't come back at all," growled Yates.

"She can get a lift back to the *Final Dawn* with us," said

scary. I get that. But sometimes it's best to let go of what's familiar. Other times, you've got no choice. And whatever happens along the way, it makes you value where you came from even more. Believe me, I know. I miss my world terribly. So, come on. Let's go save yours."

Benet glanced over Jack's shoulder at Rogan, Klik and Ginger, each gripping their rifles tight and scanning the rocks for possible threats. He let out a despondent whine and nodded.

"Okay. Follow me. Let's see if I can recall the path to the caverns half as well as I do the rest of the details in the elders' stories."

He scrambled up the loose pebbles, wincing as the course rocks scratched against his bare feet. The rest of them duly followed.

The sound of Jack's boots sifting through the fine soil carried far. Somewhere – far on the other side of the ridge, perhaps – he thought he heard the slow bubbling of something hot and sticky. A sulphur pocket, perhaps. It was pretty toasty this side of the ridge, but nowhere near hot enough to suggest they were near lava.

Yet.

There was no trail to follow, presumably because nothing ever came this way. It was hard work on the thighs. Hard on the ankles, too. A couple of times Jack stumbled climbing a patch of fine pyroxenite (according to Rogan, at least – to Jack it looked like obsidian sand) and almost twisted them. He presumed even Benet was making up his route as he went along, hoping to discover something that married their present circumstance to the stories his people had passed down from one generation to the next. But all Jack could see was black stone and black earth – an ugly, dead land gushing like a popped cyst from a lush forest overflowing with beautiful life. He was beginning to suspect they were wasting their time. There was no way they'd find anything here.

He stopped and peered back in the direction of the hidden Flo'wud city. Nothing hinted at its existence, and Jack doubted much would change even if he were standing right beneath it. Gunships equipped with heat-seeking missiles probably wouldn't have the same problem, however.

Shielding his eyes from the glare, Jack turned his gaze further upwards. He couldn't see any troop carriers descending from the planet's upper atmosphere. Their descent would be slower than the *Adeona's* – they used older, inferior tech, after all – but that didn't mean they weren't already on their way.

"There," said Benet, stopping suddenly. He pointed to a spot between a pair of large igneous boulders. "Do you see them?"

"Is something watching us?" asked Ginger, quickly aiming her rifle. "If there are targets, call them out."

"No," replied Rogan. "Not that I can see. Look closer."

Jack, never one to trust that *somebody* wasn't about to try and shoot him, crouched down behind a substantial rock and squinted where Benet was pointing. In Ginger's defence, the heat haze made it hard for human eyes to make out detail from a distance. Rogan's were artificial, whilst Klik and Benet had eyes much larger and better suited to the climate.

Finally, he spotted them.

A pair of tattered red flags drooped from wooden stakes hammered deep into cracks in the boulders. They were barely more than threadbare ribbons. Their colour had faded from years of direct sunlight. Even as elevated as they were, there was no breeze to make them flutter. Even the wind avoided the mountain, it seemed. Beyond them lay the sun-starved entrance to a narrow, rocky canyon.

"The mark of the Forgotten," said Benet. His trembling voice threatened to break completely. "That's our way into the caverns."

"They look pretty old to me," said Klik. "Maybe the Forgotten aren't here anymore. Maybe they couldn't stomach the smell."

"Or maybe the Forgotten just aren't the exterior decorating type," Rogan replied. "It's a territorial warning. Could be we're signing our own death warrants by going in there."

"But it's either that or give up and walk all the way back again," said Ginger.

Benet couldn't understand a word Ginger said, but Jack could tell from the expression on his face that he hoped the latter was still an option.

"Not to sound cocky," said Jack, "but we have guns. The Forgotten don't. We go in, we find out if the legend is true, and then we get out of there. Fast. Maybe it's stupid. But if we don't even try, the Flo'wud won't last a minute."

They stepped out of cover and cautiously approached the mouth of the hollow.

15

THE FORGOTTEN

Cliffs of glassy, crystalline rock towered over them like the gemstone walls of an ancient, stone-cut temple. The sun-drenched sky ran like a narrow, blue river above their heads, small clouds drifting along its length like empty rowboats. Down in the depths of the narrow gulch, their path was dark and strangely damp.

They moved much slower than Jack would have liked, but for good reason. The air was still, yet the echoes of their movement raced ahead of them with boundless enthusiasm. Sometimes the natural corridor opened up into a spacious gully; other times, they had to squeeze through cracks in single-file. If the Forgotten were present and decided to attack from the top of the lava-furrowed channel, they would be trapped. Everyone kept an eye on the ridges above, but the higher the sun rose in the morning sky, the harder watching for ambushers became.

Jack wiped a soggy film of sweat from his brow. He felt a little... woozy. The heat was having a weird effect on him. The fumes, too.

Flashes of ruby and zircon sparkled in every crevice they

passed. The gorges and caverns of the volcano must have been worth a fortune. Jack wondered why the Flo'wud and their exiled brethren had never considered mining it. Perhaps their kind placed no value in precious minerals. Perhaps, on New Eden, those minerals were too abundant to be worth anything.

"Can somebody ask our little green friend how far into this hellscape we're supposed to find that forest deity of his?" asked Ginger. Her words came out muffled; she'd covered her mouth with a rag. "We could be here for days scouring every last nook and cranny. Presuming it's even here."

"I doubt even he knows," said Rogan. Her body may have been metal, but she sounded as tired as the rest of them. "Do you know what would have delayed the invasion better than this? Flying back to the *Final Dawn* and telling that admiral of yours where to stuff her fleet face-to-face. I'm sure the sight of our crew strolling onto her bridge would have had her frozen to the spot."

Jack laughed, which turned to coughing when he accidentally inhaled too much of the putrid air.

"I'm sure it would," he replied. "Are you all right, Rogan? You sound more miffed than usual."

"It's just always the same," she replied. "Fleshies putting automata to work, then trashing them for scrap when they're done with us. The Mansa enslaving the entire Kretelian race and erasing their culture as well as their freedom. And now *your* kind have turned up, and already they're preparing to wipe out a whole civilisation just for a bit of land. Humanity's no better than the rest. And can someone please explain to me how we always end up in the middle of it all, trying to put the whole galaxy to rights?"

"Well... if you'd spent your whole life around humans,

you'd know it wouldn't make any difference. They'd throw me in a cell, dismantle you and Tuner to figure out how you work, dissect Klik to figure out how *she* works, and *still* have time for a genocide or two before dinner."

"Wow. Phrase it like that and humans sound much better."

Jack shrugged.

"Sorry. It's not how most of us would like it."

"Oh, I know it's not your fault. And besides, I know why we always end up in situations like these – because it's the right thing to do. Because it's better to help than turn our backs. But let's take some time off after this and enjoy ourselves for once, okay? Please?"

"Sounds good to me," said Klik. "I've barely spent a moment since getting my freedom where I haven't been chasing after an unhinged theoretical physicist or stuck in my quarters with nothing to do."

"Room for one more?" said Ginger, sarcastically. She was the only one still paying proper attention to the rocks above them. "I've only spent one day in active service and already I could use a vacation. *Psst.* Check it out. Up there. More flags."

Jack cast his gaze upwards again. The sun glanced off the polished black rock and stung his eyes, but not before he spotted another pair of raggedy red banners hanging from the precipice like medieval drapes. There was some reassurance in knowing they were still headed in the right direction... even if there was no other direction they could actually head.

"Over here!" hissed Benet from around the next bend. "I told you this was a sacred place!"

The rest of them shared a quick and nervous glance, then followed Benet under a suspiciously unnatural archway. They all stopped short on the other side. Ginger almost shot what they were all looking at in surprise, clearly more jittery than her stoically marine exterior let on.

"Is it just me," Rogan whispered to Jack, "or does that look familiar to you?"

Carved from the wall of glassy, obsidian rock was a statue at least ten metres tall. The craftsmanship was incredible, the sculpturing so fine and so detailed that Jack hardly blamed Ginger for thinking it might be alive. A tall, slender alien with an engorged cranium stared out over the ridge opposite with a cold, academic expression, its delicate hands clasped together in front of its sweeping, regal robes.

Of course it looked familiar. It was a spitting image of the bronze statues he saw in the abandoned Library archive back on Kapamentis.

"Don't tell me the same people who built that treetop city also carved this," said Ginger.

"No, they didn't." Rogan ran her metallic hand across the base of the statue. "This is older. *Much* older. I guess the ancients were here, too."

"Well, you did tell me they conquered the whole galaxy before they suddenly upped sticks and disappeared," said Jack. "Should we really be surprised?"

"I guess not," Rogan sighed. "You just don't expect to find their ruins in a place like this, that's all. Then again, an unspoiled planet is probably the only place left you *would* find them."

Klik sidled up next to Ginger, who continued to stare at the giant statue.

"Creepy, right?"

Ginger, who still couldn't understand a word anyone except Jack and the automata said, jumped in surprise and slowly backed away down the gully. Klik chittered to herself in amusement.

"Look what the savages have done," said Benet, sitting down hard on the floor. He raised a dismayed finger and pointed further along the path. "Hallowed ground. Tarnished!"

A colossal skeleton lay blocking much of the rocky corridor ahead. A *mammoth* skeleton, perhaps, for the recently deceased creature still sported a pair of breath-taking tusks. Fresh organs steamed in the heat. Blood dripped from the stones. Patches of leathery meat still hung from the head and ivory.

And pikes still jutted from gaps in the beast's ribcage.

"Eyes up," said Jack, grabbing his rifle. "The kill's fresh. The Forgotten can't be far."

"Probably heard us coming," said Klik.

"Probably watching us as we speak," Rogan added.

"How far the lost have fallen." Benet despondently rose to his feet. "Feasting on flesh. Slaughtering the innocent. Heathen barbarians. Savages!"

"Can somebody shut that little green freak up?" Ginger hissed through gritted teeth. "He's gonna get us all killed!"

Jack shook his head. Benet's tribalistic prattling was getting exhausting. Sure, the Flo'wud saw the Forgotten as beneath them. But humanity saw the Flo'wud as beneath them. And the various species within the Ministerium of Cultured Planets would surely look upon humanity as a bunch of primitive apes playing at space travel once they caught wind of all this.

All that endless judgement, and for what? It wasn't as if the galaxy's prejudice formed a ladder. It looked more like a goddamn wheel from where Jack stood, one where everyone was connected to everyone else by a hundred different bigoted spokes.

"Keep pushing forward," he said, refusing to pull his eye from the sights of his rifle. "Could be they ran off because they're afraid."

"Yeah?" said Ginger. "Well, let's keep it that way."

She fired her rifle into the air twice. Everybody winced, especially Benet, who fell backwards onto the stone again in horror. The sound of each gunshot ricocheted through the narrow canyon walls harder than any bullet could – it was a good five seconds before the last echo was out of earshot.

"Jesus Christ!" Jack grabbed Ginger's arm, but she'd already lowered her rifle. "What the hell was that?"

"A warning," she said, pushing pushed past him. "Either they now know to leave us alone, or *we* know they're not even there anymore. So let's pick up the pace, yeah? Let's find this Sky Devil and clear the skies so we can head home."

"Clear the skies?" Jack grabbed her arm again; he soon let go after the look Ginger gave him. "We're taking control of the Jörubor from the Forgotten and using it to slow down the incoming drop ships, not caging it even further. Or did you have something more permanent in mind?"

"Wisen up, Jack," Ginger snapped. "You're following a damn folk tale as if you actually think it's true! This creature you're talking about – it's killed six people already. Almost killed me and my friends, too. And you're seriously thinking of setting it on our fellow humans as they descend through the atmosphere, completely unaware? Jesus Christ. Did you really think anyone in my fireteam would actually be on board with that? Where do your loyalties lie?"

Jack's face burned red. He turned to Benet. Oblivious to

their discussion, the gangly creature stared miserably at the bloody remains of the slaughtered beast.

Was he being an idiot, siding with the Flo'wud over the human fleet? Were his priorities all messed up from being off Earth for so long?

"As much as I'd like revenge, I'm not saying we should kill this thing," Ginger continued before Jack could reply. "And I'm not saying I agree with the UEC driving tanks up to the aliens' doorstep, either. For the record, I don't. But I'm not going to let you do anything that'll get my brothers and sisters killed. I'll always put humanity first. Always. You should think about doing the same."

"I *am* putting humanity first," he said, hurriedly following Ginger through another narrow crack in the rocks. "Do you realise the trouble we'll be in if—"

"Guys?" Rogan squeezed through the gap behind them with Klik and Benet in tow. "What's all the shouting for? And why in the galaxy have you stopped...?"

"Oh," said Klik, flaring her mandibles. *"That's* why."

They'd emerged from the crevice into a round cavity carved deep into the black rock. More statues, each identical to the last and spread evenly apart from one another, stood around the cavity's edge, though none was more than half the size of the original they passed before. But it was neither these nor the scores of red banners hanging from the statues' clasped hands that turned Jack and the rest of their party to stone.

The entrance to more than twenty clumsily-excavated tunnels pock-marked the periphery of the pit, and from half of these alcoves crept uncanny cousins of Jack's simian companion. Their dwellings were adorned not with wood like the Flo'wud but with all manner of bones, bleached white from the sun and inscribed with beautiful runes so fine Jack couldn't believe they'd been carved without a laser chisel and microscope.

From a glance, nothing separated the Forgotten from the Flo'wud save for their preference of building material. But then they grinned.

They'd filed their teeth, turning molars into canines.

All the better for eating meat.

Which makes them no different to me and half the galaxy, Jack reminded himself. *Jesus Christ. Is this what Benet thinks when he looks at me?*

The Forgotten advanced from their network of tunnels and descended staircases of rock and bone. In their hands they wielded ornate daggers also fashioned from tibias and femurs. Rubies had been hammered into their hilts.

"So b-brutish, so vulgar," Benet stuttered. "They're even worse than the elders said!"

"I think we ought to be on our way," said Rogan, turning back to the fissure through which they came.

"Agreed," said Ginger, before Jack could say the same. It was beginning to feel like he wasn't in charge of the mission anymore.

But the way back was blocked. More Forgotten snarled at them from the other side, pikes grasped in their scrawny hands. Jack knew there was no use in trying to fight them. The bottleneck would only get them all killed.

"Do they speak the same language as the Flo'wud?" he asked Rogan. "Maybe we can reason with them."

"Do they *look* reasonable to you?" asked Klik.

"We come in peace," said Rogan, raising her hands so that her rifle was pointed at the sky. "If you let us pass, we can help keep you safe – keep the whole *planet* safe."

The Forgotten roared with indignation.

"I don't think they appreciate the offer," said Rogan, bringing her rifle down again.

"See?" Benet shrank behind Jack and Ginger. "I told you they wouldn't understand. They're imbeciles. They know nothing but violence."

"Are you kidding?" said Jack. "They think we're invaders here to kill them and steal their land. This is exactly how we want *you* to react!"

"The only other way out is up there." Rogan nodded towards the far end of the pit. A narrow set of steps ascended through the black rock of the ridge. "Unless anyone fancies crawling through the Forgotten's tunnels, that is."

"No thanks," said Ginger. "I'm not a huge fan of the dark. Or of confined spaces, actually."

"And you voluntarily got on a spaceship?" asked Jack, snapping the reticle of his rifle from one Forgotten to another. "Why?"

"This all makes for great conversation," said Rogan, back-stepping between them, "but do you think we could focus on the matter at hand?"

The Forgotten continued to stalk forwards. Another few seconds and they'd be within stabbing distance... and as such, too close to shoot.

"Ah, screw this." Klik swung her rifle over her shoulder and deployed her bone blades instead. "I say we just kill them and get on with the plan."

"Klik, no!" Jack could see the yarn of his plan unravel before his eyes. "The whole reason we're here is to *stop*—"

But in the end, the Forgotten drew first blood. One of the banished Flo'wud near the back of the mob yelled something Jack couldn't understand and threw her pike in Klik's direction. Klik saw the weapon coming and leapt to the side.

She was quick... but not quite quick enough. The bone-sculpted tip slashed past her shoulder before clattering to pieces against the stone wall behind. Purple-red blood splashed down the side of her borrowed t-shirt.

"Seems like they engaged first, if you ask me," said Ginger, aiming at the nearest Forgotten and pulling the trigger.

The Forgotten in question somersaulted onto his back, a bloody hole in the centre of his chest. His dagger skidded across the polished rock floor and stopped at the feet of his fellow tribe member, who hungrily snatched it up. Ginger swung her rifle towards them and a second later they were gone, too.

"Klik? *Klik?"* Jack crouched down beside her. "God-dammit, tell me you're all right."

"I'm fine," she replied, wincing. Her bone-blades had retracted. Jack tore open the sleeve of her shirt to get a better look at the wound. It wasn't as deep as he feared.

"Ouch," she said, glancing down at it. "That's gonna leave a nasty scar."

"You need to control that temper of yours," Jack said, pulling her to her feet.

"No, I need to remember to shoot first and cut later."

Klik raised her rifle with her good arm and fired a couple of shots at the Forgotten who threw the pike at her. One shattered an elephantine femur hanging beside the banished Flo'wud's head. The other caught the creature in the neck and sent her tumbling – she was dead before her skull cracked on the rocks below.

Most of the Forgotten fled back to their alcoves after the first couple of shots. The few that remained were slowly closing in on Ginger, who responded by swapping her rifle for her sidearm.

"Back the hell off."

She spat the words out like bullets. When they had no effect, she fired a few actual rounds at them. One unfortunate Forgotten fell in a violent spasm, but her two companions continued their advance unperturbed, slashing with their blades as if hacking away at a wall of invisible vines.

Rogan, behind whose metal chassis Benet insisted on cowering, hesitated for a moment before coming to her aid. Still against using firearms in all but the most unavoidable situations – the Rakletts had it coming, if you asked her – she raised the butt of her rifle and slammed it down hard on the nearest Forgotten's head. The sharp-toothed simian fell to the floor, out cold but still breathing, the stubby fins on its back twitching.

The only remaining Forgotten realised he was on his own and, after scowling at the intruders one final time, made an attempted escape through the crack in the rock behind them. Ginger spun around and let rip with her pistol. He never even made it to the wall.

Jack stared in dismay at the scene of carnage their short skirmish had left behind. Five corpses, plus one unconscious survivor whose skull may never recover from Rogan's blow. The stench of fresh blood drying under the hot sun was suffocating.

"Jesus Christ. How did this happen? We came here to stop a slaughter, not cause one."

"Let's get moving," said Ginger, sweeping the gaze of her rifle across the myriad of alcoves and tunnel mouths. "We held them off for now, but there's no telling how many more the others will come back with."

They raced up the stone steps and out of the pit. Despite the urgency of their pace, and despite his tremendous guilt regarding the violence behind them, Jack couldn't help noticing there were intricate networks of metal installed amongst the rocks. The higher they climbed, the more that cybernetic lattice seemed to consume the obsidian... and the better their view of what lay beyond the ridge became.

They paused at the top to catch their breath, only to have it unceremoniously snatched away from them again.

"Okay – what on God's green Earth is *that?*" asked Ginger.

"I don't know," said Jack, looking to an equally perplexed Rogan for answers. "But something tells me it's not supposed to be here any more than we are."

16

PAST CONTROLS FUTURE

They stood at the summit of the volcano and stared down into its crater. Jack had never seen a crater with his own two eyes before, but it didn't take an expert to know they weren't supposed to look like this one.

It also didn't take an expert to know that the volcano was still active. Pockets of boiling lava bubbled away in artificial vents down at the bottom. Jack found himself a little disoriented. There was even more heat on his face from the fires below than from the scorching, direct sun above.

Or perhaps it was just the fumes.

Klik tapped her bare foot against the floor where the crater began. It made an odd clinking sound.

"Is a volcano supposed to be made of this?" she asked.

"No," said Rogan, shaking her head. "None are. None that anyone's ever discovered before, at least."

Almost the entire surface of the crater was covered in the same intricate, cybernetic lattice Jack saw creeping up the rocky stairwell behind them – an enormous plate of armour pulsing with an eerily biotic electricity. In the absolute centre of the metal crater stood a dark tower built from the same foreign, inorganic material.

Benet pushed past them to reach the front with a look of horror scrawled across his face.

"What have those heathens done?" he moaned.

"Oh, I don't think your Forgotten friends are responsible for this," said Jack. "Sorry, Benet. I've got a suspicion the story your elders told you was missing a few chapters."

"Yes, this is much older than Flo'wud civilisation." Rogan crossed her arms and gave Jack a knowing look. "As old as the Libraries and Ministerium, perhaps. We ought to reconsider this. There's no telling what we'll find down there."

Jack was about to reply when something small and dark caught his eye. He turned his head to the heavens and his heart sank. Three drop ships and two tank-carriers silently pierced the thin blanket of clouds. They cut five neat, white trails through the sky as they plunged towards the forest.

Nothing rose to stop them.

"That'll be Fireteam Omega," said Ginger. "Looks like Kaine's been put in charge of a whole squad. Slimy toad. They've brought panzer tanks with them this time, too."

"More than enough to wipe out the entire Flo'wud city, if Benet's neighbours don't bother putting up a fight," said Jack. "It can't be a coincidence that this ancient structure is exactly where the Flo'wud believe their protector lives. We'll find something here that can help them. I just know it."

"Eurgh." Ginger rolled her eyes in mock exasperation. "Stop it, Jack. You're chasing after a damn Bigfoot. Or did you use to believe in him, too?"

"You said it yourself. *Something* tore through your drop ship."

"Yes, *something* did. But this planet could be filled with all manner of different predators. Doesn't mean any of them are magical guardians of the forest. Definitely doesn't mean any of them are gonna be inclined to help *us*."

Rogan bowed her head.

"I hate to say it, but I think Ginger is correct. Look at this place. It's a hyper-advanced relic of a civilisation that's long dead. I can't believe we'll find anything here alive, let alone of any use to the situation at hand."

"If we leave now, we'll be gone before any more Forgotten show up." Ginger nodded back down the stone steps. "Might even reach the treetop city before Kaine, too."

"I can't believe I'm hearing this," said Jack, stepping backwards to block their retreat. "After coming all this way, after being forced to kill Forgotten to reach the summit... you want to give up?"

"Be realistic, Jack." Rogan gestured to the abandoned alien structure. "There's nothing here. We're not giving up. We failed. There's a difference."

"Well, *we* failed. You, me and Klik. Ginger didn't. *She* wanted to give her fellow troops a clear path to the jungle." He patted Ginger sarcastically on the shoulder. "Well, you got what you were after. Hope you're happy, Private."

Jack stopped talking and looked around the top of the ridge.

"Hang on a second. Have either of you seen Benet and Klik?"

It took only a second for the three of them to spot the two aliens shuffling down the slope towards the structure in the centre of the crater. Jack called after them in as loud a whisper as he dared.

"What?" said Klik, throwing up her hands. Jack winced at how easily her voice carried. "You said it yourselves – there's nothing we can do to stop the invasion. If that's true, we may as well take a look around while we're up here."

They continued walking down. Jack turned to Rogan and shrugged.

"She's got a point," he said, hurrying after them.

"Hey, I never technically said we should head back." Rogan easily kept pace with him. "I only said we wouldn't find anything up here that would help."

Back on the ridge, Ginger groaned... and then followed.

The metallic floor of the crater clunked as if Jack were walking across the exterior hull of a spaceship. He guessed it was only a narrow plate stretching across an otherwise hollow volcanic shaft. Well, not *quite* hollow. Given how he could see bright yellow bubbles churning through the exposed vents off to the sides, there couldn't have been more than a few feet separating his boots from the tumultuous lava beneath.

He shivered despite the heat and concentrated on catching up with Klik.

The crater was wider than the volcano was tall, which made its cyber-industrial overhaul all the more impressive but also meant the walk to its centre was much further than it first appeared. The farther the five of them descended, the more the intricacies of its layout revealed itself. Sporadic, black obelisks. Chrome panels that shifted from one axis to another, turning like the hands and gears of a giant clock and releasing intermittent jets of steam. Transparent pipes between sections of metal floor that alternated between flashes of fiery red and bursts of blue lightning. One thing became quickly apparent, however, despite Rogan's earlier observation.

They were not alone.

Close to the central tower – which Jack now appreciated was nearing a staggering hundred metres in height – were dozens of Forgotten. Dozens of dozens, perhaps. But they the rocky silt floor if he wanted. As the bridge sloped down, the ridge of the volcano reared up before them.

It wasn't the sort of volcano that pierces the clouds like the raised fist of some ancient, hellish god. It was wide and squat like an ancient meteorite crater. The ridge was steep and littered with sharp rocks scorched blacker than their own shadows. Jack began to suspect he might be in for a harder climb than the average cliffside path. The sun danced behind a thick, exotic haze.

Jack stopped at the foot of the bridge and tried to listen for possible threats, but got nothing. Nothing at all. Gone were the songs of alien birds, the buzzing of bees and high-pitched whine of New Eden's native mosquitos. All was silent.

No life dared venture where they stood.

One by one they stepped off the last wooden plank and onto the Forgotten's turf. Jack was a few steps up the rocky slope when he realised Benet was no longer with them. He turned around and found the sorry creature cringing a few metres further up the bridge than before. His breathing had grown erratic, his green skin glistened with a nervous sweat, and his fins were spread out low.

"Can't do it," he said, scanning the rocks with panic-stricken eyes. "Can't go any further."

"Yes, you can." Jack hurried back. "Your people are counting on you, whether they realise it yet or not. You *have* to go further. We won't know what it is we're looking for without you."

"Urgh." Klik groaned and dug her heel into the dirt. "We don't have time for this..."

"Hey. Don't listen to her." Jack ducked down slightly so that his eyes were level with Benet's – Benet's larger pair, at least. "Leaving the safety of your home for the first time is posed no threat. Standing in perfect rings around the tower, facing inwards with their arms hanging loose by their sides, they seemed to barely exist in anything but the physical sense at all.

Jack, pre-empting another attack, pointed the barrel of his rifle straight at the face of the first Forgotten they came across... but the Forgotten simply stared past it – *through* it, even. Its permanent smile of bliss didn't budge an inch.

"Jesus, that's creepy." Jack checked the next one along. They were just as hypnotised as the last. "What do you think got into them?"

"It's as if they're stuck in a religious trance," said Rogan. She gave one of them a tentative prod. "Like the tower has some kind of hold over them."

"Coveting technology they don't understand." Benet shook his head, but there was no mistaking the awe in his voice. "So primitive."

"Because we don't know anyone else who would do that," said Jack, thinking of how the Flo'wud revered the comm scrambler.

"Nope, nobody comes to mind." Rogan cast a curious expression in Jack's direction. "Wait, what was it you said humanity would do to Tuner and me? Oh, yes. *Dismantle us to see how we work*. No, your species doesn't sound obsessed with advanced technology *at all.*"

Jack would have been the first to admit there was something mesmerising about the tower. The blank ruggedness of its walls. The alien blackness of the metal and rock from which it was built. Its monolithic majesty. He didn't know if he could describe the sensation it summoned. It was only something he could feel. Not just in his gut, but in his bones. In his blood.

"Are you even listening to me?" he heard Rogan ask.

"Huh?"

"There's an opening at the base of the structure," Rogan repeated, eyeing Jack with mild concern. "I say we take a look, see if we can't figure out what's responsible for all this."

"Sorry, yes." Jack blinked slowly and shook his head clear. "Absolutely."

Rogan studied him for a couple of seconds longer, then led their group further towards the tower. Closer they came, until its grand walls filled the open sky with black.

The concentric rings of Forgotten grew tighter around its base. The volcanic fumes grew thicker. And Jack's legs felt... slower.

"Something..." The sharpness had left Ginger's voice. She sounded distant. "Something about this place ain't right."

No disputing that. He'd known the place was off the moment he laid eyes on it from up on the ridge. Proximity only seemed to amplify it. That sensation the tower summoned inside Jack's blood and bones? It wasn't peace. It wasn't pleasure.

It was terror.

And yet despite everything, Jack found himself wanting to smile.

ROGAN STOOD in the shadow of the great tower and looked up. Its peak eclipsed the near-midday sun, wore it like a golden halo. Secrets of a forgotten empire waited for them inside, but the darkness that yawned from the mouth of the structure was far from inviting.

"We ought to step carefully," she said, tearing her gaze

away. "The Libraries posed no threat to early explorers, but—"

There was no use in finishing the sentence. Nobody was listening to her. They may have been listening to something – or some*body* – but if they were, she sure couldn't hear it.

Jack, Ginger, Klik and Benet – all of them stood facing the tower, their bodies relaxed yet fixed rigidly to the spot, masks of ignorance and bliss painted across their dumb faces. It was deeply unnerving – not least in regard to Ginger, who up until that moment had refused to wear any expression besides wary, gritty contempt.

Now they all looked like they were on the receiving end of a five-star spa treatment.

"What in the galaxy has got into you?" she asked, shaking Jack. "Snap out of it!"

She could move him, knock him on the forehead with a metal fist, probably even topple him over if she really wanted... but nothing seemed to shake Jack from his numb stupor. He didn't know she was there. Klik was little better, letting out a distracted moaning noise when Rogan tried to move her. Benet was worst. Like the Forgotten standing in rings behind them, the green-skinned Flo'wud was practically drooling. She didn't even bother trying to wake him.

"Bolts. This isn't good."

Whatever caught the banished Flo'wud in its trap had done the same to her companions. The question was, why hadn't it done the same to her? Rogan had her suspicions. She was both the only automata in the group and the only person unaffected. It could hardly be a coincidence.

But the cause was still no less a mystery. Perhaps it was a toxin in the air, which her system could filter out – not that toxins would affect her anyway, neurologically-speaking. Or speaking of neurology – maybe it was a transmission of some sort, one that could only influence fleshy brains and not digital code. Oh, the possibilities. Organic beings were such fragile things, sometimes.

Well, it was clear she couldn't wake them up. Maybe she could carry them out of the crater, but what would she do if *that* didn't work? Drag them all back to the city, one by one? And besides, that would hardly answer the question of why it had happened to them. Or what a strange, hyper-technological ruin was doing in an "undiscovered" volcano in the first place...

She lingered beside Jack and tapped her foot impatiently. He looked gormless.

"What would you say if I were the one stuck in standby mode?" she asked him. The question was rhetorical, but she really wished he would answer all the same. It would solve a lot of her problems. "Press on with the plan, probably. Even if the plan *is* stupid."

Rogan faced the maw of the dark tower, uncrossed her arms, and got walking.

"Pressing on, then."

NO NATURAL LIGHT reached the tower's hollow interior, yet even without activating her night vision sensors Rogan had no trouble processing the layout of her surroundings. The cybernetic lattice glowed within the structure just as it did without, flowing like neon blood through stone veins, casting the foreboding hall in a dark, purple light.

Her metal footsteps rang out like funeral bells through the cyber-gothic cathedral. She detected the sound waves of her own echoes as they rose higher and higher, raised her head and saw nothing but thick shadow shrouding the tower's ceiling a hundred metres above. If there was anything of use in here, it wouldn't be found by going up.

But as far as Rogan could tell, there were no other doors or openings around the tower's circumference. Of course, she knew her own perception couldn't be fully trusted. Jack had told her about the Ministerium's inner chamber – how it was far too massive to possibly fit inside the Ministry's headquarters. The ancient forerunners who built these ruins developed technology the galaxy's present menagerie of species could barely dream of. For them, it seemed, physical space had been no less malleable than its digital counterpart – a canvas to play with, not a rulebook by which to abide.

She stepped carefully.

It was a good thing she did.

Rogan was moments from putting her right foot forward when she realised she stood only inches from the edge of a giant hole occupying most of the tower's base. Leaning over the precipice, she discovered a vertical shaft burrowing deep into the volcano's lava core. Magma churned at its bottom – far below the level at which it bubbled through vents outside on the crater, Rogan noted.

The structure had to be tens of thousands of years old, at least. Was it the volcano's geothermal reactions that kept it powered all those years? The Libraries had been restored and retrofitted for modern power supplies by the Ministry centuries ago, before they were abandoned again years later due to budget cuts. Nobody had ever come to New Eden to do the same.

The hole wasn't a perfect circle. A relatively small platform – almost diamond in shape, but with its longer sides softly curved – clung onto one side like the silhouette of a moon just beginning to eclipse a sun. As with the rest of the hole, it possessed no handrails or security barriers, only a black stone pedestal sporting a single grey button.

Rogan stared around the rest of the hall, cycling through every video, audio, chemical and electromagnetic filter her arsenal possessed. No luck. The platform was her only lead.

She came no closer than ten feet from the pedestal when something glided through the opening behind her. Rogan threw herself to the ground, anticipating a tremendous, flying beast that would snatch her up from the floor and dash her to pieces against the adamantine walls... but it was only a drone, and one as utterly oblivious to her presence as her four companions still stood daydreaming outside.

The hovering robot – trapezium in shape, the size of a picnic hamper and as black as the structure it now entered – stopped a few metres above the hole and whirred to itself. Rogan could hear its processors clunking. Given the number of scratches and dents across its otherwise featureless shell, it was a wonder the poor thing still functioned.

"Hello?" she said in binary as she picked herself up off the floor. "Do you know what this place is? Can you even understand me?"

Forget understanding her – Rogan suspected the ancient robot couldn't even *hear* her. It wasn't an automata, that was for sure. She detected no sign of sentience, could match its design to no model in her memory banks, and, if it was anywhere near as old as the tower, it predated the first recorded manufacturing run of their kind by a good many millennia.

She wondered if it would be quite so docile if a fleshy had breached the tower's walls instead of her.

The drone finished its computational efforts with a heavy clanging noise not dissimilar to an old boiler shuddering to life. Then it descended into the shaft. Rogan watched as it dutifully followed a spiralling counter-clockwise path down towards the magma below.

She took another look at the platform with the pedestal. Guess she knew where it went, then.

Rogan stepped onto it, anxiously tapping her thigh with her finger. She needn't have been concerned. Though she couldn't see any visible supports connecting it to the shaft, the platform felt no less sturdy than the rest of the tower. Her hand hovered inches from the button. She worried less about where the platform might take her and more about whether it would be able to bring her back up afterwards.

"An automata descending into a pool of lava," she sighed to herself. "Yes, this definitely seems like a 'Jack' kind of idea."

The button depressed easily. Without so much as a whisper, the platform sank into the heart of the volcano.

17

THE JÖRUBOR

The borehole went twice as deep into the volcano as the tower rose above it, yet the elevator platform wasted no time in reaching the bottom.

It soon overtook the doddery drone. Rogan gripped the pedestal tight and leaned over the edge to get a better view of her fast-approaching destination. She could see the magna churning and spitting like geysers, feel the sizzling heat from the planet's violent innards. That she couldn't see another platform onto which to alight, however, was more than a little concerning.

Still, the elevator had to lead *somewhere* safe. Right? Why install a button if they didn't expect someone to ride it?

She found herself wishing that Maximilian, her old master (her *first* master, if her memory banks were to be trusted), was with her. He'd studied the ancients, once upon a time. If there was ever anyone who could know what to expect in a place such as this, it would have been him.

But those days were long gone.

She sensed the platform slow down as it neared the end of the hole. With wide-eyed alarm, Rogan suddenly realised there was nowhere further the platform could go – the right-hand side of the shaft ended a good thirty feet above the lava, with no suggestion that the elevator could continue its descent of its own accord. Yet as she watched, the platform began to gracefully follow the circular wall around in a similar counter-clockwise path to that of the drone above, then continued to do so even after the left-hand side of the shaft curved outwards from the borehole and morphed into a narrow rail that snaked through the wider caverns beyond.

Rogan stared around in wonder.

The subterranean chamber was simultaneously vast and claustrophobic, the ocean of fire connected to the cave's endless ceiling by bridges and pillars of rock. Luminous waves, dozens of feet in height, crashed against them in an untiring rage. Great indestructible generators rose from amongst the lava like mechanical islands, channelling the volcano's power and converting it into the blue energy she saw coursing through the rest of the structure's veins.

So close to the fire, Rogan's metal body shimmered a hot and angry red colour. Her sensors told her she didn't need to worry about the heat warping her chassis quite yet – not unless she happened to fall off the platform, at least.

The platform slowed further. Rogan spotted what she believed might finally be the end of the winding, magnetic track it followed, and, next to it, a flat bed of rock untouched by the fire and sporting an uneven pyramid of obsidian monoliths similar to those she saw back on the surface. Sure enough, her ride followed the rail to its conclusion, where it sank slowly downwards and then stopped.

Rogan took a good twenty seconds to summon enough courage to step off. Much to her relief, the elevator platform stayed where she left it. She hoped there wasn't a way someone could accidentally call it back from up top.

This had to be it, then. Whatever was causing Jack, Klik, Ginger and scores of the Forgotten to stand in a catatonic state outside *had* to be here. She had no idea what she'd do if it wasn't.

The rocky monoliths formed a black carapace over yet another ancient structure, almost as if the pyramid beneath had grown a thick, gnarly shell to protect itself from the passing millennia. Once more, nothing but suffocating darkness welcomed her from inside its colossal open doorway. No purple neon this time.

The drone, having finally caught up with Rogan – though still as oblivious to her existence as ever – floated over her shoulder and into the strange temple, where it was soon consumed by the shadows. Rogan waited a short while, but it didn't come back out.

She stood there wondering what lay within. Not anything computational, surely. It would overheat in an instant. But then again, since when did the ancients' tech follow the rules?

She clenched her fists and steeled her nerves until they were as hard as the rest of her.

Only one way to find out, she supposed.

Rogan followed the drone inside, the lenses of her eyes instantly adjusting to the gloom. But even with her optical filters, the back of the hall remained as dark as ever. Once more, she found herself wondering if things wouldn't be different had she been born of flesh, blood and bone. Would the structure have detected her presence and switched on the lights for her? Perhaps, given how the structure responded to the fleshies that crossed its crater, she wouldn't have lived long enough to find out. Or perhaps...

Stop it, Rogan. Focus.

She knew she had a tendency to overthink things when

the stakes were high. If she didn't know the answer to something in that massive supercomputer brain of hers, she went crazy trying to put every little piece of the puzzle together... even when she knew she didn't have all the pieces to hand yet. Especially then.

There isn't time.

The drone circled the entrance twice before haphazardly descending into a sunken slot beside another mysterious podium over on Rogan's right. It connected with a thud. A familiar blue static flickered over its body, criss-crossing in ever-more complicated networks until the machine's shell resembled a Kapamentis street map. A prehistoric charging port, of all things. She guessed that was how the decrepit robot remained active after all those years left unattended.

She quickly crossed to the podium. Her metal footsteps rang clearly through the great alien hall. This podium had no button, but it *did* have a screen. Rogan dared to hope. There was evidently still plenty of power inside the volcano – with any luck, the relic of a terminal would still be operational too.

A keypad of indecipherable hieroglyphic symbols extended as she approached. A good start. She considered jacking into the terminal, then thought better of it. The servers in the Libraries had been restored by some of the brightest minds in the galaxy, and even their collective genius could barely crack the surface of the ancients' secrets beyond unlocking a few NavMaps. A direct link to the forerunners' technology might scramble her systems, fry her digital synapses, or worse. And besides, it was a moot point – there almost certainly wouldn't be a compatible port she could use. The old-fashioned way would have to do.

Not that she had a clue what any of the hieroglyphic

symbols before her meant. Almost every aspect of the Libraries had been retrofitted for modern galactic use – their user interface most of all. Even Jack could operate them with the help of a translator chip.

Not wanting to accidentally press the wrong button, Rogan tried placing her hand on the screen instead.

Now the temple lit up.

But not in purple. Rogan took a horrified step backwards as, one by one, hidden strips of light running through the ceiling and walls cast the entire hall in a deep, bloody red. But it wasn't the light filling the hall that surprised her.

It was seeing what *else* filled it.

Coiled up in the centre of the otherwise empty chamber was a gargantuan beast formed of a hundred thousand interlocking plates. Every dazzling inch of its body was as chrome as Rogan's. She struggled to identify the creature's exact form, given its position curled upon the floor and the abundance of steel fins sticking out at odd angles along its spine... but there could be no mistaking what she had discovered.

The Jörubor.

The legends had been true... they just hadn't told the whole story.

She approached slowly, arms held out in front of her as if she were trapped in a cage with a slumbering lion.

"Hello?" she whispered. The last thing she wanted was to startle it. "Can you hear me?"

Nothing. Not so much as a stir. One of the Jörubor's enormous eyes stared in Rogan's direction, but it was dull and lifeless. She didn't think it was dead, however, only deactivated. On standby, perhaps.

The Flo'wud were adamant that the Forgotten had captured their sacred Jörubor and put it on some kind of leash. Evidently, that age-old belief couldn't have been further from the truth. If anything, the Jörubor and its temple had captured the Forgotten – those unlucky enough to wander too close to the crater, that is.

"Well, the Forgotten sure aren't keeping you down here," she muttered to herself as she returned to the ancient terminal. "Nor the Flo'wud, for that matter. How long have you been active? Twenty thousand years? *Thirty* thousand? Is that how long you've been programmed to guard this world?"

The screen was scarcely more comprehensible than the keypad that extended beneath it, but at least it had diagrams familiar to anyone with a rudimentary understanding of planetary geography and astrophysics. She tapped an isometric model of what she assumed was New Eden, hoping it would expand further. It did.

What she saw next was far from reassuring.

As the isometric model grew in size, small dots began to pop up across the planet's surface. These too started to grow, and with sudden horror Rogan recognised each one as a symbolic version of the dark tower rising from the crater's surface. There were dozens of them dotted around the planet. *Dozens*. Most of them blinked a disconcerting red, but many – including the one representing hers, she believed – were still lit up in green.

"There are loads of you," said Rogan, shaking her head in disbelief. She tapped on the symbol for the tower under which she presently stood. "Or there used to be, at least. And I bet each Flo'wud city thinks that theirs is the only one."

As the screen changed again, the drone released itself from its docking port beside her. It hovered in front of the Jörubor's colossal head, clunked a few times (Rogan guessed it was running some kind of a diagnostic test, but who knew), and then drifted back out through the temple's opening.

"Bye, then."

Rogan turned back to the terminal. A green geometric grid now overlay the image of New Eden – or Benet's tribe's little patch of rainforest, at least. It spread out from the volcano's location in a perfectly even circle, covering an area of land – if Rogan were to hazard a guess, based on the surface area of the planet – about a few hundred kilometres in diameter.

"Bolts alive. I wish I could understand this better." She gripped each side of the podium and called upon every last piece of linguistic and programming knowledge she had in a bid to make sense of what lay before her. "I guess... I guess this is the Jörubor's territory. And this," she added, watching the grid pulse rhythmically as the planet turned, "must represent how frequently it makes its patrols. It used to go out once every hour or so, by the look of things... but now it's down to just twice every New Eden day. Poor timing on Fireteam Alpha's part, I guess."

She glanced up at the giant inert robot.

"Protector of the forest? More like an old planetary guard dog left behind by its owners. The Forgotten haven't put a leash on you – *time* has. Ought to be put out of your misery, if you ask me."

She tried accessing more granular details and controls, or even to discover anything pertaining to the mysterious psychic disorder afflicting Jack and the others. Yet she only found herself growing more confused and frustrated by the system, at one point landing right back at the main menu and having to start from scratch all over again. She came quite close to punching the blasted thing and storming off.

But eventually Rogan arrived at a dashboard of some kind, one dominated by three white, vertical bars. Each one filled the screen from top to bottom, though Rogan hadn't the slightest clue what any of them actually represented. It wasn't as if they were labelled. She guessed it was unreasonable to expect the ancients who designed it to leave behind a handbook.

If she'd learned anything in her hundreds of years spent fiddling around with anonymous electronic controls, however, it was that doing so usually had significant consequences. The question was, what would those consequences be? Would they shut the Jörubor down permanently, as Ginger would prefer? Or would they disable its subroutine inhibitors and let the mechanical guard dog off its digital leash instead?

Rogan remembered the terrible gashes in the side of Fireteam Sigma's crashed drop ship. But she could also all too easily imagine legions of human marines massacring the Flo'wud city. She couldn't see a third, more favourable option in which everyone walked away unscathed. Leaving the Jörubor to its mindless and mostly ineffective patrolling solved nothing at all.

"I wish I could spend longer learning why all this is even here," she sighed. "But as research goes, I suppose this will have to do."

One after the other, she swiped the bars down to zero.

There was a loud, unnerving hum as she switched the second of the three bars off, but she didn't let it stop her. A terminal-sounding *thunk* followed the third. Something, somewhere, had switched off rather permanently.

Rogan waited. For a while, nothing happened.

And then the Jörubor opened its eyes.

Or rather, a harsh and angry red light bloomed behind their lenses as the mammoth robotic sentry reactivated. The deafening sound of a thousand steel plates grinding against one another filled the temple as it staggered to its feet. It was like listening to an orchestra of knives being sharpened ready for carving. Rogan wondered if this was the first time the creature had ever possessed full control over its own body.

Which begged yet another question – was the Jörubor sentient, or just another mindless drone finally let loose from its directives?

The robot stretched itself out to fill the hall. Its head was that of a great bird, complete with giant, pneumatic beak, though there were clear influences from prehistoric reptiles in the way "bony" ridges ran along the cranium and around the eyes. From its armoured torso emerged two resplendent wings, each coated in a hundred steel feathers as large and sharp as broadswords. It was easy to see how its talons could carve through a drop ship's flank. Each one of them was the size of Rogan. And its tail... Almost a snake-like beast in its own right, it couldn't have been less than fifty metres in length. The *Adeona* could have laid beside it and still not reached its spiny tip.

It jerked its massive, battle-scarred head towards her and let out a mechanical roar like two battlecruisers grinding past one another.

"Oh dear," said Rogan, backing away.

It jerked its body to the right and swung its prehensile tail around like a giant whip. Rogan could hear the interlocking segments tightening and shifting. She leapt out of the way just in time. The spiny, armoured tip bulldozed through the podium, smashing it into pieces. The sparking wreckage in its wake smelled of ozone.

"There goes every secret of the universe," said Rogan, sitting up. "Bolts. I hope Jack and Klik are all right..."

The Jörubor let out a second almighty roar before it spread metal wings and charged out through the open entrance. Rogan picked herself up and tried out one of Jack's favourite curse words. Unfortunately, it didn't make her feel any better.

As per usual, everything was getting out of hand.

They'd come to the volcano with a simple goal: take control of the Jörubor from the Forgotten and use it to frighten the human forces away from the Flo'wud city. Keep them at bay, if only for a little while. Instead, she'd set the monster loose. The best they could hope for now was that this would have much the same effect.

Rogan hurried out of the temple after the Jörubor. Experiencing freedom for the first time, it swept across the ocean of fire in a mad fury. The flames licked its belly and its wings sheered through each rocky cave formation it passed, but the titanic beast didn't appear to notice.

It was searching for a way out. She ought to do the same.

The elevator platform was still where she left it. Thank goodness. She slammed her fist down on the pedestal's single button and the platform immediately began to follow the winding rail back towards the surface.

Suddenly, Rogan had a horrible thought. What if the controls she disabled were also responsible for keeping the elevator's magnetic track running? Or for regulating the magma chamber's internal pressure, somehow? Had she inadvertently set the volcano to erupt? The Jörubor smashing the terminal probably hadn't helped matters...

The platform picked up its pace. Soon it was skimming the lakes of lava as quickly as it had before. The mechanical escapee thrashed in frustration as it swept around the ancient generators ahead. Rogan guessed the creature's subroutines had been responsible for guiding it out of the caverns the past couple dozen millennia. With them removed, the poor thing had no idea where to go.

Finally, she saw it – the central shaft leading back up into the hollow tower. Twenty, maybe thirty seconds longer and then she'd be outside again. What she'd do if Jack and company were still in a dribbling stupor, she had no idea. Carry Jack and Klik and leave the other two behind, most likely.

She told him it was a bad idea to get involved, but did he listen? No. Did he ever? And now, thanks to him, she wasn't even taking her own advice!

The platform followed the rail around its last bend before the final, vertical climb. Unfortunately, the Jörubor decided upon a similar trajectory. It swung a hard right, dipping the very tip of its wing into the bubbling magma as it turned, and crashed into the track ahead. Rogan shielded her eyes. When she opened them again, the Jörubor appeared unharmed... but an entire stretch of the magnetic rail was missing.

And still the platform kept moving.

If she couldn't find a way to stop it, the platform would almost certainly launch off the end of its broken track and crash into the lava. More importantly, so would she. Rogan pushed the button on the pedestal over and over again, but nothing happened. She couldn't even slow the damn thing down.

Then she spotted it – the drone. Despite departing much earlier than both the platform and the giant beast to which it served as custodian, it was much slower and hadn't yet made it out of the chamber. It was floating along a few metres down and to Rogan's right, still as oblivious to all the chaos going on around it as ever.

It was headed up and out.

Rogan looked to the wreckage where the platform's track had been, then back at the doddery drone. It was risky. There was no guarantee the old thing could even support her weight. But it didn't look like she had much choice.

She calculated her velocity and trajectory, and then jumped.

The drone amended its flight path at the last second. Rogan came close to tumbling past it into the fire. But she managed to get a precarious grip on its left side, and locked both of her hands into clamp-tight positions once the startled drone levelled itself out again.

It could carry her... just about.

She chanced a glance below her dangling feet as the drone slowly carried her up through the borehole, and wished the decrepit old thing would hurry. The Jörubor made sweeping pass after sweeping pass around the bottom of the shaft, each time letting out another one of its frustrated, mechanical roars. They rang out with a force that made her chrome shake.

Rogan doubted the beast would take long to figure out its own way up. It had done it a hundred thousand times before. The only difference was that this time it was free.

Free... and all the more furious for it.

18

BEST LAID PLANS

Jack's eyelids felt leaden, as if he'd woken from a deep and restful sleep. For the life of him, he couldn't remember what he was dreaming about. Something pleasant, he reckoned.

The moment of serenity passed quickly. He startled awake, frightened and confused, his eyes wide and his skin covered with goosebumps. He wasn't where he was supposed to be.

The last thing he remembered was walking towards the dark tower in the centre of the volcano's crater with everyone else. Yet to his horror, Jack now found himself standing amongst the third ring of Forgotten worshippers about thirty degrees around to the tower's east. They too were stirring from their collective trance, though they seemed to be having a little harder time breaking free than he did.

How did he even get there? He struggled desperately to recall the time he'd lost, but it was like trying to clasp his fingers around a whisper. Every time he thought he had it, he'd open his hand to find nothing there.

The Forgotten nearest him let out a long and noisy yawn. Jack's stomach twisted and climbed up into his chest cavity. He sidled past the alien before they could fully regain consciousness. Who knew which side of the bed they'd wake up on after all this time.

Much to his relief, he discovered Klik wandering down the central aisle leading towards the tower. She must have woken up before everyone else, though she still looked about as lost and confused as he felt.

"Klik!" He rushed over to her, then put his finger to his lips before she could reply. "What the hell happened? Where are the others?"

"Over here," whispered Ginger. She deftly navigated her way out of her own ring a few rows further back, dragging Benet behind her as if he were a muddy dog refusing to bathe. He stumbled about like a bad drunk. "No idea where your chrome friend is, though."

"Oh, I might have an idea," said Klik, rubbing her eyes.

Jack turned around to spot Rogan legging it up the path from the tower, an expression of alarm welded onto her metal face.

"Run!" she screamed at them. *"Run!"*

A few of the still-slumbering Forgotten stirred at the sound of her voice.

"Be quiet!" Jack anxiously hissed back at her. Even the most softly spoken word seemed to carry across the crater like a gunshot. "You'll wake—"

Jack wasn't totally sure what happened next. It all went by too fast, and his groggy mind still wasn't quite as sharp as it ought to be. But one thing was pretty hard to misinterpret.

The top half of the tower exploded.

For a moment Jack was convinced the volcano itself had erupted. Huge chunks of rock and metal wall flew into the sky like birdseed. A few of these blocks crashed down on top of hypnotised Forgotten, splattering them across the floor of the crater. A particularly large chunk shattered one of the vents near the perimeter, spewing a spout of molten lava into the air like a burst faucet.

Those that survived woke up pretty quickly after that. They ran screaming past Jack towards the rocky ravines without even stopping to see what had blown up their precious tower.

Jack *did* see, however. And quite frankly, he felt like doing the same.

At first, as it spread a pair of magnificent metal wings bigger than those of a jumbo jet and let out a tooth-rattling screech through its pneumatic, upturned beak, he thought it was a gigantic clockwork bird. Not an *automata* exactly, but some kind of automaton nonetheless. Harsh sunlight glinted off every intricate plate of its silver body. But then it sprung from the peak of the ruined tower, and Jack watched a seemingly endless tail unravel behind it. The creature was as much a snake as a bird – a mechanical dragon born from hell itself.

"Is that your doing?" he asked Rogan, pointing an accusatory finger at the beast as it tore upwards through the sky. "Did you figure out how the Forgotten were manipulating it and take over control?"

Rogan hesitated. Jack's face fell.

"Rogan. Please tell me that thing's on our side."

"Well, about that. Not exactly..."

They watched as the metal devil hung suspended as a silhouette against the sun. Then it let out another terrible roar and soared down towards them.

"The Jörubor," gasped Benet. Each syllable seemed to

plop out of his mouth like a marble. "But it's... That's not... It's supposed to be..."

"Not quite how you imagined, huh?" screamed Ginger, shoving Benet back up the crater's path. "Don't care. Do what the nice robot says – run!"

They turned and sprinted up the slope towards the ridge. The whole crater seemed full with a tinny whistling noise that grew louder and higher in pitch the closer the Jörubor came.

"Everyone, down on the ground!" Ginger yelled, just as the sound grew unbearable.

They all did as instructed, even Benet. Jack was grateful for Ginger's military attitude, even if her experience in the field was little better than his own. Unlike him, she had *training*. She knew how to handle a crisis without resorting to suicide runs and sheer blind luck.

The Jörubor pulled up only metres from the ground. Had they still been running, it most likely would have cleaved their heads off or snatched them up in its talons and dashed them against the black boulders below. Its tail, whipping about like an Indian urumi blade, demolished numerous obelisks behind them and then followed its owner back up into the open sky.

They slowly climbed to their feet and watched it grow smaller from the rocky ridge at the edge of the crater.

"Well, it's heading towards the forest," said Klik. Her voice was thick with fake optimism. "Maybe it *is* going there to protect it..."

Jack stormed up to Rogan in a fit of panic.

"What the hell happened in there?"

"That colossus was programmed by the same ancients who built everything else here," she replied testily. "I'd like to see *you* do a better job of deciphering that tech! The only option I had was to shut the systems down. I didn't know if it would disable the Jörubor or set it free."

"Here's another option for you," said Ginger. "You could have left it the hell alone!"

"Oh, I'm sorry!" Rogan marched up to Ginger so that they stood face to face. "Those same defensive systems had the four of you in a hypnotic coma. My mistake for thinking you'd want out of it!"

"Careful, robot. I'll be more than happy to locate your off-switch for you."

"Then again, humans apparently aren't the sharpest of species," Rogan continued, storming off. "Maybe if I'd left you as a vegetable, nobody would know the difference!"

"Look!" Benet's bright, innocent voice snapped everyone free from their arguments. He pointed towards the forest. "Over by the tallest tree where the elephant vines fall. Do you see it?"

"I dunno, Benet," sighed Jack, squinting. "What am I supposed to be looking at?"

"Its one of our lookout posts," Benet replied. "It's where we watch for visitors. And the Jörubor, of course," he added uneasily. "It was one of our watchers who first spotted your ships arrive and later alerted us to your plight with the Rippers. Normally they're very well hidden, but from up here you get a pretty good view."

Jack thought back to when he'd stood on the clifftop the day before, moments after the crashed spaceship had gone tumbling over the side of the waterfall. He *knew* he saw someone following them!

Exasperated but grateful for Benet's interruption, he searched the forest canopy for the hidden lookout post. One tree was clearly taller than the others, and even from kilometres away Jack could make out a curtain of gargantuan root climbers hanging from its upmost branches. They each had to be as thick as a subway tunnel. But no matter how hard he strained his eyes, it was ridiculous to think anyone could spot any wooden outpost at that distance, let alone a secret one.

He glanced over at Rogan. They both shrugged.

"Okay? And what does that have to do with anything, Benet?"

"The Jörubor is flying straight for it."

Jack spun around to face Ginger.

"Give me your binoculars."

"What? No!"

"Hurry up! For God's sake, I'll give them back!"

Ginger retrieved her binoculars from one of the satchels around her waist and begrudgingly handed them over. Jack turned back to face the tree and fumbled with the focussing wheels. In his haste, everything became even more of a blur.

"Oh, give it here." Ginger snatched the binoculars back, adjusted the focus so that the tree in question was crystal clear, then slammed them into Jack's hands again. The horrid ordeal lasted three seconds from start to finish.

"Thanks," he replied, hiding his embarrassment behind the binoculars' lenses.

Yes, there was the tallest tree in the rainforest. He could see it now. The vines draping from its branches weren't just immensely thick and multiple kilometres in length – they bulged from giant seed pods growing within them, too. With their dark, grainy and tightly-knotted appearance, each vine sort of reminded Jack of a long, braided beard.

"Behind the vines," said a worried voice from down near his chest. "Near the knot-hole that looks like a cave."

Jack followed Benet's instructions and quickly found what he was looking for. The knot-hole Benet mentioned didn't simply look like a cave – it *was* a cave, just one that opened into a dark network of wood and sap instead of rock and underground streams. There were smaller ones just like it all the way up the gigantic tree's trunk. But only the largest of them possessed a watch tower – a wide, multi-storey viewing platform supported by hefty oak buttress arches. Jack thought he could even make out a few tiny Flo'wud figures racing along its wooden parapets.

He turned his magnified gaze towards the sky, and this time he managed to get the focus right himself. The sight of the Jörubor took his breath away once again. It looked like a sentient, silver fighter-jet, one outfitted with a hundred whetted blades along its wings in place of missiles. Though already nothing but a sharp glint of sunlight when viewed with the naked eye alone, the binoculars showed it making an unmistakeable dive-bomb towards the lookout post.

"No, no, no," he muttered under his breath. Everyone else waited in silence. "Pull up, for Christ's sake. You're supposed to go after the drop ships, not the villagers..."

"Jack?" Benet tugged desperately at his arm. "Why is it—"

The mechanical Jörubor didn't pull up. Free from the restrictions of its programming yet still following its sole directive to destroy any and all intruders, it continued its suicidal plummet towards the lookouts. Even as its talons wrenched the upper platforms apart, it didn't stop. Even as its scimitar wings severed the rope supports and cleaved a white gash through the trunk of the great tree, it didn't stop. It simply charged right through as if nothing were even there. Benet let out a horrified scream as the entire watch tower went crashing down through the vines.

"Oh, that's not good," said Klik.

"Still think that monster cares about saving the forest?"

said Ginger, grabbing her binoculars off Jack. "I told you not to put your faith in fairy tales."

"It was Benet's idea." Jack replied quietly and without conviction. His whole body felt numb. "I just wanted to help."

"Yeah? Well if you wanted to help, you should have left everyone the hell alone." Ginger marched past him to the rocky steps leading down into the Forgotten's canyons. "You're not helping humanity and you're sure as hell not helping the locals."

"Where are you going?" Jack shouted after her.

"Back to the city," she replied over her shoulder. "Back to my bloody fireteam."

"Don't be ridiculous," said Rogan. "That's a two hour walk. Ninety minutes if you're lucky. It'll be quicker if I call Adi to come and get us."

"What about the giant flying death-mech?" asked Klik.

"Something tells me it won't be paying much attention to us anymore," Rogan replied, stepping away from the group. "Adi, can you hear me? We need you to pick us up from this position. Yes, I know I said the skies weren't clear. That's kind of why we need you..."

Ginger reluctantly stomped back up the stone steps.

"I'm only sticking with you lot for expediency's sake," she grumbled. "The sooner I'm back on the *Final Dawn*, the better. This planet can do one."

"You won't hear me complaining," muttered Jack.

"The *Adeona* is on her way," said Rogan, also returning to the group. "Should be a couple of minutes out at most."

"Thank the gods," said Klik. "I can't wait to be as far across the galaxy from that pissed-off scrapheap as possible. Never let me complain about being bored on the ship again."

"Erm, guys?" Jack stood watching the ancient statue-filled clearing from the top of the ridge. "Not to alarm anyone, but I don't think the Jörubor's the only one who's pissed."

Dozens more of the Forgotten streamed out from their alcoves and tunnels around the pit. Jack had no doubt some of them had been "liberated" from the dark tower's influence only minutes before. Judging by the bone blades and pikes they carried, they weren't coming back to thank them.

"Oh, come *on*," said Ginger.

"What have they got to be annoyed about?" asked Klik, clutching her rifle. "We saved them! If it hadn't been for you, Rogan, they'd still be drooling over that tower!"

"Saved them? Really?" Rogan shook her head. "I think a few of us need to get some perspective on what's actually happening here, because if there's one thing we're *not* doing, it's saving anyone."

"What's the ETA on that ship of yours?" asked Ginger, checking how many rounds she had left in her magazine. By the look on her face, not nearly enough.

"Let's be optimistic and say eighty seconds," said Rogan, staring up at the blistering sky. The apertures of her lenses contracted into dots.

"Oh, great." Ginger slammed the magazine back into her rifle with a grunt. "Because I give us thirty before we're overrun."

She aimed at the top of the stone steps. Rogan gently pushed the muzzle of her rifle away.

"We killed their friends and then blew up something sacred to them," she said. "Perhaps we could *try* not to make things any worse?"

"Do whatever you want, Madam Toaster." Ginger shook

Rogan off and resumed aiming. "But I don't plan on dying up here."

They backed down the slope of the crater towards the shattered wreckage of the ancient tower, cradling their rifles or, in Benet's case, his head in his hands. As Jack's eyes darted to the left and right, he spotted more Forgotten breaching the rocky banks all around. There was no use in running the opposite way. They were surrounded... or at least, they soon would be.

"Steady," said Jack, flexing his sweaty fingers around his weapon's grip. "Let's not antagonise them any further."

"Another great plan," said Ginger. "Let's not defend ourselves. I'm sure they'll get real tired of hacking us to death after a little while. Then we can be on our way."

"You're not the one who got hit by a spear already," said Klik, snapping her mandibles at Ginger and forgetting she still couldn't understand a word coming out of her insectoid mouth. "Someone else can be the target this time. Any bright ideas, Jack?"

Jack shook his head.

"No. I've got nothing."

"That's unusual," said Rogan. "You're normally full of them, presumably because they undergo such a poor vetting procedure."

"Really? Now?"

"Sod it," said Ginger. "I'm the highest ranking marine here—"

"You're the *only* marine here!" said Jack.

"—and I say offence is the best defence. If we shoot, they attack. If we don't shoot, they attack! So why the hell shouldn't we at least get the first shot in?"

"She does have a point," Klik reluctantly conceded. "It

does seem like somebody's getting stabbed or shot either way."

The Forgotten continued to stalk further inwards from all around the crater. The four intruders bunched together around Benet, each facing a different point of the compass. Save for jumping down the borehole under the tower, there was nowhere left for them to go.

Jack swallowed hard. The faster his heart beated, the harder it was to resist the temptation to open fire. And once the first of them pulled the trigger, the rest of them would have no choice but to follow suit. If they wanted to live, that is.

"Why don't we try—"

"Hostile on your three o'clock," Ginger yelled, snapping her rifle towards a sprinting attacker on Jack's right. "Engaging n—"

Ginger's sentence was cut off as the sound of roaring thrusters flooded the volcano. She looked up – everyone on the volcano did, including the dozens of banished Flo'wud. But only Jack, Rogan and Klik broke into smiles.

"Am I too early?" The *Adeona* spoke through Rogan's speakers. "Shall I do a loop and come back in a minute or two?"

"Jesus Christ." Ginger kept her rifle trained on the nearest batch of Forgotten, who stood gawping up at the *Adeona* in awe. "Your pilot sure knows how to make an entrance. Almost gave me a heart attack."

"Not a pilot. Ship. She's..." Jack shrugged and gave up. "You know what? Never mind."

Dust and rubble quaked as the *Adeona* slowly descended to within a few metres of the crater floor. Her loading ramp opened with a mechanical whir and clunked to a stop against one of the toppled monoliths.

"Everyone inside!" Rogan shouted over the din. "Move!"

Klik hopped up without a second thought. Ginger glanced at the renovated mining ship's alien design, hesitated, then followed Klik in. Jack and Rogan had to practically carry Benet, the poor creature was so reluctant to climb on board.

A bone spear clattered harmlessly against the *Adeona's* hull as she brought her ramp back up.

"What was that?" she asked through her cargo bay speakers.

"Nothing," Jack quickly replied. "Just get us out of here."

The *Adeona* rocketed forwards. Even with her artificial gravity generator softening the blow, they all felt the acceleration. Benet struggled the most, falling onto his backside and staring in open-mouthed terror at his cold, inorganic surroundings.

"Thank God for that," said Ginger. She pulled off her helmet and ran a trembling hand through her oily hair. "Get us back to the *Final Dawn* for a debrief, pronto."

"Where is this?" asked Benet, his big eyes glistening with fear. "What's happening, where are you taking me? I want to go home."

"Tell Benet not to worry, Rogan." Jack tore the lid off the same UEC crate that once stored their battle rifles. "We're still going back to the city."

"I'm sorry, what did you say?" Ginger laughed in disbelief as she sank against the hull. "Back to the city? In this thing? Are you out of your damn mind?"

Jack ignored her.

"Rogan, you were right. This wasn't our fight to begin with, and we should never have got involved. Not with the UEC, not with the Flo'wud, and certainly not with the bloody Jörubor. For what it's worth, Benet, I'm sorry."

He pulled out a bunch of fresh rifle magazines and chucked one of them over to Ginger. Surprised, she caught it.

"But this is one problem we did create," he added, "and now it's our job to fix it."

19

OMEGA

Sergeant Kaine grimaced as his boot sunk into yet another hidden pocket of swamp water. Ten minutes on humanity's new world and already he hated the damn place.

It was hot. It smelled. And the mosquitos were the size of bloody dragonflies. The sooner they established an air-conditioned base camp, the better.

Twenty three marines marched behind him, spread out evenly amongst the ferns. Joining him were the other three members of Fireteam Omega, of course, as well as the five other fireteams constituting Tango Squad. Two hulking great tanks rolled through the undergrowth to either side of them, crushing trees beneath their treads and spoiling the humid air with the stench of guzzled diesel.

Kaine wrenched his boot free, then ground his teeth in irritation. It was a big honour, being chosen to lead the colonisation effort. He wasn't about to mess it up like those idiots in Alpha and Sigma.

"Onwards, soldiers." He checked the beacon tracker on his data pad and pointed further into the dense rainforest.

"The morning's already lost. We'd better hustle if we want to secure this place before sundown."

Not that it mattered hugely if they didn't. Command would be on his back about the delay, sure, but if the suits up top didn't consider a nocturnal incursion acceptable, why had they outfitted Kaine's unit with flares and floodlights?

But no, it wouldn't take that long. Kaine grinned as he stomped through a bed of purple heather. From what that idiot civvy – *what was his name? Jack something?* – had told the admiral, the local population consisted entirely of tree-huggers. Absolute cakewalk. Absolute joke. Omega could probably march right through the gates of their stupid tree-house city – burn it to cinders, even – and still meet zero resistance.

Kaine secretly hoped they did, though. He hadn't enlisted in the UEC just to bunk in a tiny, ice-cold space-coffin and guard some godawful jungle latrine. He was a soldier, not like all the runts and cowards who signed up for no reason besides saving their skin.

A real marine didn't sign up for their own sake.

No.

A *real* marine did it for the thrill.

AS KAINE privately contemplated what constituted proper military duties, Tuner fled down a winding, wooden staircase as fast as his cumbersome legs would carry him.

The whole Flo'wud city was in disarray.

He'd spent hours trying to convince the elders to evacuate their population ahead of the human invasion, all to no avail. "Nothing could ever make us leave our home," the elders had told him. "These trees define us. They make us who we are."

Of course, now that a giant, metal snake-bird was turning their watch towers and bridges into match sticks, the Flo'wud couldn't scarper fast enough.

Typical.

Tuner threw himself to the floor as a massive black shadow swept overhead, and scrambled to keep from sliding off the walkway altogether. The planks groaned and split under his weight. One snapped off in his hand. He rolled onto his back just in time to spot the monster's long, armour-plated tail swim through the blue sky like a silver sea serpent before it disappeared once more behind the trees.

A Flo'wud and her two young children raced past him, skipping gracefully over the gap his fall had left in the walkway. He stumbled to his feet and hurried after them, listing this way and that as the whole treetop network shook.

He found Sergeant Yates, Ghost and Duke standing on one of the lower platforms, rifles in hand. They weren't alone. Hundreds of Flo'wud city dwellers huddled together in the shade, trembling and staring up in terror at the pencil-thin rays of light piercing through the leafy canopies and platforms above.

"Hey, look," Ghost said in a deadpan voice. She nodded in Tuner's direction. "It's the robot. Yay."

"Before I embarrass myself," said Tuner, choosing to ignore Ghost's robot comment, "that thing up there's not one of your weird human weapons, is it?"

"Like hell it is," said Sergeant Yates. "It's like nothing from R&D I've ever seen. Not that they'd show us grunts, of course. I was hoping *you'd* recognise it."

"Isn't it obvious?" Duke jabbed a thick thumb towards

the heavens. "That's the forest guardian the locals told you guys about. What was its name? The Your-a...? The You...?"

"The Jörubor?" Tuner tilted his body upwards as he tried catching another glimpse of the thing.

"Yeah, that's it. The Jörubor, or something. I guess it's not quite as friendly up close."

"That's the thing Ginger and the others went after?" Ghost chewed her lip as she shook her head. "Jesus Christ. I hope our girl's okay."

"She'd better be," said Yates. His voice softened. "Don't worry, guys. If there's anyone who can face down a flying mech and come out unscathed, it's Ginger."

"Plus, she's with Jack," said Tuner, optimistically. "Jack is practically made of luck. Well. *Bad* luck as much as good, but still."

Ghost made a harrumphing sound.

"Quiet," said Yates, raising his hand. Everyone fell silent, not that it made much difference. The whole treetop city swelled with the sound of panicking Flo'wud and collapsing wooden walkways.

"Do you hear that?" he asked.

Tuner's audio receptors weren't as good as Rogan's (or the ones in his old chassis, for that matter), and he couldn't isolate the specific noise to which Yates was referring. But he *could* sense a growing rumble beneath his mechanical feet, reverberating up through the trees from the forest floor below.

"Tanks," said Duke, his face stony. "Pair of Challenger Fours, by the sound of it."

"Goddammit," said Yates. He exhaled sharply through gritted teeth. "It's Kaine. The drop ships carrying Omega and the rest must have landed before that guardian thing took to the skies. So much for your friend's plan, eh?"

Flustered, Tuner looked at all the Flo'wud cowering in the shadows around them.

"They can't be here yet!" he said. "We're not ready! Many of the Flo'wud have taken secret bridges to other settlements nearby, but there are still plenty who refuse to leave. Others who are frightened and don't know what's going on. If they—"

Duke laid a big hand on Tuner's flank.

"Hey. Buddy. Don't be so hard on yourself. This invasion's happening whether we like it or not. There's nothing more any of us can do."

"Duke's right," said Yates. "Our orders were to wait here until Fireteam Omega arrived with the first wave and then head back for debriefing. It's out of our hands. Nothing we can do to stop it."

"With all due respect, Sergeant," said Ghost, "those orders came in before a giant flying robot started terrorising the LZ. If Command thinks I'm getting in another drop ship with that thing still in the air, they've got another thing coming."

Yates contemplated this as somewhere overhead the Jörubor let out another of its terrifying metallic shrieks. A tree toppled through the forest with a hearty crunch.

"It does look like we're grounded for the time being," he eventually said with a sigh. "And I suppose we do owe these people a favour, what with them saving Duke's life and all. How long do you think they need to evacuate?"

Tuner shrugged.

"However long we can give them. It's not like any of them listen to me. Some of the elders won't leave no matter what, but..."

"But the more we can slow the invasion down, the more lives we can save," said Duke, nodding.

"The least we can do is buy them a little more time," agreed Yates. "Not that I'm promising anything, of course. It's not like Kaine will want to listen to me."

"Oh, I don't know." Ghost rolled her eyes. "That bone-headed *pendejo* will take any opportunity to gloat."

"Then let's go give him one." Yates nodded towards one of the rickety, pulley-drawn elevators leading down to the forest floor. "Fireteam Sigma, move out."

Tuner took one last look at the Flo'wud city.

Such a waste.

"I'm coming with you," he said, stomping after them. "We're going to need all the distractions we can get."

THE EARTH beneath the Flo'wud city was cold and brittle and damp. Little to no sunlight made it past the thick layers of leaves and branches and structures carved inside the trees, so the ground was carpeted with mushy, black leaves and plagued by pale, spectral mushrooms.

Yates, Ghost and Duke jogged towards the approaching sound of tanks and troops. Tuner lagged behind. His legs were built for clamping into the earth for support, not running across it.

Something vaguely hut-shaped crashed to the rainforest floor behind him, spraying out splinters like shrapnel. A few of these wooden shards scratched against Tuner's shell.

What a fine sorry mess this was turning out to be, he thought to himself. Even if they *could* hold off the human invasion for a while longer, what difference would it make? The Jörubor was making quick work of reducing the city to firewood anyway.

He supposed there were a great many other Flo'wud

communities across New Eden. The Jörubor might stop at one, but the humans? No, the humans wouldn't stop until the whole planet was under their control.

And Jack wanted to go *live* with these people?

Yikes.

As they sprinted out from under the city's shadow and into the wider rainforest, the foliage returned to its luscious, overgrown self. Vines and roots coiled like anacondas. The petals of extraterrestrial tulips grew as large as palm leaves. Barbed toadstools grew to grotesque heights, with stems as hardy as beech trees and red sap that fizzed as it dripped from their caps. Even the local wildlife grew more abundant the further they left the settlement, though much of it appeared to be fleeing the advancing attack force and scarpered in an even greater panic when they saw the shambling form of Tuner coming the opposite way.

All the while, the rumble of the tank treads grew louder, until almost nothing else in the forest could be heard at all.

Tuner closed the distance between him and the three remaining members of Fireteam Sigma before too long, but not because they were waiting for him to catch up. The marines were walking out into a clearing of long grass with their rifles raised above their heads. Rather than follow them, Tuner decided to keep watch on proceedings from a safe spot behind the treeline instead.

"Hold your fire," he heard Sergeant Yates shout. "It's us, Fireteam Sigma. That you, Sergeant Kaine?"

Tuner peeked out from behind his hidey-hole formed of two fallen logs and a moss-cloaked boulder. If those big armoured tortoises were what humans classified as tanks, then Duke had been right. There *were* two of them, and their cannons gave his own hand a serious run for its money. Their engines rumbled idly. He spotted about two dozen soldiers standing spread out amongst the grass, all of whom had their rifles trained on Sigma.

A marine with a jaw like an anvil advanced from the crowd and raised his hand.

"At ease," said Kaine, smirking. "It's just Yates and his crew. These guys are no threat to anyone."

He pretended to search behind them.

"You're one short, I see. Lose someone?"

Sergeant Yates smiled sarcastically.

"Private Rogers is accompanying another team on a recon mission. Identifying potential threats. As is our job," he added firmly.

"Ah, yes. The civilian sent down to rescue you. Well..." Kaine gestured for his unit to press on. "Thank you *so* much for all your help. You picked a *great* spot for colonisation." He patted Yates on the shoulder. "Really great. The grown-ups can take it from here."

Yates gritted his teeth and refrained from shrugging Kaine's hand off his shoulder. They may have both been sergeants – though staff sergeant or an even higher rank was surely on the horizon for anyone commanding his own mini-platoon, if it hadn't been bestowed already – but he needed to placate Kaine, not piss him off.

"Woah, hold on a sec." Yates raised his hands in the air and laughed as if everything was a-okay. "Don't you want to know what we found in there before you go charging in?"

"Whatever it is, my marines can handle it."

"Come on, Kaine. This is your first incursion into non-terrestrial territory, just as it was ours. Are you sure you want to go in unprepared?"

Without taking his eyes off Yates, Sergeant Kaine raised his fist. Both tanks and the two dozen soldiers grunted to another stop without complaint.

"Out with it, Yates. What's in store for us? Little grey men with particle lasers? An army of giant lizard people? What?"

Ghost and Duke took turns alternately looking at the skies and their shoes. Tuner could sense the awkwardness even from his spot behind the trees.

"Well, no. Not exactly. More like a civilisation of intelligent, vegetarian pacifists. But they're no threat. You don't need to go in there guns-blazing. Hell, you don't need to go in there at all."

Kaine's jaw tightened further.

"No threat, eh? Sure glad you alerted me to that one, Yates. Would have been an absolute disaster otherwise."

"There's more!" Yates quickly stepped in front of Kaine before he could march onwards. "There's a forest guardian of some kind, a flying steel mech the size of an old troop carrier. It's tearing the city apart as we speak."

"Bollocks is there," said Kaine. "You've gone soft in the head, Yates. Sun's got to you. Always knew you weren't cut out to be a soldier."

"He's telling the truth, Kaine," said Ghost, shrugging. "I wouldn't go in there if I were you."

"No, *you* wouldn't. But that's why Omega's in charge of this mission and Sigma isn't. We actually get the job done."

"Do you guys hear that?" said Duke, tightening his grip on his rifle.

"Don't tell me," Kaine said sarcastically, this time with much less humour than the last. "It's this metal monster of yours coming to get us, right?"

"No." Duke furrowed his brow and shielded his eyes. "Whatever it is that's coming, it's sure got a hefty pair of thrusters on it."

Suddenly the *Adeona* burst into view above the clearing, casting them all in shadow. The surrounding trees swayed and bent in the wind. The turrets of the tanks quickly swung towards it.

"What the hell is *that?"* yelled Sergeant Yates, his fatigues flapping around his chest as the ship descended.

"Everyone stand down," shouted Kaine, gesticulating madly. "I said *stand down!"*

"You recognise that thing?" asked Ghost, holding onto her helmet.

"Of course I do," Kaine snapped. "I saw it docked in the hangar of the *Final Dawn* yesterday. No idea what division that rusty monstrosity belongs to, but it's piloted by that civvie who came to rescue you. I'm surprised you haven't seen it already," he added, somehow managing to turn even *that* into a boast.

As the *Adeona* neared ground level, she swung to the side, burying herself as much amongst the trees as possible. A few of the thinner ones snapped during the impact and spread a loose disguise of leaves and broken branches across the top of her hull.

Her engines fell to an idle rumble and her loading ramp descended. Tuner watched in relief as Jack, Rogan and the others hurried down its length. He hadn't a clue what had happened to them and the Jörubor up in those caverns, but he sure was glad they all made it out again in one piece.

"Fireteam Sigma," Jack said in greeting, nodding to Yates, Ghost and Duke. He breathlessly marched up to Kaine. "Sergeant Kaine, wasn't it? Listen, Sarge. You've got to hold off on this invasion. There's a much bigger threat—"

"You bloody bet there is." The cold grip of fear frosted over Kaine's eyes. He whipped his rifle up and aimed it at the *Adeona's* loading ramp. "Hostiles at two o'clock!"

All twenty-something marines snapped their weapons to face the enemies in question – Klik and Rogan, guiding

20

THICKER THAN WATER

Sergeant Kaine slowly turned his eyes to look at Jack. The rest of him didn't move an inch.

"Are you sure you want to do this?" he asked.

"Not even remotely," Jack replied. "There's two dozen of you and one of me. But that doesn't change a thing. You're pointing a gun at my friends. I can't let that happen."

"They're friendlies," said Yates, stepping forward. "I can vouch for them."

"Like your word means anything," Kaine replied, still glaring at Jack. "They're not friendlies. They're goddamn aliens."

"Then take *my* word," said Ginger, stepping off from the end of the loading ramp. "After all, I just rode in a ship with them. You won't find any threat here. And we've got much bigger problems, believe me."

Jack and Kaine continued to stare one another down. A fresh stream of sweat ran down Jack's spine. He couldn't expect Kaine not to notice the way his gun shook. And he was bluffing, of course. If any of the marines *did* take a shot at his crew, he wasn't about to blow a fellow human's head off. He was an idiot, not a bloody psychopath.

Of course, for all Kaine knew he was a rogue human with a crew full of robots and aliens. Perhaps the sergeant would be a little less keen to call his bluff than he thought.

"Do any of those... *things*... belong to the local population?" Kaine eventually asked, turning his gaze back to the aliens.

"One of them," Jack replied slowly. "But I'm sure as hell not telling you which."

"The one not carrying a UEC-issued rifle, I'm guessing." Kaine dropped his voice so only Jack could hear him. "Pacifist, right? Christ, it's one unfortunate looking creature. Heck, the whole lot of them are. I won't ask you where you found them."

Jack took a deep breath and ignored the sharp twinge growing in his neck.

"For crying out loud. Lower your goddamn guns, *now*."

Sergeant Kaine took another long look at Rogan, Klik and Benet, then raised his hand. One by one, the marines lowered their rifles... though not without considerable hesitation. A few towards the back were either too distracted to see Kaine's orders or much too frightened to follow them.

Jack half-lowered his own rifle in return.

"Thank you," he said, not bothering to hide the relief in his voice. "Where's Tuner, by the way? We tracked his signal to this location."

"I'm over here," came a familiar voice from the bushes.

More rifles shot up, including Jack's own.

"Lower your weapons," Kaine shouted at his marines, spinning around in a mad circle. "Christ Almighty. Bring him out and get him to stand with the rest of them."

Tuner hesitantly emerged from his hiding spot of his

own accord, arms raised. His already semi-gored chassis was covered with fresh scratches from the forest. He sidled over to Rogan, who put an affectionate arm around him.

"Is that it?" asked Kaine. He seemed to grow more hysterical by the second. "Got any more surprises you want to tell us about?"

Jack took a step backwards, then chucked his rifle to the ground.

"Yeah, that's it."

"Good," said Ginger, and socked him in the mouth.

Jack fell to the floor like a sack of cement. He could taste iron in his mouth, could feel the blood sticking to his gums. He clutched at his jaw and spat a red globule of phlegm into the dirt.

"Wha...?" he spluttered. "What on earth was *that* for?"

"For not getting your priorities straight," Ginger replied. She flexed her fist open and closed as she spoke. "What the hell's wrong with you, Jack? Humanity finally has a chance to start fresh after decades of hardship and death, but you seem hell bent on holding us back. First it's calling off the colonisation, then it's releasing the Jörubor to attack human drop ships, and now you're pointing rifles at our fellow marines!" She pointed at the crew of the *Adeona*. "You ought to be on *our* side, not theirs!"

"I *am* fighting for humanity, you idiot." Jack sat up and rubbed his tongue along his teeth, checking none were loose. "Do you want to go toe-to-toe with the Mansa armada, huh? How about a private fleet of Ghuk destroyers? Do you really think these are fights we can win? There are rules, even in as lawless a galaxy as this. If you'd been here for more than five minutes, you'd know that."

"Private Rogers!" snapped Yates, red with embarrassment

from his fellow marine's behaviour. "Stand down and fall in line."

"Shame." Kaine raised his eyebrows and let out a sigh. "I was actually starting to enjoy myself."

"Private Rogers?" Jack's insides turned to ice. Surely the name was just a coincidence. "I thought your name was Ginger."

"Erm, yeah." Ginger looked at him like he was an idiot. Even more so than before, that is. "That's just a nickname, obviously. Private Rogers, Ginger Rogers, Ginger. Ask Duke – he gave it to me. There was some famous actress by that name or something. I'd never heard of her before. My full name's actually Elizabeth Rogers, after my maternal grandmother."

Jack's guts went from frozen to a sloshing bucket of ice-water. He suddenly felt like throwing up.

"Your mother." He staggered to his feet, already knowing the answer to his next question. "What was her name?"

Ginger awkwardly looked at the members of her fireteam.

"Erm, Amber? Amber Rogers. Why?"

This time Jack *did* throw up. Ginger jumped.

"Jesus, Jack. I didn't think I hit you *that* hard."

Jack's mind raced as he heaved the meagre contents of his stomach into the grass. Could it be possible? Surely not. She inherited Amber's surname, not his. As much as he hated to think about it, anyone could be the father. He had been gone twenty-nine Earth years, after all. But Ginger looked to be in her late twenties, didn't she? He guessed the timeline matched up, but...

Oh God.

The day he left home for the last time, when he said goodbye to Amber without telling her about the experiment... she'd been sick. She checked her blood for radiation poisoning, but it came back negative.

He wondered if a different test might have come back positive instead.

"Did I break something?" asked Ginger, who started to look nervous. "Are you sick?"

"It's not that," he said, coughing as he wiped his mouth with the back of his hand. "It's just... It's just I think you might be my daughter."

There was silence amongst the grass. For a long, tense moment, only the faint sound of crashing trees and mechanical shrieking could be heard in the distance.

And then Ginger broke into laughter.

OVER BY THE *ADEONA*, Tuner sidled up to Rogan.

"What's going on?" he whispered. "Is this all part of the distraction, or...?"

"No, I think this is real," Rogan replied with a sigh. "Poor Jack. Things have been ever so confusing for him lately."

"Well, I hate to mess up the reunion, but do you think we should move things along a bit?" Tuner shifted from one foot to the other. "Maybe not stand out in the open so much?"

"Do *you* want to be the one to go out there and suggest it?" said Klik, nodding to the two dozen marines still staring daggers at them.

"I suppose it'll wrap itself up sooner or later," he quietly mumbled to himself.

But as Jack's conversation went on, Tuner couldn't ignore the haunting way in which the long grass at the back of the clearing swayed...

...even though no wind blew through it.

"YOU'RE MESSED UP, MAN." Ginger shook her head in disbelief. "Seriously. I'd never met you before last night. And how could you possibly be my father? We're the same age, you idiot!"

"Biologically, yes." Jack laughed. He knew how ridiculous it sounded. "But I disappeared in twenty-forty-two. I bet you were born eight or nine months after that. Three decades have passed for you, but for me? For me, it's been just a few months."

"What a load of bull," said Kaine, sneering. "What the hell are we doing even listening to this crap? Everybody, move out. We've got a settlement to secure."

"You can ask Admiral Blatch if you want," said Jack, ignoring the troops as they pushed forward. It was only Ginger to whom he spoke. "She knows. She was there when I went through the wormhole. It's classified, but to hell with it. I don't see why I should keep her secrets if she won't even tell *me* the truth."

"No, I don't believe it." Ginger clenched her jaw and backed further away from him. "What you've said proves nothing. I don't know you. I don't *want* to know you. And—"

"Erm, guys?" said Ghost, awkwardly interrupting. "Does anyone else hear that whistling sound?"

"I thought I was the only one," said Sergeant Yates, stiffening.

Slowly, as if dreading what he might see, Duke raised his face to the sky.

"Everybody down!" he bellowed.

Duke threw Ghost to the floor as a pair of metal talons

like construction excavators swept across the clearing mere feet from their heads. They clamped down on one of the tanks so hard its armour plating buckled inwards, crushed it like it were an empty soda can, and then dragged the whole sorry vehicle up into the air with them. One of the unlucky marines inside climbed out the hatch only to fall thirty feet to his death.

Jack looked up from the dirt just in time to see the Jörubor drop the broken tank into the forest and sweep around for another pass.

"At least it's not attacking the Flo'wud city anymore," he said, accepting Yates' outstretched hand. The sergeant pulled him back onto his feet. "That's progress, I guess."

"Except now it's attacking us," said Yates. "Forgive me if I don't think that's any better."

Kaine's soldiers were in a panic. Nobody had trained them for this. Jack suspected they hadn't been trained for anything they might encounter out in the cosmos, really. Flustered, they spun around pointing their rifles at anything that moved. Often birds taking flight from the trees. Sometimes each other.

At least the marines operating the one surviving tank were a little more experienced in dealing with armour-plated enemies, albeit not usually ones capable of Mach Three. They slowly rotated their turret to aim at the incoming bird of prey.

"You'd better have a plan to stop that thing," Ginger shouted over the sound of indiscriminate rifle fire.

"More of a loose idea, if anything," said Jack, grimacing. "Look, Ginger..."

"Don't. Just fix this, goddammit."

Jack nodded then sprinted back towards the *Adeona* through the crowd of confused marines. It was at that moment the tank fired a single 120mm shell in the Jörubor's direction. Jack's ears rang so hard from the shot, he didn't even hear the explosion that followed. But he sure as hell saw it... just as a second later he saw the Jörubor's untarnished silver beak pierce the fiery black cloud as it continued its unrelenting dive towards them.

"Jack!" Tuner ran into the clearing and dragged him into cover. "What do you want us to do?"

Everyone ducked as the Jörubor swept overhead, decapitating a great deal of the surrounding trees with its razor-sharp wings. The tank fired a second shot, though this shell detonated harmlessly in the open air dozens of metres behind it. Its snaking, serrated tail mangled a couple of unsuspecting soldiers in its wake.

"Get the hell out of here for starters," Jack replied. "The three of you need to take Benet back to his city."

"There's not much of it left," Tuner replied, lowering his voice so that panic-stricken Benet couldn't hear.

"It's still going to be a lot safer there than here. Besides, maybe he can help you with the evacuation efforts. Who knows how long the invading force will be distracted for."

"What about you, Jack?" said Klik. "What will you be doing?"

Jack was about to answer when a reptilian roar filled the clearing. One of the vicious theropod creatures the Flo'wud called Rippers leapt out from the long grass and wrapped its jaws around a marine at the back of the crowd. Dark blood sprayed across the green blades. Her screams were sharp but short-lived.

Half a dozen more pounced soon after. Some pinned hapless soldiers to the ground and started eating; others swam through the grass like brown, leathery sharks. The remaining marines – including a horrified Kaine, whose carefully sculpted stoicism was fast crumbling – blindly emptied their clips into the foliage.

"As if we didn't have enough to deal with," said Jack, turning back to his crew. "Stick to the plan. Fall back and get Benet to safety. But, erm, try to make sure Ginger makes it back in one piece too, okay?"

"Of course, Jack." Rogan ushered the petrified Flo'wudian behind her. "Are you sure you're okay?"

"I'm fine," he said, glancing over his shoulder. "I'm going to take Adi and see if I can put a stop to the Jörubor. Or at least get it as far away from anywhere populated as possible."

"What?" Tuner rushed forwards. "But the Jörubor is designed to *destroy* ships! That's—"

"I know, buddy." Jack patted his metal arm. "But it's my mess – my job to put it right. Don't worry. I'll see you when it's done."

"You'd better," said Klik, her mandibles clacking nervously.

"I will."

"We don't have a way off the planet otherwise."

Jack sighed.

"Thanks, Klik. I'll keep that in mind."

The Jörubor roared by overhead. Somebody in the clearing screamed as a Ripper disembowelled them.

"What are you waiting for?" Rogan shouted at him. "Go!"

Jack turned and sprinted up the *Adeona's* loading ramp. He briefly paused to look back at his friends from the top.

His gut told him it might be for the last time.

21

FROM ABOVE AND BELOW

Jack scrambled up to the *Adeona's* cockpit and threw himself into his captain's chair. He fumbled with the straps.

"Is everything all right, Jack?" the ship asked.

He took a deep breath.

"I've been thrown decades out of sync with humanity, my wife – who no doubt spent her whole life wondering why I straight up vanished one day – has been dead for years even though I only saw her a few months ago, and I think I have a daughter who's almost the same age as me and hates my guts. So yeah, everything's bloody great."

"Yes, that does sound emotionally turbulent."

Jack tapped his fingers against the dashboard.

"I need to stop the Jörubor," he said, "but I can't do it without you. It's your call. It's going to be dangerous – if you want no part in this, I'll understand."

"Don't be ridiculous. You're the captain. Where you go, I go. Usually by necessity, but even so. There is one thing, however."

"Yes?"

"You'll need to do the flying. My reflexes aren't sharp enough for a dogfight right now. I still have full command of my weapon systems, though."

"Not a problem." Jack grabbed the flight stick. "I'll focus on where we're going, you concentrate on hitting that steel dragon with everything you've got. Deal?"

"Deal."

"Right." Jack whistled. "Here goes nothing."

The *Adeona* rose from her spot hidden amongst the trees. Loose branches and clumps of leaves slid off her hull, brushing past the cockpit windows on their tumbling path to the earth below.

A few of the Rippers flinched at the roar of her thrusters. Jack watched as a group of marines surrounded one of the reptiles and peppered its thick hide with what must have been close to a hundred rounds. It collapsed in a bloody spasming mess, but there were still plenty more of its kind hunting through the grass.

Jack searched the airways. The Jörubor had just made another sweep over the clearing, so it couldn't have gone far. He spotted it perhaps a kilometre away – a bright glint of metal in an otherwise bright and blue summer sky.

He jammed the accelerator lever forward and chased after it.

It suddenly occurred to Jack that he'd never actually piloted the *Adeona* inside a planet's atmosphere before. Or any other kind of flying vehicle outside of a simulation, for that matter. The cracked planet belonging to the Ceros system had been different – its gravity was weaker, the shifting corridors between its floating chunks of rock a lot more claustrophobic. All of the heavens were open to him, and he could *feel* the force from the ship's thrusters pushing him harder into his seat as they went.

If it hadn't been for the fear of getting decimated by a giant mechanical snake-eagle, it would have felt good.

He tightened his grip on the control stick as they hurtled closer and closer. The whole dashboard shook like it was coming loose... much like the rest of the *Adeona*.

If only they hadn't come to New Eden straight from a near-catastrophic space battle. Something to think about next time.

As they neared their target, the shaking lessened. The Jörubor was so big they could actually ride in the creature's slipstream.

"We're within optimum firing distance," said the *Adeona* in a voice far too cheerful for their present situation. "Target locked. Hold me steady."

Jack did as he was told. After all, he had the easy job. All *he* had to do was keep his nerve and not point the ship towards orbit in a cowardly panic. He wasn't altogether sure he wouldn't once the flying mech figured out they were on its tail.

The rotary cannons on either side of the ship let rip. Jack jumped. It should have been obvious, but the guns were so much louder when fired inside an atmosphere than out in space! It was as if he'd buried his head between a pair of jackhammers. He could feel every single shot thunder through the *Adeona's* metal hull.

Jack gritted his teeth to keep them from rattling and tried not to let the quaking of the ship steer him off course.

The majority of the *Adeona's* ballistic rounds sprayed against the Jörubor's massive, sweeping tail, but a few got past and peppered the beast's silver hide. Most were mere ricochets – scratching, scuffing and even denting its chrome shell... but nothing more.

Yet Jack could have sworn he saw one of its many interlocking panels snap off and glint in the sunlight as it spun past their ship.

Either way, their attack didn't go unnoticed. The Jörubor let out its harshest screech yet – a shrill, anguished cry that pierced Jack's frontal lobe like a lobotomy needle and set his teeth on edge – snapped its colossal head to the left, and fixed the *Adeona* with a crimson, cybernetic eye.

It was a good thing Jack was sat down, because he felt his legs turn as watery as his bladder.

The huge metal falcon took a sharp left, banking on its side and lacerating the air with its gloriously resplendent wings. The bird's turning circle was incredibly tight – far more impressive than anything with a pair of thrusters could achieve. Jack ignited the *Adeona's* airbrakes and did his best to follow it around. The last thing he wanted was for the Jörubor to end up on *their* tail rather than the other way around.

"That's it, Jack!" said the *Adeona*. "I've got a great shot at the Jörubor's flank. Firing another burst now."

Jack clenched his jaw, but there was nothing he could do to block out the sound of the rotary cannons. Once more their rattles and booms drowned out everything inside the cockpit. He didn't even realise he was screaming through gritted teeth until their barrels whined to a stop.

Leaning as far forward across the dashboard as he could without sacrificing his paralysed grip on the joystick, Jack tried to gauge the damage. He'd lost sight of the target – thank goodness he had a sentient ship manning the guns.

"What's happening, Adi? Did you get it?"

"I estimate an approximate shot-on-target success rate of sixty-two percent," she replied. "Unfortunately, it appears that the damage I inflicted was largely superficial. A few of the 'feathers' on its back shattered, but that's all. I'd hate to be a frog on the rainforest floor when *they* come crashing down."

"Goddammit." Jack strained as he wrenched the joystick as far to the left as it would go. "I'll try to catch up with it again."

"Oh, I wouldn't worry about doing that."

"No?"

"No." The *Adeona's* usual cheerfulness suddenly carried a sarcastic edge. "The Jörubor has been kind enough to catch up with us instead."

Multiple video screens bloomed across the cockpit windows. The ship magnified the rear-view feeds so Jack could better see behind them. He rather wished she hadn't.

The Jörubor raced towards them faster than any jet fighter Jack had ever seen – perhaps even faster than the *Adeona*, too. Its stubby, mechanical beak looked strong enough to tear the rear of the ship off in a single bite. From the cold glare of bloodlust in its synthetic eyes, the mech planned to do just that.

"Well, at least you've got a good line of sight on its head," he yelled up at the cockpit's speakers. "For God's sake, hit that thing with everything you've got!"

For a third time, the Adeona's rotary cannons whirred into life. And for a third time the cockpit was filled with ballistic fire... for a few seconds, at least. They spluttered to a stop.

"What are you doing?" Jack screamed, teetering on the verge of hysterics. "Why aren't you still shooting at it?"

"Because that was everything I've got, Jack," the ship replied matter-of-factly. "I've depleted my ammunition reserves."

"Ah," said Jack, swallowing hard. "Bugger."

ROGAN AND KLIK fired their battle rifles through the long grass, whilst Tuner used his plasma cannon to obliterate the grass completely.

"Did I get it?" he asked in a mad panic. "I can't tell!"

The Ripper in question burst out from the clump of ferns beside them. It came close to clamping its jaws around poor Benet's head before the three of them blasted one of its hind legs into a red mist. Klik quickly stepped forward and plunged one of her forearm blades through its beady yellow eye to finish it off.

The clearing was in total chaos.

Most of the marines were dead. Besides those crushed in the first tank and the two soldiers decimated by the Jörubor's prehensile tail, all of the losses were a direct result of the theropod pack. The reptiles must have tracked them ever since their rescue at the hands of the Flo'wud.

The second tank had been of little use. It couldn't fire its 120mm cannon at such close range and its smaller turrets had limited fields of view. The Rippers covered its shell in a swarm. Its crew may have survived had the gunner not opened the top hatch to unload her rifle at them. She was torn apart in an instant, and a few of the smaller, younger raptors hopped inside a moment later. There had been screaming for a short while; now, the tank was silent.

Sergeant Kaine, Sergeant Yates, Ghost, Ginger, Duke and the last few surviving marines from Fireteam Omega were bunched up together in the middle of the clearing, keeping the remaining Rippers at bay with a firestorm of bullets. The crew of the *Adeona,* closer to the treeline and therefore the Flo'wud settlement beyond, tried desperately to get their attention.

"We need to fall back to the city," Rogan cried out. "The Rippers won't be able to follow us. We'll be safe up there."

"I vote we leave them behind," Klik snapped. She fired a couple of rounds at a reptile stalking around the clearing towards them. "It's kinda their fault we're in this mess anyway."

"Erm, guys?" Tuner took a break from blasting away chunks of earth with his cannon to frantically search their group. "Has anyone seen Benet?"

A scratchy scrambling noise made them all look up. Benet was climbing the narrow trunk of a nearby tree with ease. He disappeared amongst the bushy canopy only to reappear moments later about half a dozen metres away, racing along the branches back in the direction of his home.

"Well at least *someone's* got the right idea," Klik grumbled. "Can we go now?"

"Not without Ginger," said Rogan. "You heard Jack. She's important to him."

"Don't see why. He hardly knows her."

"She's his family. Probably. Imagine if you lost your partner and then, within minutes of finding out you have a child, you lose them too. Jack can be glum enough as it is."

"Yeah, well. I've got no-one except you lot, and Jack's probably ditching us after this. A few minutes seems plenty to me."

Rogan gave up trying to get Fireteam Sigma's attention from afar.

"It's more than *I'd* choose to spend with Ginger, I'll give you that. Come on. Let's go help the stupid humans."

No longer burdened with the responsibility of keeping Benet safe, the three of them hurried through the grass towards the group of marines. Duke and Ghost were startled by their approach and very nearly fired in their direction, but the others were too busy shooting into the field to even notice.

"You know something?" Duke shouted over his shoulder. "I'm starting to think New Eden isn't the paradise we were hoping for."

"Really? You think?" Ghost sprayed into a worryingly leathery patch of ferns with her submachine gun. "What's the matter, can't see someone setting up a Starbucks here?"

"Didn't you idiots hear me?" said Rogan. "This place isn't going to get any safer the longer we stay here. We need to fall back to the Flo'wud city."

"We heard you fine," Ginger snapped, casting a fleeting, incredulous look at Rogan. "But it's not our call to make."

Rogan would have rolled her eyes if she had the time.

"Who gives the orders?"

"Yates."

Rogan peered around. Everyone was wearing helmets – it was hard to tell one marine from another.

"And where in the galaxy *is* Yates, then?"

"Other side of us," said Duke. "With Kaine."

Rogan pushed past them both and found herself in the middle of the marines' circle. Tuner and Klik merged with the defensive ring and helped keep the Rippers at bay. Rogan found the two sergeants standing beside one another on the opposite side.

She irritably tapped Yates on the shoulder. He nearly had a heart attack.

"What the hell do you want?" he screamed.

"To keep you and your fireteam alive," Rogan replied. "Kaine and his troops too, if they want. We need to head—"

"—back to the city," said Yates, nodding erratically. "Yes. Good idea, if we can make it. You coming, Kaine?"

Kaine finished unloading his rifle at the hulking reptiles

stalking around them and switched out his spent magazine for a fresh one. He didn't appear to hear him.

"Kaine!" said Yates.

"What?" he spat. "Blindly follow a bunch of robots and aliens into hostile territory? Are you out of your mind, Yates? It could be a trap! They could slaughter us!"

One of the marines to their right was stood a few feet out from the circle. One second he was firing at the surrounding Rippers, the next he was yanked out of sight. The long grass rustled as a raptor dragged him towards the trees on the other side, his screams turning to gurgles as his lungs filled up with blood.

Yates grabbed his fellow sergeant's shoulder.

"We're getting slaughtered right now, Kaine!"

Sergeant Kaine fired off a couple more shots, then grunted.

"Fine." He aggressively gestured back the way Rogan came. "Everybody push forward! Continue on to the objective as planned!"

Not exactly what Rogan had in mind but, given the circumstances, it would have to do. She hurried past Duke to regroup with Tuner and Klik as everyone made a hasty push towards the Flo'wud city.

"Stick close to Ginger if you can," she told them. "But don't do anything stupid just for her sake. All of us are getting out of here in one piece."

"I don't need protecting," Ginger shouted, but Rogan noticed she didn't exactly pull away from them, either.

"You can guard me if you want," said Duke, firing slug after slug from his rifle's shotgun undercarriage. He sent one of the Rippers chasing after them crashing into the dirt. "I'll take all the help I can get."

Ghost paused as they neared the broken treeline where the *Adeona* had once parked.

"Where's Sergeant Yates?" she asked.

Rogan found him towards the back of the fleeing squad. Kaine was alongside him. Both were holding the pursuing reptiles back while the rest of their marines escaped.

They were doing surprisingly well. Rogan actually thought they had a real chance of making it... until she spotted one of the Rippers clambering up the side of the inert, bloodstained tank beside them. The two marines were so focussed on the monsters ahead that neither of them were paying attention to their flank.

"Yates!" screamed Ghost. "Watch out!"

Sergeant Yates' reflexes were much too slow. Luckily for him, the Ripper lunged at Kaine instead. One second he was firing precision shots into the thick hides of the beasts before him; the next he was pinned to the ground, his arms broken and his ribcage caved inwards. The Ripper fed. Flesh spurted into the air as if someone had just punched a bowl of red jelly.

Fireteam Sigma charged back into the clearing to defend their sergeant, who now found himself staring down two more Rippers alone. Rogan tried to stop them – or to stop Ginger, at least – but she doubted even the Jörubor could have held them back. She begrudgingly chased after them.

Kaine continued to scream. Yates put his rifle to the head of the Ripper feasting on him and pulled the trigger. He didn't let go of it until nothing but empty clicks came out and the hungry beast was dead. But by that point, so was Kaine.

Ginger stopped beside him and fired round after round at the remaining two Rippers – the last two anyone could see above the grass, anyway. Duke and Ghost caught up and did the same. For a moment, a ceaseless wall of lead appeared between mankind and beast.

The reptiles snarled in pain, bowed their heads as if about to charge through the barrage, and then turned tail and bounded off in the opposite direction.

Rogan slid to a stop in the wet dirt. She looked down and wished she hadn't. There wasn't much left of Kaine's torso. It was like a hand grenade had gone off in his stomach.

Fleshies sure were messy.

"No time for that," she said to Duke as he started to gag. "You can be sick all you want once you're back at the city."

"Rogan's right." Sergeant Yates tore his eyes away from Kaine and pushed Duke forward. "Fall back, fireteam. That's an order."

Once more they sprinted back through the clearing, past more ravaged corpses and body parts, through bloody mud and trampled plant life.

Once more they only got so far.

Rogan reached the treeline first with Klik and Tuner. Ginger, Ghost and Duke followed close behind. Sergeant Yates jogged backwards after the rest of them, erratically swinging his rifle to and fro.

He stopped and gave the clearing one final, cursory sweep.

"Good," he said, turning back to his fireteam. "I think we made—"

The Ripper that mauled Kaine suddenly pounced from behind him. Its left eye was gone and half of the flesh had been blasted from its skull, but its two-inch teeth and the claws on its stubby forearms were just as sharp as ever. It threw Yates to the floor, bit down hard on his leg and dragged him screaming into the undergrowth.

"Yates!" screamed Ginger, running after him. "No!"

"He's gone," said Rogan. She grabbed Ginger around the middle to hold her back. "You can't save him."

She thought it probably best not to add that with her superior audio receptors, she could already hear the snap and crunch of bone.

"She's right, Ginger." Ghost ran around front and started pushing her back towards the forest. "Yates wouldn't want you dying, too. You know that."

"He's not dead," Ginger whispered.

"Come on." Rogan pleaded to the others. "We can't stay here. They'll be back in even greater numbers."

Ginger fought against them, but it was with grief, not fury. There was no strength in it.

None of them had any strength left.

22

SPLASH DAMAGE

Jack pushed the accelerator lever as far forward as it would go. Even with the *Adeona* helping as much as she could, they weren't going fast enough.

"What do you mean, we're out of ammunition?"

"I'm not sure I can be any less ambiguous," the ship replied. "We never restocked after the battle for the Iris. Actually, we never restocked since Brackitt first installed my weapon systems back on Detris. I'm not *actually* a warship, remember."

Jack risked another glance in the rear-view video feed. The Jörubor was still behind them, gaining fast.

"Don't you have anything else on board we can use?"

"It appears I left my proton torpedoes in the garage," the *Adeona* sarcastically replied.

"What about an electro-magnetic pulse?" Jack grew desperate. "The Jörubor's electronic, I think. We could disable it for a while, at least."

"And what do you think would happen to us? That we'd hang in the air like an anti-gravity brick? We're not in space,

Jack. If we hit the Jörubor with an EMP, we'll be going down with it."

"Well..."

"Besides, I don't have one," the *Adeona* continued. "Not without shorting out all my drives. Not advisable even if we were sure it would have any effect. Which we're not."

"Then what *do* you suggest, Adi?"

The ship went silent for a few seconds. Splitting his gaze between the cockpit windows and the video feed of their pursuer, they felt like some of the longest seconds of Jack's life.

"Adi? What are you doing? Say something!"

"I'm scanning the local geography with everything I've got," she replied. "Radar. Sonar. X-Ray. Infrared. *Everything*."

"And?"

"Keep heading east. There's an ocean – or possibly a very large lake – a few dozen kilometres from here. At our present velocity, we should reach it in less than a minute."

"An ocean? What good is that? What are we gonna do, drown—"

"Watch out for that mountain, please."

Jack thrust the joystick to the right and threaded the *Adeona* between the two snowy peaks of a mountain that seemed to sprout out of nowhere. They were flying so fast, terrain came and went in snapshots. Jack glanced down past the wispy clouds, but the ground below was nothing but a blur. He couldn't even tell if they were flying over forest anymore.

Yet still the Jörubor kept chase, driven by the echoes of its original directive. They were a ship – a planetary intruder – in need of swift eradication. It swept between the two mountainous peaks, elegantly twisting its silver body sideways without ever taking its unblinking red eyes off its target. Even when the tip of its steel wing sliced through an overhanging outcrop of icy rock, it didn't so much as flinch.

"Adi," Jack said once he'd caught his breath, "I'm not sure—"

"Trust me. Reduce your altitude to three-hundred feet. Slowly."

"But we'll be so much slower that close to the ground!"

"*Trust me*," the *Adeona* insisted. "This is my body. I think I know how best to use it."

Jack gradually brought the ship closer to ground level and maintained their previous velocity as much as he could. The atmosphere was thicker at lower altitudes, and as such it was inevitable that air resistance would slow them down. Following in their slipstream, the Jörubor wouldn't have as much trouble... and it was already gaining on them as it was.

There. Ahead of them was a thin streak of blue that seemed to stretch from one end of the world to the other. It turned out they were still flying over the rainforest, though the trees grew more sparse and its green canopies were intermittently replaced by patches of unspoiled golden sands.

"You know," said Jack, whose shirt was glued to his seat with sweat, "that bird's getting pretty close..."

"Good. The closer the better. Now take us down right above the water – a few dozen feet should do it. And when I give the signal, fly us upwards as hard as you possibly can."

"Are you going to tell me what's going on?"

"No. If I did, you might not do it."

Jack thought back on all the mad plans he'd dragged the *Adeona* into. She'd always followed without question.

"All right," he said, flexing his stiff fingers. "Fair enough."

He guided the *Adeona* over the sands and down towards

the serene water. Twin waves erupted and crashed in her wake. Fine salt water sprayed against the cockpit windows.

"Keep going," said the ship. "Steady..."

Jack tried to concentrate on the horizon and not the image of the Jörubor only a dozen or so metres from their fiery thrusters. Its metal head glowed a scolding red, but if the heat was having any detrimental effect on the mech, it wasn't showing it. As if it knew Jack watched through the cameras, it let out another furious caw.

If it *did* catch them, there was nowhere they could go.

"Adi...?"

"Not long now, I promise."

The peaceful waters and empty skyline helped Jack remain cool. All he could do was keep the ship moving forward. In a sense, all he had to do was keep from doing anything at all.

Until the *Adeona* gave the word.

And then he saw it – what looked like an underwater cave just below the surface. It was enormous. A gulf of submerged blackness at least a hundred metres wide. That had to be what the *Adeona* picked up on her scanners, and they were approaching fast.

"You want me to dive into that thing?" Jack asked. "Do your thrusters even work underwater?"

"No!" the *Adeona* screamed. Her speakers practically crackled. Jack had never heard her so on edge before. "Up! When I give you the signal, I want you to fly *up!"*

"Okay, okay!" Jack took a deep breath. "I just don't see—"

"Now!"

Jack pulled the control stick towards himself as hard as he could, at the same time triggering every one of the air thrusters on the *Adeona's* undercarriage. She violently tilted upwards. The seawater beneath them bubbled and hissed.

But the ocean was already churning plenty without their help, Jack noticed.

The Jörubor almost flew right into them, they changed trajectory so quickly. Had it done so, it probably would have cleaved the ship in two. Yet despite its size it pulled off a mid-air pirouette, spinning like a whirlwind as it swept up after them.

"Whatever your plan is, it's not working," said Jack, pinned into his chair by the force. "The Jörubor's still after us."

"Wait for it..."

Jack glanced at the rear-view video feed and gasped. But it wasn't the flying mech that took his breath away.

It was the other creature coming at it.

Bursting up from the water was the largest fish Jack had ever seen. It could have fit a whole megalodon in its gawping mouth and not even had to chew. It was scaly, ugly, prehistoric... and rising from the depths at an alarming rate.

"My God! That thing's a colossus!" Jack rammed the accelerator lever forward again, but it wouldn't go any further. "If you've been holding any juice back, now's the time to use it!"

The darkness of its gaping, tendril-covered maw grew to fill the entirety of the video feed. Soon even the Jörubor was drowned in its shadow.

And then the fish clamped its fleshy mouth shut.

To Jack's relief, it missed the *Adeona*. It also missed the Jörubor... or at least, the main bulk of it. Its fifty-something metre tail was a whole other matter. It caught in the giant fish's mouth like a fisherman's hook. And the fish, suspended at the peak of its jump, dragged the flailing mech back down to the water.

They crashed into the ocean together and quickly disappeared amongst the dark depths. No evidence of the fish or the Jörubor remained.

Jack deflated as he let out the breath he'd been holding for the past minute. He slowly levelled the *Adeona* back out again.

"Jesus Christ. Did you know that would happen?"

"I had reason to suspect," the ship answered. "My scans picked up something massive lurking beneath the waves. From its mass, shape and internal physique, I deduced it was either hibernating or lying in wait. My guess is that it normally preys on unsuspecting flocks of those flying reptiles we saw when we first got here."

"If humanity *does* settle here, remind me never to take up fishing," he sighed, sinking into his seat. "Or rowing. Or even swimming, for that matter."

"Feel safer on land, do you?"

"Huh. Good point."

Suddenly, the whole ship shook. Jack sat bolt upright. The *Adeona's* red warning lights switched on, though she didn't appear to have suffered a direct hit.

"What the hell was that?" asked Jack.

"Oh, that's not good," the ship replied.

The Jörubor rocketed past the cockpit, splashing the windows with seawater. Its shockwave buffeted the ship for a second time. Large chunks of flesh hung from the multi-bladed segments along its tail.

"I'm guessing the fish had trouble digesting it," said Jack. "Got any more bright ideas?"

"Besides finding another fish? No."

The Jörubor swung around in a wide loop, shaking its tail back and forth like a steel whip. Jack doubted the third pass would be as genial as the others.

"Right," he said, launching the *Adeona* into another upward climb. "Well, I do."

"What are you doing? Are you heading for orbit?"

"Heat doesn't bother it and water can't slow it down either. I don't know if we can freeze it, but at least in space it'll be out of harm's way."

"And what if it doesn't follow us out of the atmosphere?"

"Then at least *we'll* be out of harm's way."

They rocketed in a near-vertical ascent. Predictably, the Jörubor chased after them. New Eden's size was only marginally smaller than Earth's, which meant there was approximately a hundred kilometres between space and sea level. Maybe a little less. At maximum velocity, it would only take them a few minutes to breach the thermosphere... presuming the Jörubor didn't catch them first.

It was a harrowing flight. The *Adeona* rattled worse than ever. All Jack could see before him was blue sky getting thinner and fainter. Each time they passed through a patch of white cloud, he'd glance over at the feed to see the Jörubor burst through after them.

He almost switched the feed off. There was nothing they could do if it caught up with them anyway. But he needed to know it was still following them. No matter how terrified he grew, he couldn't let it fly back to the Flo'wud city.

The higher they flew, the thinner the atmosphere became. And the thinner the atmosphere became, the more the stars came into focus, until it was as if the fading blue sky was covered in a hundred thousand morning dew drops. And then Jack spotted them, circling New Eden in a tidal-locked orbit – a couple of Arks and their UEC fleets. Whether either of them was the *Final Dawn*, Jack couldn't tell.

Something bashed into the rear of the ship. Jack immediately detected a drop in the *Adeona's* speed. He glanced at the feed and felt sick. The camera showed nothing but a shuddering plate of fire-blasted chrome. The Jörubor was no longer only figuratively on top of them – it had one of their thrusters quite literally gripped in its beak.

When the *Adeona* sealed the cockpit door to keep it from depressurising in the event of a breach, Jack knew they were in trouble.

"Come on," he muttered to himself, his hands shaking. He couldn't get the image of Fireteam Sigma's savaged drop ship out of his mind. "Not when we're this close..."

"Shall I prepare the skip drive?" the ship asked. The panic was gone from her voice. Now she sounded scared. *Really* scared.

"I hadn't thought of that," replied Jack. "Yes. Just in case. Let's see it hold on in subspace."

Any semblance of New Eden's sky was gone; the black cosmos lay before them in all of its infinite majesty. Surely they'd crossed into the thermosphere already... but it wouldn't be until they hit the Kármán line that they'd escape the last of the planet's gravity.

A horrifying crunching noise came from the rear of the ship; Jack could hear its metal screech resonate through the very walls of the *Adeona*. It sounded like a trash compactor or a car crusher. He guessed the Jörubor hadn't the reach to attack them with its talons or its wings – thank goodness – but from the sound of it, its beak was more than capable of tearing the hull apart.

"Do something!" the ship screamed.

"I'm trying!" he screamed back. "We're not—"

"It's coming through, Jack! Do something *now!*"

There was no way of knowing if they'd climbed high enough. It wasn't as if the Kármán line was a visible metric.

If the Jörubor let go or simply decided not to chase them any longer, there was no guarantee that gravity wouldn't drag the blasted machine back towards the planet's surface.

But the *Adeona* was right. There was no time to be certain of anything. Ready or not – whatever he did, he needed to do it now.

He cut the primary engines, spun the *Adeona* about ninety degrees with her air thrusters so that she lay approximately parallel to the planet's surface, and then boosted forwards again.

The effect was such that the Jörubor was whipped upwards, carried away from New Eden by its momentum, while the *Adeona* continued in a whole different direction. It was dangerous, not least because Jack hadn't counted on the Jörubor being physically attached to the ship when he'd hastily come up with the plan.

But it worked...

...for the most part.

There came a short, sharp crack as the mech took part of the *Adeona* along with it.

"What was that?" Jack yelled. "Adi, are you okay?"

"Exterior heat shield," replied the ship, audibly relieved. "Hull integrity hasn't been compromised. Though we'll need to get the shield repaired as soon as possible, especially with its proximity to my rear thrusters."

"And the Jörubor?"

Without Jack touching any of the controls, the ship slowly turned to face back the way she came.

"See for yourself."

The steel guardian floated up and away from the *Adeona*, thrashing and flailing. Jack sank back into his chair with relief. Somewhere on the way up, they'd crossed gravity's threshold. It didn't matter how hard the Jörubor struggled.

Outside the planet's atmosphere, it lacked the propulsion to fly.

As they watched it grow smaller outside the windows, pockets of ice began to form along its length. The crystals shattered and exploded as the mechanical bird flapped its wings over and over again, but after a few minutes the robot's motors juddered to a stop. The red light of its eyes dimmed and died as it spiralled away into the frozen aether.

"Thank Christ that's over," Jack sighed. "At least the Flo'wud city will be safe for a little while longer."

He sat up, suddenly alert again.

"Everyone else is still down there!" he said, scrambling at the dashboard controls. "Bloody hell. I hope they escaped from that Ripper ambush okay."

"I'm still tracking Tuner," said the *Adeona*, already racing back towards the planet. "Want me to take us down? It might be best, given I'm missing a heat shield and all. Re-entry could get a little rough."

"Yes. Thank you, Adi."

As they rocketed back towards New Eden, Jack gazed out at the grey armada of Arks and battlecruisers. The last remnants of humanity, drifting on the edge of a new world.

All those people. Hoping. Waiting.

Praying for a place to call their home.

Jack slumped back into his chair and buried his head in his hands.

If not for a home, what *was* he fighting for?

23

GOOD INTENTIONS

The *Adeona* found a suitable drop-off point near the top of the Flo'wud city. The moss-drenched platform looked stable enough – the cuts of wood were a few metres thick and installed across two humungous tree branches – but considering the damage already caused by the Jörubor, putting her weight on it wasn't worth the risk. She hovered patiently beside the treetop canopy while Jack disembarked.

Rogan and Klik waited for him at the bottom of her loading ramp. Tuner barrelled his way past them and gripped him in a mighty hug.

"We thought we lost you," he said.

"Almost," Jack replied, barely able to breathe let alone get the words out. "I think we owe Adi a bit of a makeover after the ordeal I just put her through."

The *Adeona* fired jets from her air thrusters in approval.

"How is everyone?" he asked, staring around the empty platform. "Did everyone make it?"

Rogan and Tuner looked at each other. Klik looked down at her bare feet.

"There were quite a few casualties," Rogan replied,

before quickly adding, "Ginger's fine. So is Benet. But... well, you might want to go speak to people yourself."

They escorted him to the other side of the platform and up a rickety winding staircase. Each plank was suspended by ropes from the branches above like a swing. Tuner took one look at the climb and decided to stay with the ship.

Jack spotted a whole host of Flo'wud citizens busying themselves at the top, fixing whatever they could. At least they wouldn't be short of building materials, he supposed. With the Jörubor gone, many of the city's inhabitants were already making their way back home from neighbouring settlements... potential human invasion be damned.

Benet stood near a few of the elders Jack recognised from their time with the comm scrambler. None of them looked very happy, but Benet looked the most miserable of all.

"Thank goodness you're alive," Jack said as he hurried over. "The damage to the city – how bad is it?"

Benet sighed, shook his head and wandered off without another word. The elder who had healed Duke's wounds approached him instead.

"We can rebuild what was broken, but there's no fixing the Flo'wud lives we lost," she said. "Nor can we so easily repair our faith. The Jörubor was supposed to protect us. Instead, it almost brought about our end."

Jack hung his head and tried to explain.

"I'm sorry. We thought that—"

"You thought you knew better," she said. "You thought that with your spaceships and your walking machines, you had answers we did not. No, Jack Bishop. Evidently, you knew nothing. Nothing at all."

Jack kept quiet as a second elder approached.

"Young Benet told us what happened." He spoke in a

sterner tone of voice than his companion. "The Jörubor was trapped in an eternal cycle, he says. Kept on a leash that *you* dared release. And for what? To stop this invasion you talk about? I see no invasion." He pointed a gangly finger at Jack's chest. "The only one I see causing destruction here is you."

"I'm sorry!" Jack repeated, but the elders were already walking away. "I didn't mean... There really is an invasion coming..."

He sighed and gave up.

"Oh, what's the use?"

Rogan laid a hand on his shoulder.

"Don't let them get to you," she said. "They don't know about the ancient tower up in the volcano, or how it held you and the Forgotten under its spell. And they still don't comprehend the full scale of what's coming their way."

"No, everything they said is true." Jack slumped back in the direction of the *Adeona*. "If we hadn't got involved, none of this would have happened. All we did was make everything worse. A *lot* worse."

He waited for a reassuring response, but Rogan had nothing to say. That's how Jack knew he was right.

By the time they got back to the ship, a small contingent of surviving human marines were stood waiting beside it. There were fewer than Jack hoped. At least he wasn't to blame for the Ripper attack... though he supposed he *had* fed Klik's ration bar to one of their offspring, thus getting their attention. For Christ's sake. Now he felt more guilty than ever.

To his relief, he spotted Ginger leant up against the *Adeona's* port side hull. She was deep in conversation with Ghost and Duke. All three of them glanced up at him as he drew close.

"Hey," said Jack. "Glad you... Wait. Where's Sergeant Yates?"

Ginger pursed her lips and bowed her head. Ghost said nothing, only glared at him. Duke shrugged his considerable shoulders.

"Oh, goddammit," said Jack. The bottom dropped out of his stomach and his face turned red. He suddenly felt like he'd disturbed a hornets' nest. "I'm so sorry. Honestly. Yates seemed like a really decent guy."

"Yeah." Ginger stepped away from the hull with both her fists and jaw clenched. "He was. And now he's dead. Got anything to say, Jack?"

Duke sighed and shook his head as a pained expression crossed his face.

"Ginger..."

"No, Duke. Sure, Kaine and his squad might have died trying to cross the clearing with or without the Jörubor turning up. But Yates shouldn't have been there. None of us should've. Those weren't our orders."

"You were happy to disregard orders when you came up that volcano with us," said Rogan.

"To stop you from sending that giant killing machine after human drop ships!" Ginger shouted in disbelief. "How is that the same as deliberately obstructing the colonisation effort?"

"Which the sergeant chose to do of his own accord," said Duke. He sounded as exhausted as he looked. "Nobody forced his hand. Not Jack. Not his robot buddy. Yates decided it was the right thing to do. And Ginger... we agreed."

Ginger turned to Ghost, who reluctantly nodded.

"I mean, the creatures here saved Duke's life," said

Private Flores. "The least we could do was give them a chance to escape. Didn't see any harm in it at the time."

"I'm sorry, okay?" said Jack, throwing up his hands in lethargic defeat. "I messed up. Big time. It's all I seem to be good at, apparently. I couldn't help humanity, and I sure as hell couldn't help the Flo'wud, either."

He raised his eyes to the heavens and groaned.

"And apparently none of it made any difference anyway."

A few of the larger UEC battleships were just about visible as grey specks in an otherwise azure sky – the same faded way the Moon could sometimes be seen in the daytime back on Earth. But far closer to their location, and far more alarming, was a flock of small, black dots perhaps a dozen strong. They could have been mistaken for birds if it weren't for their formation. A second and even larger wave of tanks and drop ships was headed straight for the treetop city.

Rogan stepped forward and contracted her eye lenses.

"Oh, I wouldn't be so sure of that."

Jack squinted past the reinforcements. If he hadn't felt so guilty, he might have laughed. He ran up the *Adeona's* loading ramp, grabbed his helmet (and with it, its telescopic view) and returned outside for a better look.

More ships were blinking into existence around the UEC fleet as they jumped out of subspace. One by one they emerged at a standstill, until a huge swathe of the sky was full with them. Enormous, clunky and burdened with outdated tech, they fit right in alongside Earth's colony ships.

It appeared the Ministry had got his message.

"Took them long enough," said Jack. "Right. Let's show Admiral Blatch how a *proper* first contact is done."

24

HOMECOMING II

The hangar of the *Final Dawn* was cleared of all but essential personnel. Only those directly involved in the New Eden incursion were present. That meant Jack and the crew of the *Adeona* (who remained inside the ship, for the humans' sake), but also the three surviving marines from Fireteam Sigma and the Ark ship's high command – Captain Dyer and Admiral Blatch. A line of suited UEC board members stood in silent apprehension quite some distance behind.

On the opposite side of the hangar to them, just inside the sealed pair of industrial bay doors, a lone Ministry shuttle was parked. Its occupants had yet to disembark.

The tension was borderline unbearable. The others – Rogan, Tuner and Klik – couldn't wrap their heads around it. The galactic community had existed for so long before any of them were built or born that the idea of two space-faring species meeting officially for the first time was nothing short of bizarre.

None of them could understand the gravity surrounding the situation. The implications this would carry for every member of the human race going forward. But Jack could. It was like his first step onto Kapamentis, but this time magnified for all mankind.

That gravity, however, could be clearly seen in every weathered line on Admiral Blatch's face. She wore her smartest, grandest military uniform. Her cold, stately expression hadn't shifted the whole time they stood waiting; neither had her gaze left the shuttle ahead of her. When the envoy did finally arrive, whomever the Ministry had sent, she would be the one to greet them.

First Contact.

Officially, at least. As far as the history books were concerned, Jack and Everett's little escapades wouldn't count. Given the damage done, Jack supposed this was probably for the best.

The door at the front of the shuttle hissed open. Jack didn't think it was possible for anyone in the hangar to stiffen further, but they managed it. Blatch looked as if she'd turned to stone.

Three figures emerged from inside. Two of them were humanoid in figure – a deliberate choice, Jack reckoned – though the details of their appearance were hidden beneath their black Executor uniforms. They carried plasma rifles. The envoy walking between them not only sported the trademark black robe worn by all members of the Ministerium of Cultured Planets, but also a gold emblem possessed only by the seven Grand Ministers who presided over the council. The matter of humanity's arrival in the galaxy was being taken very seriously indeed, it seemed.

Jack allowed himself to relax a little. It was Grand Minister Heram who walked across the hangar to meet them – with a translator-bot scuttling up onto his shoulder, no less. Had one of the others come, things may not have played out so smoothly. It was hard to start a dialogue with something that looked like a giant, oil-black sea urchin.

The slender, seven-foot Oortilian stopped a couple of metres away from Blatch, who Jack could tell was struggling to maintain her composure. He had no doubt she'd practiced for this eventuality since long before departing Earth, but nothing can prepare you for an alien face so close to your own. Especially one with large, pupil-less eyes and slits for a nose.

Remembering herself, Blatch held out an old, trembling hand.

"Greetings from the people of Earth," she said.

Heram looked down at the offered appendage, glanced *almost* imperceptibly at Jack, and then took it in his own.

"Welcome to our galaxy," the bald alien replied, smiling politely as Duke awkwardly snapped a photo for posterity.

Everyone inside the hangar breathed a sigh of relief, but the pervasive tension never quite dissipated. Meeting an extraterrestrial for the first time wasn't something one got over quickly, and there was an unshakable sense that humanity was about to be put on the Naughty Step.

Heram retrieved a data pad from the folds of his robe and drew himself to full height.

"You are in direct violation of the Observer Accord," he announced, reading from the screen. "I must ask you to withdraw your forces and vacate planet EY-1993 at once. Given that you are not yet affiliated with the Ministerium and therefore ignorant of its regulations, the council has generously waived any penalty for your actions, should you comply within the next planetary rotation."

He pocketed the data pad again. Once it was clear that Heram was finished speaking, Admiral Blatch cleared her throat.

"I understand, your excellency." She maintained her composure, but there was no hiding the nervousness in her voice. "But this is—"

"*Very* generously waived any penalty, I should perhaps reiterate," said Heram, bowing his head scholarly.

Blatch swallowed hard but continued nonetheless.

"For which the United Earth Collective is extremely grateful. But this is our only chance to start anew. Our entire species has been displaced. It took everything we had just to get out here. We lack the propulsion technology to reach any other system with a planet suitable for colonisation."

"A predicament, indeed. One that perhaps the Ministry can assist with. However, the Accord stands. Planet EY-1993 is a reservation world, which means nobody is allowed to so much as *visit* it until its dominant species reaches a point of spacefaring capability – should it ever wish to, that is. We monitor the Flo'wud from afar with satellites, but it's illegal to even set up a base on the surface. Colonising it – even a small part of it – is completely out of the question. I'm sure you understand."

"Of course, but—"

"Speaking of satellites – I noticed that you damaged one of your rear thrusters upon exiting your wormhole. I presume this was also what destroyed one of our relays? We'll have to address the cost of replacing it once your currency is synonymous with our own."

Admiral Blatch went as if to protest, then steeled herself and changed tact.

"But where, if not EY-1993, does this 'Ministry' of yours suggest we go?"

"Where?" Heram allowed himself a rare, humourless laugh. "Anywhere you like, providing you don't break any more laws and accords. There are thousands of cities in which members of your species could choose to live, perhaps even thrive. Jack Bishop here certainly hasn't struggled to fit in."

There came a bout of concerned murmuring from the suited UEC board members huddled behind them.

"I was thinking more of a homeworld," Blatch replied. "Humanity can't afford to go its separate ways. Not yet, at least. There are too few of us. We need a planet to call our own."

Heram silently contemplated this request. Jack knew why it gave the Grand Minister trouble – if there was a planet close to the galactic centre not already colonised or purchased by a mega-corporation for its resources, there was usually good reason for it. At last, Heram looked up with a sly, satisfied smile and put his alien hand on Blatch's arm. She bristled with obvious discomfort. Still unaccustomed to human emotion, he didn't seem to notice.

"I think I may have a solution," he said, guiding the admiral in the direction of the alarmed UEC board members. "Let me tell you about Ennakis..."

And that was it – humanity and the Ministry had been introduced. Captain Dyer and Heram's twin guards followed their respective bosses across the hangar, while Jack and the three members of Fireteam Sigma stood respectfully where they were until everyone else had left.

"Christ, that was tense," said Ghost as soon as they were alone. "I thought the admiral was gonna have an aneurism."

"You're telling me." Duke showed her the picture he took on his data pad. "I could barely keep my hands still enough to get it in focus. Look all right to you?"

"It's no Ansel Adams," she said, slapping him on the back, "but it'll do."

"Who?"

They looked up as Jack approached, then glanced across at Ginger. She nodded her approval.

"We'll give the two of you some space," said Ghost, ushering Duke towards one of the empty drop ships.

Jack and Ginger only made eye-contact for a split second before both of them elected to stare at their boots instead. Neither of them said anything for quite some time.

"So..." said Jack.

"Yep," Ginger replied.

Jack chewed his lip. There was nothing else for it. He just had to come out and say it.

"I confronted Admiral Blatch as soon as we got back. She confirmed everything. She knew you were my daughter even before I volunteered to head down to New Eden and find you. Told me she kept quiet on account of not wanting to freak me out if... well, if you were dead."

"Right," Ginger replied. "Okay. I can't tell if that's considerate of her or if she straight up used you."

"Oh, it's the latter. After the experiment in the lab, she knew your mother was pregnant. She implied as much when I asked if the, erm, timelines matched up. But she never told Amber what happened to me – why I suddenly disappeared one day. Which meant *you* grew up not knowing, too. She could have said *something*, but she didn't. Not even that there'd been an accident. All to keep Everett's project secret. I'm sorry. For not being around, I mean."

Ginger said nothing.

"This is pretty weird, right?" said Jack.

"Just a little."

The second lull in conversation was even longer and more awkward than the first.

"I'd like to get to know you better." Jack scratched the

back of his neck. "I guess I've missed a lot during the last twenty-something years."

Finally, Ginger looked him in the eyes.

"I'm not sure I want that," she replied.

Jack was taken aback. For a moment, he didn't know what to say. Luckily, Ginger got there before he could embarrass himself further.

"It's nothing personal," she continued in earnest. "I just... I just don't know you. Like, at all. You might biologically be my father—" she looked uncomfortable even saying the word "—but you're a stranger to me. And to be honest, I grew up without a dad just fine. I'm certainly not looking to get one now."

"Oh. Yeah. I guess that makes sense."

She smacked him on the arm.

"Hey. Maybe when this is all over and humanity gets itself settled, we can grab a drink. As friends, or something. I dunno. Start from there."

Jack smiled, though not without some sadness.

"Yeah, I'd like that. Thanks."

Ginger nodded curtly and then made for the drop ship Ghost and Duke were leant against. Jack kind of hoped she'd look back at him over her shoulder... but she didn't.

He understood.

By the time he'd walked back to the *Adeona's* open loading ramp, Heram and the human contingency had already left the hangar and its regular docking operators were returning to their posts. He quickly hurried inside the ship. It would be just his luck to still be hanging about in a t-shirt when those giant industrial doors opened up onto the vacuum of space again.

He found Rogan and Klik up in the cockpit. Tuner was down in the engine room, double-checking the interior panels in case any hairline fractures had gone unnoticed following the Jörubor's attack.

"Ka'heet is only a couple dozen star systems over," Rogan said, consulting the holographic NavMap. "Shouldn't take more than eight or nine hours, presuming Adi can handle the trip."

"I'm perfectly fine," the ship replied. "It might get a bit bumpy, that's all."

Klik looked up disappointedly from her swivel-chair as Jack entered.

"Hey, Jack. I guess this is it, then. You've come to say your goodbyes."

Jack shambled past them and collapsed into his captain's seat.

"Nah, you're stuck with me for a while longer. If you'll have me, that is."

"Of course," said Rogan as Klik's face lit up. "But... why? Think of everything you went through trying to get back to your people. Here we are, and now you want to leave? Already?"

Jack gazed out of the cockpit windows. The hangar was abuzz with pilots and engineers in cruddy cosmonaut gear. Behind its walls lay an industrial network of dank tunnels and sterile corridors and shuddering elevators – he could still recreate some of it in his mind from his earlier trip to Blatch's office. And beyond that flimsy web, a whole city of survivors. Thousands of families huddled in cramped dormitories. Fake promenades filled with nervous smiles and the beautiful stench from a hundred different cuisines. Digital archives of history and culture. Echoes of an Earth now lost.

He'd miss it, sure. But he was nothing but a stranger

now, and missing something was never a good enough reason to stay.

"Nah, there's nothing for me here anymore." He ran his hand along the ship's controls. "I know where my real family is."

Klik smiled at him as she climbed up onto Brackitt's old chair and put her feet up on the dashboard. Rogan crossed the cockpit and squeezed Jack's shoulder. He covered her hand with his own.

"Well, Tuner will be pleased," she said.

An alarm began to blare outside as the hangar doors rumbled open. Taking this as her cue, the *Adeona* ignited her landing thrusters and slowly rose from her bay. She paused facing the cosmos as if giving Jack one last chance to stay.

"Permission to depart, Captain?"

Jack leaned back and folded his arms behind his head.

"No need to ask, Adi. Today, I'm just a passenger."

For the first time, there was nowhere he needed to go.

He was already home.

The FINAL DAWN series will continue!

If you'd like to be alerted when the next book in the *Final Dawn* series is released, sign up for T.W.M. Ashford's mailing list at the website below.

www.twmashford.com

Continue reading for a preview of *Sigma*, the first book in the *War for New Terra* spin-off trilogy (coming soon).

25

SIGMA

PREVIEW CHAPTER

Sergeant Elizabeth Rogers swung her legs off her bunk and groped blindly for the data pad on her dresser. It was barking out an oh-six-hundred alarm. She slapped it until it shut up.

Before she could so much as rub the sleep dust from her eyes, there came a loud and abrupt knocking at her bunk room door.

"Yo, Ginger." The female voice belonged to Private Flores, more commonly known as Ghost amongst the squad. "You up yet? Baker expects us down for briefing in twenty."

"Yeah, yeah. I'm awake." She waved at the closed door. "Go on ahead – I'll catch up."

Her instruction was met with indifferent silence. Good. Ginger buried her head in her hands and groaned. She wanted to believe that her grogginess was because she'd yet to acclimatise to the *UECS Invincible's* artificial atmosphere, but that was a load of crap. It was the old whiskey the squad had passed around last night. She could still smell it on her breath.

Well, it didn't do to turn up at a briefing looking – or smelling – worse for wear. Especially when you were the new fireteam leader and all. She got up and noticed that the bunk above hers was already made.

"Jesus Christ, Flores. You really are a ghost."

She grabbed her combat fatigues from her locker and headed for the showers.

THE BRIEFING ROOM was on the deck directly below the bunk rooms. Ginger arrived with her hair still wet from her shower and the upper half of her fatigues tied around her waist. She wore a white vest top beneath. Her watch read 06:19. Just in time. She punched the button beside the doors to open them.

Almost everybody else was already inside. It wasn't hard to tell. A dozen fold-out chairs were laid out in front of a large display screen set into the back wall, and only two of them were empty. Flores had saved one for Ginger next to Duke and herself.

She hurried over and took her seat before Staff Sergeant Baker could make a snarky comment.

"How nice of you to join us," said Flores, smirking. "Duke didn't reckon you'd make it. Maybe he was right. You still look a little queasy..."

"How in God's name are you so chipper this morning? You drank twice as much as I did." She slicked her undercut hair back so it didn't hang in her face and tried to make herself look a little more presentable. "And thanks, Duke. Your confidence in me is making me all teary-eyed."

Duke, who officially went by Private Sampson, was a giant of a man. Unlike Ghost, who specialised in long-range marksmanship, Duke preferred to get up close and personal – shotguns and explosives. He responded to Ginger with a big, toothy smile.

"Practise." He gave her a hearty slap on the back, and she felt her stomach heave. "Makes perfect, right? Maybe if you spent more time drinking and less time writing in that journal of yours, you'd be able to keep up."

Ginger rolled her eyes and pointed at the other empty seat in front of them.

"Where's the new guy?"

Ghost and Duke shrugged in unison.

"Maybe he isn't on board yet," said Ghost. "He's being transferred over from the *Constellation*, apparently."

"This close to deployment?" Ginger raised a hungover eyebrow. "Cutting it a bit fine."

The door to the briefing room hissed open and everyone stiffened. When they saw that it was just Staff Sergeant Baker, they relaxed again. Baker outranked everyone else in the room but, despite his slightly cantankerous disposition, meetings with him tended to fall more on the relaxed side. He didn't like the three fireteams in his squad standing to attention any more than they did.

"Yes, stay seated," said Baker, coming to a stop beside the display screen. He brandished a data pad at them. "You'll want to be sitting down when you see what you're going up against."

He swiped at the pad and a three-dimensional image of a blue-green planet appeared on the screen. Before he could continue speaking, the doors hissed open again.

A young man of about eighteen years of age burst into the room, looking wide-eyed and out of breath.

"Sorry," he spluttered, wilting under everyone's gaze. "Got lost, sir."

"Private Bradley, correct? The new recruit." Baker tutted and nodded to the only empty chair in the room. "Hurry up and take a seat before you hold up the entire war effort."

"You have got to be kidding me," Ginger whispered to Ghost. "Look at him. He's as green as they get. What the hell's he doing with us?"

"*Everyone's* green, remember?" Ghost sounded almost as pissed off as she did. "Most of the UEC's armed forces have barely seen combat with other humans, let alone whatever we're gonna find out here. Still, you're right. They could have sent somebody a little more experienced to replace Yates."

Ginger bristled at the name. Yates had been the Sergeant before her. It was his death back on New Eden – the last planet humanity tried colonising – that had led to her taking over as leader of Fireteam Sigma.

"He'll be dead in five minutes."

"Then you won't have to worry about him for very long," Ghost replied.

Duke shuffled his chair to one side so that Private Bradley could squeeze his apologetic way through to the front. A few of the privates from Fireteams Tau and Upsilon smirked as he sat down.

"This," Baker continued, pointing at the planet, "is Ennakis. Command have renamed it New Terra. Some of the more observant of you will have noticed we've been sitting just outside of its orbit for the past thirty-four hours. Ladies and gentlemen, you're looking at humanity's new home."

"That's what they said last time." The cocky voice belonged to Private Jackson over in Tau. "I don't see why we couldn't just take New Eden. Who cares about some dumb little alien reservation, anyway?"

Ginger rolled her eyes. Unlike Jackson, she'd actually been down to New Eden and met some of those "dumb little aliens" first hand.

"Funnily enough, the United Earth Collective doesn't believe that humanity's first interstellar act should be one of war against the entire galactic community," replied Baker. "Like it or not, this is the world the Ministerium of Cultured Planets is letting us take. The atmospheric and geological conditions are remarkably similar to that which we experienced back on Earth – before everything went to hell, that is."

"If this New Terra is so great," asked Ghost, "why hasn't anyone else colonised it yet?"

Ginger nodded thoughtfully. Now *that* was a good question. Humanity was a relative latecomer to the planetary party, after all. Many worlds were already taken.

"They have. That's the catch." Staff Sergeant Baker crossed his arms and inhaled deeply. "According to our contacts at the Ministry, New Terra used to be inhabited by a non-spacefaring race whose society rose to a stage we might have considered pre-industrial back on Earth. But, a few years back, an invasive species found its way onto the planet. Nobody's quite sure how. By the time anyone in the Ministry realised what was going on, the planet had been overrun and the original inhabitants completely wiped out."

"I'm not sure I like where this is going," grumbled Duke.

"New Terra is ours, providing we eradicate the invasive species first," Baker confirmed.

"But the aliens at this Ministry place – they can help us, right?" Jackson suddenly didn't sound so cocky. "Like... they've got military tech like we couldn't believe, haven't they?"

"If they were going to cleanse the planet, they'd glass it

from orbit." Baker shook his head. "Obviously that's not an option for us if we still want to live on it afterwards. I'm afraid we're on our own, boys and girls. And no, there's no third planet. New Eden was a bust, so we've gotta make this one work."

The mood of the room dropped without another word needing to be spoken. Ginger eventually broke the silence.

"These things we're exterminating. Any idea what they look like? Behaviour? Weaknesses, that sort of thing?"

Baker tapped his data pad and the picture on the screen changed from the planet to a collection of grainy black-and-white photographs. Ginger struggled to make out anything more than a few dark, menacing shadows.

"These were taken from a drone we sent down yesterday. Unfortunately, they're all we've got – the species in question tends to spend most of its time underground. From what the Ministry tells us, we should expect semi-bipedal insectoids of limited intelligence and muscular anatomy. Six, maybe seven feet in length, though we've already detected some slight variation between social castes."

"Jesus Christ!" said another private. She was sweating. "Seven feet? I thought we were gonna be clearing out cockroach nests or something – not... not this!"

"Well, a bit more like giant ants from the sound of things." Baker shrugged dismissively. "As I said before, nobody really knows that much about what we're going up against. For now, Command is simply referring to them as bugs and roaches. But we're told the hard work will come from having to systematically cleanse a whole planet rather than the threat of the individual bugs themselves. Nothing we can't handle, Private."

"So we're being sent in on a recon mission, then?" Duke's

booming voice dominated the room. "Head down there, see what we're up against and then report back?"

"You wish. I know we were trained specifically for advance reconnaissance missions, but Command wants everyone down on New Terra pronto. We're going in with the rest of the invasion."

"Pronto?" said Ghost, sitting forward. "How pronto?"

Baker checked his watch.

"Five hours and forty minutes," he replied casually. "That's when sundown hits this side of the planet. We'll take the drop ships down under the cover of darkness."

"What?" Ginger's head was suddenly pounding, and she didn't think it was just from the drink anymore. "But we were told nobody was being redeployed for another week!"

"Yes, well. What Command wants, Command gets. Right now we have the element of surprise, but we won't if we hang around in near-orbit for much longer. Not if there's anything smart down there. Now shut your mouths and open your ears. This is the important bit."

Everyone grumbled quietly to themselves as Baker switched the display to the next slide. It showed a bird's-eye view of the planet's surface. This one was in colour and far more detailed than the ones before. It must have been taken by a drone much higher up inside New Terra's atmosphere. Perhaps even from one of the ships in orbit.

"This," said Baker, pointing to a developed region in the top-right corner of the photograph, "used to be one of the previous inhabitants' most prosperous cities. Rhinegarde, they called it. Our mission is to eradicate every last bug from the city so that the UEC can begin its colonisation effort. Simple, yes? Good."

He highlighted a dark crack running all the way from one side of the satellite image to the other.

"This fissure makes the Grand Canyon look like a pothole," he continued. "It's over a mile wide. Scans won't tell us how deep it is. And it would take weeks to navigate our way around on foot. Unfortunately, we have to cross it if we're to reach Rhinegarde." He tapped an unusual marking on the map. "That's where this here rectangle comes in – the Bridge of Etmark. That's our first objective."

Bridge? Ginger shifted uncomfortably in her seat. Looked more like a bottleneck to her.

"That red circle in the bottom-left," said Duke, referring to a crude graphic overlaying the original photograph. "Is that the drop point, sir?"

"That's Rally Point Bravo. Don't worry about the drop point, private – you leave that to our pilots. If for whatever reason anyone gets separated, you make it your top priority to regroup with everyone else here. It's elevated and open. Command expects minimal resistance, if any."

"Yeah," Ghost whispered to Ginger, "but how much resistance should *we* expect?"

Baker turned the screen off and addressed the uneasy room.

"So to recap: we rendezvous with the rest of the company at Rally Point Bravo, we secure the Bridge of Etmark and then we advance on the city of Rhinegarde. That's Operation Ground Zero in a nutshell. Any questions?"

Jessie from Fireteam Tau raised her hand.

"Yes, private?"

"Is it too late to take my chances back on Earth?"

Everyone laughed nervously. Staff Sergeant Baker pursed his lips to show that even he wasn't totally devoid of humour.

"If you want to roast to death on our husk of a homeworld, be my guest. But you'll be getting there via a first-class ticket out the airlock. Any sensible questions, squad?"

A dozen solemn faces looked either back at him or down at the floor. He nodded.

"Good. That's what I like to hear. There's five and a half hours left until deployment – I suggest you all get some grub in you, pack your stuff together, and meet up on deck at eleven-hundred and thirty hours. Dismissed."

Everybody else slid their fold-away chairs aside and hurried back to their bunk rooms. Ginger sank into her seat and groaned. She'd only just gotten over her last visit to an alien world humanity wanted to plant a flag on.

"I guess that means movie night is cancelled," Ghost sighed. "Shame. I always wanted to see Casablanca before I died."

"Oh, and Sergeant Rogers?" Baker called across at her from inside the briefing room doorway. "Make sure you bring our newest recruit up to speed."

Private Bradley turned around in his seat and gave her an uncomfortable smile.

"Good luck," said Duke, beaming that big, friendly grin of his. He gave her another slap on the back, this one hearty enough to rattle her teeth. "I'll catch both you ladies on deck."

Ghost followed Duke out along with Staff Sergeant Baker and the other two fireteams. Ginger rose to her feet. Private Bradley hesitantly approached.

"Good morning, ma'am." The poor boy's voice sounded nearly as fragile as he looked. "Erm, should we perhaps—"

"Stop." Ginger raised a hand and closed her eyes. "Just stop. Whatever you're about to say, my brain is not in the mood for it. And cut out the *ma'am* crap. You've heard of the phrase, 'no man left behind', right?"

Private Bradley nodded enthusiastically.

"Well, today it means something slightly different. If you don't turn up for deployment on time later, I'll find you and throw you down to the planet myself. Understand?"

"Yes, ma'am. Sorry," he quickly added.

"Good." Ginger gave him two quick pats on the shoulder and then walked away. "Welcome to Fireteam Sigma."

Sigma – Coming Soon

If you'd like to be alerted when *Sigma*, the first book in the *War for New Terra* series is available to order, sign up for T.W.M. Ashford's mailing list at the website below.

www.twmashford.com

WANT AN EXCLUSIVE FINAL DAWN STORY?

Building a relationship with my readers is one of the best things about writing. Every now and then I send out newsletters with details on new releases, special offers and other bits of news relating to my books.

And if you sign up to the mailing list I'll even send you a **FREE** copy of *Before the Dawn*, an exclusive prequel story set immediately before *The Final Dawn*.

Not bad, eh?

Sign up today at www.twmashford.com.

Enjoy this book? You can make a big difference.

Reviews are the most powerful tool in my arsenal when it comes to getting attention for my books. As an indie author, I don't have quite the same financial muscle as a New York publisher. But what I *do* have is something even more effective:

A committed and loyal bunch of readers.

Honest reviews of my books help bring them to the attention of other readers.

If you've enjoyed this book I would be very grateful if you could spend just five minutes leaving a review (it can be as short as you like) on the book's Amazon page.

Thank you very much.

ABOUT THE AUTHOR

T.W.M. Ashford is a British novelist living in London. You can call him Tom.

He's written hundreds of scripts and copy for some of the biggest companies in the world, and provides a variety of creative content for Mark Dawson's Self Publishing Formula. He's even been known to play a bass guitar on occasion.

But, of course, his main passion is writing fiction. He's currently setting up an interconnected space opera universe called the *Dark Star Panorama*, of which *Final Dawn* is the first series.

Send him an email at tom@twmashford.com. He'll enjoy the attention.

BOOKS BY T.W.M. ASHFORD

Books in the Dark Star Panorama Universe

Final Dawn Series

- The Final Dawn
- Thief of Stars
- A Dark Horizon
- The New World

War for New Terra Series

- Sigma

Printed in Great Britain
by Amazon

24896667R00158